EVERYONE LOVES MAX!

PRAISE FOR *THE ANGEL EXPERIMENT*

PRAISE FOR *SCHOOL'S OUT—FOREVER*

For Jennifer Rudolph Walsh; Hadley, Griffin, and Wyatt Zangwill
Gabrielle Charbonnet; Monina and Piera Varela
Suzie and Jack; MaryEllen and Andrew; Carole, Brigid, and Meredith
Fly, babies, fly!

Many thanks to Gabrielle Charbonnet, my conspirator,
who flies high and cracks wise.
And Mary Jordan, for brave assistance and research at every twist and turn.

Copyright © 2005 by SueJack, Inc.
Excerpt from *School's Out—Forever* copyright © 2006 by SueJack, Inc.
Maximum Ride® is a trademark of JBP Business, LLC.
Excerpt from *Witch & Wizard* copyright © 2009 by James Patterson
Witch & Wizard® is a trademark of JBP Business, LLC.

JIMMY Patterson Books / Little, Brown and Company
Hachette Book Group
1290 Avenue of the Americas, New York, NY 10104
JimmyPatterson.org

First Paperback Edition: April 2007
First published in hardcover in April 2005 by Little, Brown and Company

JIMMY Patterson Books in an imprint of Little, Brown and Company, a division of Hachette Book Group, Inc. The Little, Brown name and logo are trademarks of Hachette Book Group, Inc. The JIMMY Patterson name and logo are trademarks of JBP Business, LLC.

The publisher is not responsible for websites (or their content) that are not owned by the publisher.

The Hachette Speakers Bureau provides a wide range of authors for speaking events. To find out more, go to hachettespeakersbureau.com or call (866) 376-6591.

Cover design by Larry Rostant

Library of Congress Cataloging-in-Publication Data

Patterson, James.
  Maximum Ride : the angel experiment / by James Patterson. — 1st ed
    p. cm.
Summary: After the mutant Erasers abduct the youngest member of their group, the "bird kids," who are the result of genetic experimentation, take off in pursuit and find themselves struggling to understand their own origins and purpose.
  ISBN 978-0-316-15556-4 (hc) / ISBN: 978-0-316-06795-9 (pb)
  [1. Genetic engineering — Fiction. 2. Adventure and adventurers — Fiction.] I. Title.
PZ7.P27653Max 2005
[Fic] — dc22   2004018623

HC 10 9 8 7
PB 30 29

LSC-C

Printed in the United States of America
The text was set in Life.

MAXIMUM RIDE

RIDE

THE ANGEL EXPERIMENT

JAMES PATTERSON

JIMMY Patterson Books
LITTLE, BROWN AND COMPANY
New York   Boston   London

To the reader:

The idea for Maximum Ride comes from earlier books of mine called *When the Wind Blows* and *The Lake House*, which also feature a character named Max who escapes from a quite despicable School. Most of the similarities end there. Max and the other kids in Maximum Ride are not the same Max and kids featured in those two books. Nor do Frannie and Kit play any part in Maximum Ride. I hope you enjoy the ride anyway.

WARNING

If you dare to read this story, you become part of the Experiment. I know that sounds a little mysterious — but it's all I can say right now.

Max

PROLOGUE

Congratulations. The fact that you're reading this means you've taken one giant step closer to surviving till your next birthday. Yes, *you,* standing there leafing through these pages. *Do not put this book down.* I'm dead serious — your life could depend on it.

This is my story, the story of my family, but it could just as easily be your story too. We're all in this together; trust me on that.

I've never done anything like this, so I'm just going to jump in, and you try to keep up.

Okay. I'm Max. I'm fourteen. I live with my family, who are five kids not related to me by blood, but still totally my family.

We're — well, we're kind of amazing. Not to sound too full of myself, but we're like nothing you've ever seen before.

Basically, we're pretty cool, nice, smart — but not "average" in any way. The six of us — me, Fang, Iggy, Nudge, the Gasman, and Angel — were made on purpose, by the sickest, most horrible "scientists" you could possibly imagine. They created us as an experiment. An experiment where we ended up only 98 percent human. That other 2 percent has had a big impact, let me tell you.

We grew up in a science lab / prison called the School, in cages, like lab rats. It's pretty amazing we can think or speak at all. But we can — and so much more.

There was one other School experiment that made it past infancy. Part human, part wolf — all predator: They're called Erasers. They're tough, smart, and hard to control. They look human, but when they want to, they are capable of morphing into wolf men, complete with fur, fangs, and claws. The School uses them as guards, police — and executioners.

To them, we're six moving targets — prey smart enough to be a fun challenge. Basically, they want to rip our throats out. And make sure the world never finds out about us.

But I'm not lying down just yet. I'm telling *you*, right?

This story could be about you — or your children. If not today, then soon. So please, please take this seriously. I'm risking everything that matters by telling you — *but you need to know.*

Keep reading — don't let anyone stop you.

> — Max. And my family: Fang, Iggy, Nudge,
> the Gasman, and Angel.
> Welcome to our nightmare.

PART 1

FLOCK FRIGHT

1

The funny thing about facing imminent death is that it really snaps everything else into perspective. Take right now, for instance.

Run! Come on, run! You know you can do it.

I gulped deep lungfuls of air. My brain was on hyperdrive; I was racing for my life. My one goal was to escape. Nothing else mattered.

My arms being scratched to ribbons by a briar I'd run through? No biggie.

My bare feet hitting every sharp rock, rough root, pointed stick? Not a problem.

My lungs aching for air? I could deal.

As long as I could put as much distance as possible between me and the Erasers.

Yeah, Erasers. Mutants: half-men, half-wolves, usually armed, always bloodthirsty. Right now they were after me.

See? That snaps everything into perspective.

Run. You're faster than they are. You can outrun anyone.

I'd never been this far from the School before. I was totally lost. Still, my arms pumped by my sides, my feet crashed through the underbrush, my eyes scanned ahead anxiously through the half-light. I could outrun them. I could find a clearing with enough space for me to —

Oh, no. Oh, no. The unearthly baying of bloodhounds on the scent wailed through the trees, and I felt sick. I could outrun men — all of us could, even Angel, and she's only six. But none of us could outrun a big dog.

Dogs, dogs, go away, let me live another day.

They were getting closer. Dim light filtered in through the woods in front of me — a clearing? *Please, please . . .* a clearing could save me.

I burst through the trees, chest heaving, a thin sheen of cold sweat on my skin.

Yes!

No — oh, no!

I skidded to a halt, my arms waving, my feet backpedaling in the rocky dirt.

It wasn't a clearing. In front of me was a *cliff*, a sheer face of rock that dropped to an unseeable floor hundreds of feet below.

In back of me were woods filled with drooling bloodhounds and psycho Erasers with guns.

Both options stank.

The dogs were yelping excitedly — they'd found their prey: *moi.*

I looked over the deadly drop.

There was no choice, really. If you were me, you'd have done the same thing.

I closed my eyes, held out my arms . . . and let myself fall over the edge of the cliff.

The Erasers screamed angrily, the dogs barked hysterically, and then all I could hear was the sound of air rushing past me.

It was so dang peaceful, for a second. I smiled.

Then, taking a deep breath, I unfurled my wings as hard and fast as I could.

Thirteen feet across, pale tan with white streaks and some freckly looking brown spots, they caught the air, and I was suddenly yanked upward, hard, as if a parachute had just opened. *Yow!*

Note to self: No sudden unfurling.

Wincing, I pushed downward with all my strength, then pulled my wings up, then pushed downward again.

Oh, my god, I was *flying* — just like I'd always dreamed.

The cliff floor, draped in shadow, receded beneath me. I laughed and surged upward, feeling the pull of my muscles, the air whistling through my secondary feathers, the breeze drying the sweat on my face.

I soared up past the cliff edge, past the startled hounds and the furious Erasers.

One of them, hairy-faced, fangs dripping, raised his gun. A red dot of light appeared on my torn nightgown. *Not today, you jerk,* I thought, veering sharply west so the sun would be in his hate-crazed eyes.

I'm not going to die today.

2

I jolted upright in bed, gasping, my hand over my heart.

I couldn't help checking my nightgown. No red laser dot. No bullet holes. I fell back on my bed, limp with relief.

Geez, I hated that dream. It was always the same: running away from the School, being chased by Erasers and dogs, me falling off a cliff, then suddenly *whoosh*, wings, flying, escaping. I always woke up feeling a second away from death.

Note to self: Give subconscious a pep talk re: better dreams.

It was chilly, but I forced myself out of my cozy bed. I threw on clean sweats — amazingly, Nudge had put the laundry away.

Everyone else was still asleep: I could have a few minutes of peace and quiet, get a jump on the day.

I glanced out the hall windows on the way to the kitchen. I loved this view: the morning sunlight breaking over the crest of the mountains, the clear sky, the deep shadows, the fact that I could see no sign of any other people.

We were high on a mountain, safe, just me and my family.

Our house was shaped like a letter *E* turned on its side. The bars of the *E* were cantilevered on stilts out over a steep canyon, so if I looked out a window, I felt like I was floating. On a "cool" scale from one to ten, this house was an easy fifteen.

Here, my family and I could be ourselves. Here, we could live free. I mean *literally* free, as in, not in *cages*.

Long story. More on that later.

And of course here's the best part: no grown-ups. When we first moved here, Jeb Batchelder had taken care of us, like a dad. He'd saved us. None of us had parents, but Jeb had come as close as possible.

Two years ago, he'd disappeared. I knew he was dead, we all did, but we didn't talk about it. Now we were on our own.

Yep, no one telling us what to do, what to eat, when to go to bed. Well, except me. I'm the oldest, so I try to keep things running as best I can. It's a hard, thankless job, but someone has to do it.

We don't go to school, either, so thank God for the Internet, because otherwise we wouldn't know *nothin'*. But no schools, no doctors, no social workers knocking on our door. It's simple: If no one knows about us, *we stay alive.*

I was rustling around for food in the kitchen when I heard sleepy shuffling behind me.

"Mornin', Max."

3

"Morning, Gazzy," I said as the heavy-lidded eight-year-old slumped at the table. I rubbed his back and dropped a kiss on his head. He'd been the Gasman ever since he was a baby. What can I say? The child has something funky with his digestive system. A word to the wise: Stay upwind.

The Gasman blinked up at me, his gorgeous blue eyes round and trusting. "What's for breakfast?" he asked, sitting up. His fine blond hair stuck up all over his head, reminding me of a fledgling's downy feathers.

"Um, it's a surprise," I said, since I had no idea.

"I'll pour juice," the Gasman offered, and my heart swelled. He was a sweet, sweet kid, and so was his little sister. He and six-year-old Angel were the only blood siblings among us, but we were all a family anyway.

Soon Iggy, tall and pale, slouched into the kitchen. Eyes closed, he fell onto our beat-up couch with perfect aim. The only time he has trouble being blind is when one of us forgets and moves furniture or something.

"Hey, Ig, rise and shine," I said.

"Bite me," he mumbled sleepily.

"Fine," I said. "Miss breakfast."

I was looking in the fridge with naive hope — maybe the food fairies had come — when the back of my neck prickled. I straightened quickly and spun around.

"Will you *quit* that?" I said.

Fang always appeared silently like that, out of nowhere, like a dark shadow come to life. He regarded me calmly, dressed and alert, his dark, overlong hair brushed back. He was four months younger than me but already four inches taller. "Quit what?" he asked calmly. "Breathing?"

I rolled my eyes. "You know what."

With a grunt, Iggy staggered upright. "I'll make eggs," he announced. I guess if I were more of a fembot, it would bother me that a *blind* guy six months younger than I am could cook better than I could.

But I'm not. So it didn't.

I surveyed the kitchen. Breakfast was well under way. "Fang? You set the table. I'll go get Nudge and Angel."

The two girls shared the last small bedroom. I pushed the door open to find eleven-year-old Nudge asleep, tangled up in her covers. She was barely recognizable with her mouth shut, I thought wryly. When she was awake, we called it the Nudge Channel: all Nudge, all the time.

"Hey, sweetie, up and at 'em," I said, gently shaking her shoulder. "Breakfast in ten."

Nudge blinked, her brown eyes struggling to focus on me. "Wha'?" she mumbled.

"Another day," I said. "Get up and face it."

Groaning, Nudge levered herself into a crumpled but technically upright position.

Across the room, a thin curtain concealed one corner. Angel always liked small cozy spaces. Her bed, tucked behind the curtain, was like a nest — full of stuffed animals, books, most of her clothes. I smiled and pulled the curtain back.

"Hey, you're already dressed," I said, leaning over to hug her.

"Hi, Max," Angel said, tugging her blond curls out of her collar. "Can you do my buttons?"

"Yep." I turned her around and started doing her up.

I'd never told the others, but I just loved, loved, *loved* Angel. Maybe because I'd been taking care of her practically since she was a baby. Maybe because she was just so incredibly sweet and loving herself.

"Maybe because I'm like your little girl," said Angel, turning around to look at me. "But don't worry, Max. I won't tell anybody. Besides, I love you best too." She threw her skinny arms around my neck and planted a somewhat sticky kiss on my cheek. I hugged her back, hard. Oh, yeah — that's another special thing about Angel.

She can read minds.

4

"I want to go pick strawberries today," Angel said firmly, scooping up a forkful of scrambled eggs. "They're ripe now."

"Okay, Angel, I'll go with you," said the Gasman. Just then he let rip one of his unfortunate occurrences and giggled.

"Oh, jeez, Gazzy," I said disapprovingly.

"Gas . . . mask!" Iggy choked out, grasping his neck and pretending to asphyxiate.

"I'm *done*," Fang said, getting up quickly and taking his plate to the sink.

"Sorry," the Gasman said automatically, but he kept eating.

"Yeah, Angel," said Nudge. "I think the *fresh air* would do us all good. I'll go too."

"We'll all go," I said.

Outside, it was beautiful, clear and cloudless, with the first real heat of May. We carried buckets and baskets as Angel led us to a huge patch of wild strawberries.

She held my hand. "If you make cake, I can make strawberry shortcakes," she said happily.

"Yeah, that'll be the day, when Max makes a cake," I heard Iggy say. "I'll make it, Angel."

I whirled. "Oh, thank you!" I exclaimed. "Okay, I'm not a fabulous cook. But I can still kick your butt, and don't you forget it!"

Iggy was laughing, holding up his hands in denial. Nudge was trying not to laugh, even Fang was grinning, and the Gasman looked . . . mischievous.

"Was that *you?*" I asked Gazzy.

He grinned and shrugged, trying not to look too pleased with himself. The Gasman had been about three when I realized he could mimic just about any sound or voice. I'd lost count of how many times Iggy and Fang had almost come to blows over stuff Gazzy had said in their voices. It was a dark gift, and he wielded it happily.

It was just another weird ability — most of us had them. Whatever they were, they sure made life more interesting.

Next to me, Angel froze and screamed.

Startled, I stared down at her, and in the next second, men with wolfish muzzles, huge canines, and reddish, glinting eyes dropped out of the sky like spiders. Erasers! And it wasn't a dream.

5

There was no time to think. Jeb had trained us not to think — just to act. I launched myself at an Eraser, spinning and planting a hard, roundhouse kick in his barrel chest. His breath went *oof,* and the odor was just awful, like raw sewage left out in the hot sun.

After that, it was like a movie, a bunch of superimposed images that hardly seemed real. I landed another blow, then an Eraser punched me so hard that my head snapped around and I felt a burst of blood in my mouth. Out of the corner of my eye, I saw Fang holding his own against an Eraser — until two more ganged up on him, and he went down under flailing clawed hands.

Iggy was still upright, but one eye was already swelling shut.

Beyond shock, I scrambled to my feet, then saw the Gasman out cold, lying facedown on the ground.

I leaped toward him, only to be grabbed again. Two Erasers pinned my arms behind my back. Another leaned in, his reddish eyes glinting with excitement, his jaw fully morphed out and snoutlike. He pulled back his hand and curled it into a fist. Then he brought it in hard, punching me in the stomach. An unbelievable pain exploded inside me, and I doubled over, dropping like a stone.

Dimly, I heard Angel screaming and Nudge crying.

Get up! I told myself, trying to suck in air. *Get up!*

As weird mutant kids, we're much, much stronger than regular grown-up humans. But Erasers aren't regular grown-up humans, and they outnumbered us as well. We were dog meat. I struggled to my hands and knees, trying not to retch.

I staggered to my feet, bloodlust in my eyes, ready to kill. Two Erasers held Nudge's hands and feet. They swung her hard, and she went sailing, hitting her head against a tree. I heard a small pained cry, and then she lay crumpled among the pine needles.

With a hoarse, blood-muffled shout, I ran up and clapped my cupped palms around an Eraser's furry ears. He shrieked as his eardrums popped, and he fell to his knees.

"Max!" Angel screamed, high-pitched and terrified, and I spun around. An Eraser had her by the arms, and I raced forward, jumping over Iggy, who now lay unconscious. Two Erasers fell on me, knocking me down, one pressing a heavy knee into my chest. I wheezed and struggled, and one of them cuffed my face hard, his ragged claws digging deep welts in my cheek.

Dizzily, I fell back, the two Erasers pinning me, and with uncomprehending horror I saw three other Erasers stuffing Angel, my baby, into a rough sack. She was crying and screaming, and one of them hit her.

Frantically struggling, I tried to scream but could make only a hoarse, choked cry. "Get *off* me, you stupid, freaking —" I choked, but I was slammed back again.

An Eraser leaned over me, smiling horribly.

"*Max,*" he said, and my stomach clenched — did I know him? "Good to see you again," he went on conversationally. "You look like crap. You always acted so much better than everyone else, so this cheers me up."

"Who are you?" I gasped, feeling cold at the center of my being.

The Eraser grinned, his long, sharp teeth barely fitting in his jaw. "You don't recognize me? I guess I've grown some."

My eyes went wide with sudden, horrified recognition.

"Ari," I whispered, and he laughed like a mad person. Then he stood up. I saw his huge, black boot come at my head, felt my head jerk to one side, and everything went black.

My last thought was disbelief: Ari was Jeb's son. They'd made him into an Eraser. He was seven years old.

6

"Max?" The Gasman's voice was very young and very scared.

I heard a horrible, low moan, then realized it had come from me.

The Gasman and Fang were leaning over me, concerned expressions on their bruised, bloodied faces.

"I'm okay," I croaked, having no idea if I was or not. Memory came rushing back, and I tried to sit up. "Where's Angel?" My voice was strained.

Fang's dark eyes met mine. "She's gone. They took her."

I thought I might faint again. I remembered being nine years old, looking out the wired-glass lab window, watching the Erasers in the semidarkness. The whitecoats had released chimpanzees onto the School grounds and let newly made Erasers loose after them. Teaching them how to hunt.

The sounds of the chimpanzees screeching in terror and pain still echoed in my mind.

That was who had Angel now.

Rage overwhelmed me — why couldn't they have taken

me instead? Why take a tiny kid? Maybe *I* would have had a chance — maybe.

Shakily, I got to my feet. My head was spinning, and I had to lean against Fang, hating my weakness. "We've got to get her," I said urgently, trying to stay upright. "We've got to get her before they —" Horror-filled images flashed through my mind — Angel being chased, being hurt, being killed. I gulped, shutting them down.

"Check in, guys — are you up for a chase?" I examined the four of them. They looked like they'd been stuffed into a blender set on "chop."

"Yes," Nudge said in a tear-choked voice.

"I'm up," said Iggy, a split lip making his voice thick.

The Gasman nodded solemnly at me.

To my horror, hot tears momentarily blurred my vision. I wiped them away with the back of one hand and called on fury to keep me going.

Just then Iggy cocked his head slightly. It was a clue for me to start listening intently. Then I heard it too: a faint engine noise.

"There!" Iggy said, pointing.

The five of us ran stiffly and clumsily toward the sound. A hundred yards through the woods brought us to a sharp drop-off maybe fifty feet above an old, unused logging road.

Then I saw it: a black Humvee, dull with dust and mud, bumping roughly over the unpaved road. My heart pounded. I knew, just knew, that my little one, my Angel, was inside.

And she was on her way to a place where death came as a blessing.

It wasn't going to happen, not while I was breathing.

"Let's get her!" I cried, then backed up about ten feet. The others scurried out of my way as I ran to the edge and simply jumped out into space.

I started to fall toward the road.

Then I unfurled my wings, fast, catching the wind.

And I began to fly.

7

You see, that nightmare I had is actually hard to tell apart from my real life. My friends and I really did used to live at a stinking cesspool of evil called the School. We were created by scientists, whitecoats, who grafted avian DNA onto our human genes. Jeb had been a whitecoat, but he'd felt sorry for us, cared about us, and kidnapped us away from there.

We were bird kids, a flock of six. And the Erasers wanted to kill us. Now they had six-year-old Angel.

I gave a strong push down and then up, feeling my shoulder muscles working to move my thirteen-foot wingspan.

I banked sharply, heading after the Humvee. A quick glance back revealed that Nudge had jumped out after me, then Iggy, the Gasman, and Fang. In tight formation, we swerved down toward the car. Fang snatched a dead branch off a tree. He dropped straight down and smashed it against the Humvee's front windshield.

The vehicle swerved, a window rolled down. A gun barrel poked out. Around me, trees started popping with bullets. The smell of hot metal and gun smoke filled the air.

I looped back into the tree line, still tracking the car. Fang smashed the windshield again. Bullets spit from several windows. Fang wisely surged away.

"Angel!" I screamed. "We're here! We're coming for you!"

"Up ahead," called Fang, and I saw a clearing maybe two hundred yards away. Through the trees, I could barely see the greenish outline of a chopper. The Humvee was bouncing heavily over the rutted road. I met Fang's eyes, and he nodded. Our chance was when they moved Angel from the car to the chopper.

It all happened so fast, though. The Humvee braked awkwardly, sliding in the mud. The door burst open, and an Eraser sprang out. Fang dropped on him, then recoiled with a yell, his arm dripping blood. The Eraser sped toward the chopper, throwing himself through the open hatch. A second Eraser, showing his huge yellow canine teeth, leaped from the car and hurled something into the air. Shouting, Nudge grabbed Iggy's hand and they pulled backward fast as a grenade exploded in front of them, spewing chunks of metal and tree bark everywhere.

The chopper's rotor was picking up speed, and I shot out from behind the trees. They were *not* going to get my baby. They were *not* taking her back to that place.

Ari jumped out of the car, carrying the sack with Angel in it.

I tore toward the chopper, fear and desperate anger making my blood sing. Ari threw Angel's sack through the open door. He jumped in behind, an incredible athlete himself.

With a furious roar, I sprang up and caught hold of the chopper's landing skid just as it took off. The metal was hot from the sun and too wide to hold. I hooked one arm over it, trying to steady myself.

The massive downdraft from the rotors almost snapped my wings in half. I pulled them in, and the Erasers laughed, pointing at me as they closed the glass hatch. Ari was right there. He picked up a rifle and aimed it at me.

"Let me tell you a secret, old pal, old chap," Ari yelled at me. "You've got it all wrong. *We're the good guys!*"

"Angel," I whispered, near tears. Ari's claw tightened on the trigger. *He would do it.* And dead, I would be no use to anybody.

My heart breaking, I let go, falling fast, just as I saw a small, tousled blond head shake itself free of the sack.

My baby, flying away toward her death.

And, trust me on this, things much worse than death.

8

We all have great vision — raptor vision. So we had the excruciating pain of watching the helicopter take Angel away for much longer than the average person. My throat closed with a sob. Angel, whom I had cared for since she was a baby with goofy chicken wings. I felt like they had chopped my own right wing off, leaving a ragged, gaping wound.

"They have my sister!" the Gasman howled, throwing himself down. He always tried so hard to be a tough guy, but he was only eight, and he'd just seen his sister kidnapped by the hounds of hell. He pounded the dirt with his fists, and Fang knelt next to him, one arm tenderly around his shoulder.

"Max, what are we gonna do?" Nudge's eyes were swimming with tears. She was bruised and bloody, her fists clenching and unclenching anxiously. "They have *Angel.*"

Suddenly I knew I was going to implode. Without a word, I pushed off from the ground, wings out, taking off as fast as I could.

I flew out of sight, out of the others' hearing. Ahead was

a huge Douglas fir, and I landed ungracefully on one of its upper branches, maybe 175 feet in the air, scrabbling to catch hold because I'd overshot. Gasping, I clung to the limb.

Okay, Max, think. Think! Fix this! Figure something out.

My brain was flooded with too much thought, emotion, confusion, rage, pain. I needed to get a grip.

But I couldn't get a grip.

It was like I had just lost my little sister.

And like I had lost my little girl.

"Oh, God, *Angel, Angel, Angel!*"

Yelling as loud as I could, I made fists and punched the chunky bark of the fir tree hard, over and over, until finally actual pain seeped into my seared consciousness. I stared at my knuckles, saw the blood, the missing skin, the splinters.

The physical pain hurt much less than the mental kind.

My Angel, my baby, had been snatched away. She was with bloodthirsty man-wolf mutants eager for her blood who would turn her over to despicable lab geeks who wanted to take her apart. *Literally.*

Then I was crying, clinging to the tree as if it were a lifeboat from the *Titanic,* and I sobbed and sobbed until I thought I'd make myself sick. Gradually, the sobs slowed to shudders, and I wiped my face on my shirt, leaving streaks of blood.

I sat in the tree until my breathing calmed and my brain seemed to be hitting on most cylinders again. My hands were killing me, though. *Note to self: Stop punching inan-imate objects.*

Okay. It was time to go down and be strong, to get everyone together, to come up with Plan B.

And one other thing — Ari's last words were still screaming in my brain: *We're the good guys.*

9

I don't even remember flying home. I felt heartbroken and numb, and when we walked into the kitchen, the first thing I saw was Angel's breakfast plate on the table.

Iggy howled and swept his hand across the kitchen counter, catapulting a mug through the air. It hit Fang in the side of the head.

"Watch it, idiot!" he yelled at Iggy furiously. Then he realized what he'd said, clenched his teeth, and rolled his eyes at me in frustration.

Tears were streaming down my cheeks, their salt stinging where the Eraser had raked me with his claws. Moving automatically, I got the first aid kit and started cleaning the Gasman's scrapes and cuts. I looked around. Nudge's cheek was bleeding; some shrapnel had burned her as it flew past. For once she wasn't talking — she was curled on the couch, crying.

The Gasman glanced up at me.

How'd you let this happen, Max?

I was asking myself the same question.

True, I'm the leader, I'm Max the Invincible — but I'm

also just a fourteen-year-old kid. And every once in a while, like when I realize all over again that Jeb is gone forever, that we're on our own, that the others depend on me and I can't let them down, well, that's when it all gets to me. Suddenly, I'm a little kid again, wishing Jeb were back — or even, hey, wishing I was *normal!* Or had *parents!*

Yeah, right.

"*You* watch it!" Iggy shouted at Fang. "What *happened?* I mean, you guys can *see*, can't you? Why couldn't you get Angel?"

"They had a chopper!" the Gasman yelled, squirming out of my reach. "And guns! We're not *bulletproof!*"

"Guys! Guys!" I yelled. "We're all upset. But *we're* not the enemy! *They're* the enemy."

I stuck the last Band-Aid on the Gasman and started pacing. "Just — be quiet for a minute so I can think," I added more calmly. It wasn't their fault our rescue mission had been such a total ditcher. It wasn't their fault Angel was gone.

It *was* their fault that the kitchen looked like it belonged to a family of hygiene-challenged jackals, but I would deal with that later. Whenever that kind of thing became important again. If ever.

Iggy moved to the couch and almost sat on Nudge. She scooted to one side, and when he sat down, she put her head on his shoulder. He stroked her hair.

"Take deep breaths," the Gasman advised me, looking concerned. I almost burst into tears again. I had let his sister get kidnapped, failed to save her, and he was worried about *me.*

Fang was darkly silent. His eyes watched me as he opened a can of ravioli and picked up a fork with a heavily bandaged hand.

"You know, if they just wanted to kill her, or kill all of us, they could have," Nudge said shakily. "They had *guns.* They wanted Angel *alive* for some reason. And they didn't care if *we* were alive or not. I mean, they didn't go out of their way to make *sure* we were dead, is what I'm saying. So that makes me think we have time to go after Angel again."

"But they were in a chopper," said the Gasman. "They're way gone. They could be anywhere." His lower lip trembled, and he clenched his jaw. "Like, China or something."

I went over and ruffled his already ruffled blond hair. "I don't think they took her to China, Gazzy."

"We know where they took her." Fang's calm words fell like stones. He scraped the bottom of the can with his fork.

"Where's that?" Iggy asked, raising his head, his blind eyes bloodshot with unshed tears.

"The School," Fang and I said at the same time.

Well, as you can imagine, that went over like a ton of freaking bricks.

10

Nudge gasped, her hand over her mouth, her eyes wide.

The Gasman looked scared, then tried to wipe it off his face.

Iggy's spine tightened, his face like ice. When he'd been at the School, they'd tried to surgically enhance his night vision. Now he was blind forever. Oops.

"They took Angel back to the School?" the Gasman asked, confused.

"I think so," I said, trying to sound together and leaderly. As if I weren't screaming with panic inside.

"Why?" Nudge whispered. "After four years, I thought maybe they had forgotten —"

"They want us back," said Fang.

We'd never really talked about this. It was like, out of sight, out of mind. Actually, more like, let's all try to forget when we were at the mercy of sadistic spawns of Satan in a place that's a total, hellish abomination and ought to be firebombed. Yeah, more like that.

"They'll never forget about us. Jeb wasn't supposed to take us out of there," I reminded the Gasman.

"Jeb knew they would do anything to get us back. If anyone ever discovered what they did to us, it would be the end of the School," Fang explained.

"Why don't we tell on them, then?" Nudge demanded. "We could go to a TV station and tell everyone and say, Look, they grew wings on us, and we're just little kids, and —"

"Okay, that would fix *them*," Iggy interrupted. "But *we'd* end up in a zoo."

"Well, what are we gonna do, then?" The Gasman was starting to sound panicky.

Fang had gotten up and left the room, and now he returned, holding a sheaf of yellowed, fading papers. The edges looked nibbled, and he shook some mouse poop off.

"Eew," said Nudge, wiping her nose on her sleeve. "Eew. Was that —"

"Here," said Fang, pushing the papers at me.

They were Jeb's ancient printed-out files. After he disappeared, we'd cleared off his desk and shoved everything in the back of a closet so we wouldn't have to look at it all the time.

We spread the papers out on the kitchen table. Just looking at them made the hairs on the back of my neck stand up. Not to mention the strong eau de mouse. I'd rather have been doing anything but.

Fang started to sift through the pile. He found a large manila envelope, sealed with a clump of wax. After looking at me, catching my nod, he popped the wax with his thumbnail.

31

JAMES PATTERSON

"What is that?" asked the Gasman.

"Map," Fang said, pulling out a faded topographical drawing.

"Map of what?" Nudge leaned closer, peering over Fang's shoulder.

"Map of a secret facility," I said, feeling my stomach clench. I'd hoped I'd never have to see it again, never break that wax seal. "In California. The School."

11

"Whaaat?" the Gasman squeaked.

Iggy went even paler than normal, if possible.

"That's where they took Angel," I said. "And that's where we have to go to get her back."

"Oh," said Nudge, her brain hitting overdrive. "Yeah. We have to go get Angel back. We can't let her stay there — with them. They're — monsters. They're going to do bad things to her. And put her in a cage. Hurt her. But there's five of us. So the rest of us have to go get *hmph* —"

I had wrapped my hand across her mouth. She peeled my fingers apart. "Uh, how far is it?"

"Six hundred miles, more or less," Fang said. "At least a seven-hour flight, not including breaks."

"Can we *discuss* this?" Iggy asked, not turning his head. "We're way outnumbered."

"No." I scanned the map, already working out routes, rest stops, backup plans.

"Can we take a vote? They had *guns*. And a chopper." There was an edge in Iggy's voice.

"Iggy. This is not a democracy," I said, understanding

his fear but unable to do anything about it. "It's a Maxocracy. You know we have to go after Angel. You can't be thinking that we would just let them take her. The six of us look out for one another — no matter what. None of us is ever going to live in a cage again, not while I'm alive." I took a deep breath.

"But actually, Nudge, Fang, and I are going after Angel. You and the Gasman — I need you to stay here. Hold down the fort. On the off chance Angel escapes and makes her way home."

There was a moment of dead silence.

"You are so full of it," said Iggy, turning toward me. "That's not why you want us here. Why don't you just say it?"

Tension was making my stomach hurt. I didn't have time for this. No — *Angel* didn't have time for this.

"Okay," I said, trying for a placating tone. "It's true. I don't want you to come. The fact is, you're *blind,* and while you're a great flyer around here where you know everything, I can't be worrying about you in the middle of a firefight with the Erasers."

Iggy's face twisted in anger. He opened his mouth but got cut off.

"What about *me?*" the Gasman squealed. "I don't *care* if they have guns and a chopper and Erasers. She's *my* sister."

"That's right. And if they want her so bad, they might want *you* just as bad," I pointed out. "Plus, you're a great flyer, but you're eight years old, and we're going to be logging major hours."

"Jeb would never have made us stay," Iggy said angrily. "Never. Ever."

I pressed my lips together. I was doing the best I could. "Maybe not," I admitted. "We'll never know. Jeb's dead. Now everyone get your gear together."

PART 2

HOTEL CALIFORNIA, SORT OF

12

"We clear on Plan B?" I asked, raising my voice so Fang and Nudge could hear me over the roar of the wind.

We were headed into the sun, south-southwest. Leaving the Sangre de Cristo Mountains behind, streaking through the sky at a steady ninety miles per hour. If we hit a nice air current, we could add twenty miles per hour to our speed. The glory of flight.

Fang nodded. *God, is he ever the strong and silent type.*

"Uh-huh," said Nudge. "If we get separated somehow — though I don't see how we could, unless maybe one of us gets lost in a cloud or something — do you think that could happen? I haven't ever been inside a cloud. I bet it's creepy. Can you see anything inside a cloud —"

I shot her a look. She paused, then quickly finished, "We meet up at the northmost point of Lake Mead."

I nodded. "And where's the School?"

"In Death Valley, eight miles due north from the Badwater Basin." Her mouth opened to add more, but I raised my eyebrows at her. I love Nudge, Nudge is a great kid, but that motormouth of hers could have turned Mother Teresa into an ax murderer.

"You got it," I said. "Good job." Did you hear that address? Could the School be located in a more perfect place? *Death Valley.* Above the *Badwater Basin.* Like, when we got there, we'd see a road paved with good intentions and have to cross the river Styx to get in. Wouldn't surprise me.

The wind was undoing my braid, and chunks of long hair whipped annoyingly across my face. *Note to self: Cut hair short.*

The Gasman and Iggy had been none-too-happy campers when we'd left, but I thought I'd made the right decision. That was the problem with this leader stuff. It didn't come with an instruction manual. Given what Angel was facing, their being unhappy was the least of my concerns.

I glanced over at Fang and saw that his face looked serene, almost — well, not exactly *happy,* Fang's never happy — but just really calm. I edged closer to him.

"On the plus side, flying is just really, really cool," I said, and he looked at me with a half smile of understanding. His dark wings moved powerfully, glinting faintly purple in the sunlight. The wind was whistling in our ears; we could see everything for miles. It was like being God. I imagine.

Oh, yeah. "On the minus side, we're mutant freaks who will never live a normal life."

Fang shrugged. "Win some, lose some."

I was too upset to laugh but gave a wry smile and looked over at Nudge. She was three years younger than us but was holding her own. Like all of us, she was tall for her age, and skinny, probably weighing no more than sixty pounds, thanks to her strong, light bird bones.

Ninety miles an hour wasn't fast enough. The "scientists" at the School could do a lot of damage in seven hours. Even so, I knew we'd have to take a break before we got there. If we were going to hit the School, we'd need to be rested, not hungry.

I checked my watch — we'd been skyborne for a good two hours. I was already feeling empty, a little shaky. Flying burned energy like nothing else, and after a long flight, I felt like I could eat a cow. Fork optional. Even needing to get to Angel, we couldn't forget the basic necessity of eating.

"Max?" Nudge's big eyes, the same tawny russet as her wings, looked over at me. "I was thinking —"

Here we go.

"I mean, right before we left? I just looked at Jeb's old files, you know? And some of them were about us. Or me. I saw my name on a page, my real name, Monique, and then, like, some people's names, and then — Tipisco, Arizona. Tipisco is right on the Arizona-California border — I found it on the map. Real tiny town, it looked like. Anyway, I was thinking, none of us ever knew our real parents, and, you know, we've always wondered, or at least I mean I've always wondered, but I guess the rest of you have too, like, whether they gave me up voluntarily or whether —"

JAMES PATTERSON

"Nudge. I know how you feel. But those names might not have anything to do with you. We don't know if we were just test-tube babies or what. Please. Let's focus on rescuing Angel."

No response.

"Nudge?"

"Yeah, okay. I was just thinking."

I knew this one was going to come back and bite me in the butt.

13

Her mouth was so dry. Her head ached — everything ached. Angel blinked several times, trying to wake up. Above her was a dark brown plastic roof. A cage. A dog crate. A Kanine Kamper, size medium. Fuzzy thoughts pushed at her brain as she struggled to a sitting position. She knew where she was — she would recognize that chemical, disinfectant smell anywhere. She was at the School.

`New new 'n' wings and new new wings`
`girl new`

Quickly, Angel turned in the direction of the thoughts.

In a crate next to hers were two other children, younger than she. Their eyes, too big for their hungry faces, locked onto her.

"Hi," Angel whispered. She didn't feel any whitecoats around — just the scrambled, incoherent thoughts of these kids.

`Mouth noise girl wings new new`

The other children stared without answering. Trying to smile, Angel looked at them more closely. She thought they were both boys. One had rough, scaly skin — literally *scaly,* like a fish, but just in patches, not all over. Not a happy effect.

The other one just looked like . . . a mistake. He had extra fingers and toes, and hardly any neck. His eyes were huge and bulging, and the hair on his head was sparse. It made Angel's heart hurt just to look at him.

"I'm Angel," she whispered again. "Do you have names?"

`Noise noise bad girl wings bad noise`

The two boys looked afraid, and they turned from her and edged farther back in their cage.

Angel swallowed hard and was quiet. What had happened to Max and the others? Were they in cages too?

A door opened and footsteps sounded on the linoleum floor. Angel felt the caged boys trembling with dread, crazed, swirling thoughts of fear crashing in their brains. They huddled together at the back of their cage. But the two whitecoats stopped in front of Angel's.

"Oh, my God — Harrison was right," one whitecoat said, hunching down to stare at Angel through the grate. "They got her! Do you know how long I've wanted to get my hands on this one?" He turned excitedly to the other whitecoat. "Did you ever read the Director's precept report about this recombinant group?"

"Yeah, but I wasn't sure I believed it," said the other whitecoat, a woman. "Are you saying this is Subject Eleven? This little girl?"

The first whitecoat rubbed his hands together with glee. "You're looking at it." He leaned forward to unhook her cage door. "Come on, little thing. You're wanted in lab seven." Oh, *yes!* Man, when I section her brain . . .

Angel winced, then rough hands dragged her out.

Pathetic relief washed through the boys that it was she who was being taken and not them.

Angel didn't blame them one bit.

14

"Max? I'm starving."

I had been ignoring my own ferociously growling innards for half an hour. There was no way I was going to break first — and give Fang the satisfaction? I don't think so. But I did have an obligation, as leader, to take care of Nudge. As much as I hated to stop and lose time, it was a reality.

"Okay, okay. We need food." How's that for incisive leadership? "Fang! We need to refuel. Ideas?"

Fang pondered. It always amazes me how he's able to seem so calm at the absolute worst times. Sometimes he seems like a droid — or a drone. Fang of Nine. Fang2-D2.

Below us were mountains — the San Francisco Peaks, according to our map.

Our glances met — it was creepy how we knew what each other was thinking so much of the time. "Ski slopes," I said, and he nodded. "Summertime. Empty vacation houses."

"Would they have *food*?" Nudge asked.

"Let's go find out," I said.

We flew in a big circle around the edge of the mountains. Small towns that came alive in winter dotted the foothills. I led us away from them, to where a few homes stood like train-set models among the trees. One house was apart from the others. No cars parked outside, no smoke coming from the chimney. Nobody home?

I banked and slowed, tucked my wings in a bit, and started to drop.

We landed a hundred yards away. As usual, after flying for hours, my legs felt a tad rubbery. I shook them out, then folded my warm wings in tight against my body.

Nudge and Fang did the same.

We crept quietly through the woods. No signs of life. The porch was covered with pine needles, the driveway hadn't been used, the shrubbery was way overgrown.

I gave Nudge the thumbs-up, and she smiled, though, amazingly, she stayed quiet. *Bless you, child.*

A quick reconnaissance revealed no alarm system I could see. No red lights blinking inside for motion detectors. This wasn't a big fancy house worth alarming, anyway. It was just a teeny-tiny vacation cottage.

With my pocketknife I slit a window screen and unhooked the latch. The screen lifted off easily, and I set it carefully against the side of the house: A thoughtful burglar, that's me.

Then Fang and I shook the old wooden window frame

until the lock at the top jiggled open. Fang climbed in first, then I boosted Nudge in, then I scrambled in and shut the window.

Dust covered everything. The fridge was turned off, its door open. I started opening kitchen cupboards. "Bingo," I said, holding up a dusty can of soup.

"Oh, yeah, pay dirt, woo-hoo!" Cans of beans, fruit, condensed milk, whatever that was — it sounded bad. The ever-popular ravioli. "We're golden!"

Fang found some dusty bottles of orange soda, and we popped those suckers open. But let me tell you — there's a reason people serve that stuff cold.

Half an hour later, we were sprawled on the musty couches, our eyes at half-mast, our bellies way too full.

"Uhhnnhh," Nudge moaned. "I feel like, like *concrete*."

"Let's take ten, rest a bit," Fang said, closing his eyes. He lay back against the couch and crossed his long legs. "Digest a minute, we'll feel better."

"I second that emotion," I muttered, my own eyes closing. *We're coming, Angel. In a minute.*

15

"Let's throw all their stuff into the canyon," Iggy said angrily, punching a door frame.

Having to listen to the rest of the flock leaving while *he* sat around being *blind* was more than he could stand. "I think even their beds would fit out the hall window."

The Gasman scowled. "I can't believe *I* have to stay home while they go off and save my own sister."

He kicked a worn red sneaker against the kitchen island. The house seemed empty and too quiet. He found himself listening for Angel's voice, waiting to hear her singing softly or talking to her stuffed animals. He swallowed hard. She was his sister. He was responsible for her.

An open bag of cereal lay on the counter, and he dug out a dry handful and ate it. Suddenly, he picked up the bag of cereal and hurled it at a wall. The bag split open, and Frootios sprayed everywhere.

"This *sucks!*" the Gasman shouted.

"Oh, did that just occur to you?" Iggy said sarcastically. "I guess you can't fool the Gasman. He might not *look* like the sharpest tool in the shed, but —"

"Shut *up*," said the Gasman, and Iggy raised his eyebrows in surprise. "Look. This sucks so bad. Max left us here 'cause she thought we couldn't keep up."

Iggy's face stiffened.

"But was she thinking about what would happen if the Erasers came back here?" the Gasman asked. "Like, they got Angel not far from here — they *saw* all the rest of us. So they know we must be somewhere in the area. Why wouldn't they come back for us?"

"Huh," Iggy said thoughtfully. "Course, it would be hard to find this place, and even harder to get to it."

"Not if they have a chopper," the Gasman pointed out. "Which they do."

"Huh," said Iggy, and the Gasman felt proud that he had thought of all this before Iggy had, even though Iggy was older — as old as Max and Fang. Nearly ancient.

"Does that mean we have to sit here and take it?" the Gasman asked, pounding his fist on the counter. "No! We don't have to wait for the Erasers to come get *us!* We can do stuff! We can make *plans.* I mean, we're not useless, no matter what Max thinks."

"Right," said Iggy, nodding. He came to sit next to the Gasman at the counter, his feet crunching over dry cereal. "Yeah, I see what you mean. So to speak."

"I mean, we're smart! We're tough as nails! Max might not have thought about keeping the camp safe, but we did, and we can do it."

"Yeah, now you're talking. Uhhh . . . But how?"

"We could make traps! Do sabotage! Bombs!" The Gasman rubbed his hands together.

Iggy grinned. "Bombs are good. I love bombs. Remember the one from last fall? I almost caused an avalanche."

"That was to make a trail through the woods. Okay. There was a reason for it. Max approved it." The Gasman pawed through a hill of ancient newspapers, piles of junk, someone's old socks, a long-forgotten bowl that had once held some sort of food substance — oops — until he found a slightly oil-stained memo pad.

"Knew it was around here," he muttered, ripping off used sheets. A similar search revealed part of a pencil. "Now. We need a great plan. What are our objectives?"

Iggy groaned. "Oh, no — years of Max influence are taking their toll. You sound just like her. You're, like, a Maxlet. A Maxketeer. A . . . a . . ."

The Gasman frowned at Iggy and started writing. "Number one: Make firebombs — for our *protection* only. Number two: Blow up demonic Erasers when they return." He held the paper up and reread it, then smiled. "Oh, yeah. Now we're getting somewhere. *This is for you, Angel!*"

16

Angel knew she couldn't go on like this much longer.

Her lungs had started burning bad an hour ago; she hadn't been able to feel her leg muscles for longer than that. But every time she stopped running, a sadistic white-coat — Reilly — zapped her with a stick thing. It jolted electricity into her, making her yelp and jump. She had four burn marks from it already, and they really, really hurt. What was worse was she could feel his eager antici-pation — he *wanted* to hurt her.

Well, he could zap her a thousand million times, if he wanted. This was it — she couldn't go on.

It was a relief to let go. Angel saw the whole world nar-row down to a little fuzzy tube in front of her, and then even that went gray. She sort of felt herself falling, felt her feet tangle in the treadmill belt. The zap came, once, twice, three times, but it felt distant, more an unpleasant stinging than real pain. Then Angel was lost, lost in a dream, and Max was there. Max was stroking her sweaty hair and crying.

Angel knew it was a dream because Max *never* cried.

Max was the strongest person she knew. Not that she had known that many people.

Ripping sounds and a new, searing pain on her skin pulled Angel back. She blinked into white lights. Hospital lights, prison lights. She smelled that awful smell and almost retched. Hands were pulling off all the electrodes taped to her skin, *rip, rip, rip.*

"Oh, my God, three and a half hours," Reilly was murmuring. "And its heart rate only increased by seventeen percent. And then at the end — it was only in the last, like, twenty minutes that its peak oxygen levels broke."

It! Angel thought and wanted to scream. *I'm not an it!*

"I can't believe we've got a chance to study Subject Eleven. I've been wanting to dissect this recombinant for four years," another low voice said. "Interesting intelligence levels — I can't wait to get a brain sample."

Angel felt their admiration, their crummy pleasure. They liked all the things *wrong* with her, all the ways she *wasn't* normal. And all those stupid long words added up to one thing: *Angel was an experiment.* To the whitecoats, she was a piece of science equipment, like a test tube. She was an *it.*

Someone put a straw into her mouth. Water. She started swallowing quick — she was so thirsty, like she'd been eating sand. Then another whitecoat scooped her up. She was too tired to fight.

I have to think of how to get out of here, she reminded

herself, but thoughts were really hard to string together right now.

Someone opened the door of her dog crate and flopped her inside. Angel lay where she fell — at least she was lying down. She just had to sleep for a while. Then she would try to escape.

Wearily, she blinked and saw the fish boy staring at her. The other boy was gone. Poor little guy had been gone this morning, hadn't come back. Might not.

Not me, Angel thought. *I'm gonna fight. Right . . . after . . . I . . . rest.*

17

"Unhhh . . ."

This bed was horrible! What was wrong with my bed?

Irritated, I punched my pillow into a better shape, then started sneezing hysterically as clouds of dust sailed up my nose.

"Wah, ah, ah, choo!" I grabbed my nose in an attempt to keep some of my brains inside my head, but the sudden movement caused me to lose my balance, and with no warning I fell hard to the floor. *Crash!*

"Ouch! Son of a gu —" I scrambled to get up. My hands hit rough upholstery and the edge of a table. Okay, now I was lost. Prying open my bleary eyes, I peered around. "What the . . ."

Where was I? I looked around wildly. I was in a . . . cabin. A cabin! Ohhh. A cabin. Right, right.

It was oh-dark-thirty — not yet dawn.

I leaped to my feet, scanned the room, and saw nothing to be alarmed about. Except for the fact that obviously, Fang, Nudge, and I had just wasted precious hours sleeping!

Oh, my God. I hurried over to Nudge, who was sprawled across a recliner. "Nudge! Nudge! Wake up! Oh, man . . ."

I turned to Fang, to find him swinging his feet over the edge of a couch. He sneezed and shook his head.

"What time is it?" he asked calmly.

"Almost morning!" I said, terribly upset. *"Of the next day!"*

He was already moving toward the kitchen cupboards. He'd found an ancient, stained backpack in a closet, and now he methodically started to fill it with cans of tuna, sealed bags of crackers, zip-locked bags of trail mix.

"Wha's happ'nin'?" Nudge asked, blinking groggily.

"We fell asleep!" I told her, grabbing her hands and pulling her upright. "Come on! We've gotta go!"

Dropping to all fours, I raked my shoes out from under the couch and blew dust bunnies off them. "Fang, you can't carry all that," I said. "It'll weigh you down. Nothing's heavier than cans."

Fang shrugged and pulled the backpack on. Stubborn kind of fella. He moved soundlessly across the room and slipped through the window like a shadow.

Now I was jamming Nudge's shoes onto her feet, rubbing her back, trying to wake her up. Nudge was always a reaaallly slow waker. Usually I appreciated the lack of word-spew, which would begin when she was fully functioning, but right now we needed to *move, move, move!*

I practically threw Nudge through the window,

slithered out myself, then propped the screen back in place as best I could.

A quick run down a country road and we were off, stroking hard, pushing to get airborne.

Sorry, Angel. Sorry, sorry, sorry, my baby.

18

Okay. Despite the imminent sunrise, I felt better once we were flying above the treetops.

But still! How stupid was that? What kind of a loser was I, to let us fall asleep in the middle of a freaking *rescue!* I thought about Angel waiting for us, and my heart clenched. With a sense of dread, I banked and set us going about ten, twelve degrees southwest. Anxiety fueled my wings, and I had to remember to find good air currents, set my wings at an angle, and coast when I could.

"We *had* to rest," Fang said, coming up beside me.

I shot him an upset glance. "For ten *hours?*"

"Today we've got another four hours to go, maybe a bit more," he said. "We couldn't have done it in one shot. It was late when we left. We're going to have to stop again anyway, right before we get there, and refuel."

There's nothing more annoying than cold logic and reason when you've got a good fit going.

Fang was right, of course — sigh — and of course we'd have to stop again. We hadn't even hit the California border yet. Far from it.

"We going to storm the place or what?" Fang asked an hour later.

"Yeah, Max, I was wondering what your plan was," said Nudge, coming up alongside. "I mean, there's only three of us, and a whole bunch of them. And the Erasers have guns. Could we, like, drive a truck through the gates? Or even into a building? Or maybe we could wait till nightfall, sneak in, and sneak out with Angel before anyone notices us."

That crazy thought cheered her up. I kept silent — I didn't have the heart to tell her we had about as much chance of that as we did of flying to the moon. But if worse came to worst, I had a secret Plan C. If it worked, everyone would escape and get free. Except me. But that was okay.

19

Despite my growing anxiety, it was glorious up here. Not many birds flew this high — some falcons, hawks, other raptors. Every once in a while some of them would come check us out, probably thinking, *Man, those are some dang ugly birds.*

This high up, the land below took on a checkerboard effect of Robin Hoodsy greens and browns. Cars looked like busy ants moving purposefully down their trails. Every once in a while I picked something small down below and focused on it. It was cool how some little tiny thing, like a swimming pool, a tractor, whatever, would ratchet into focus. At least those maniacs at the School hadn't had time to "improve" my vision like they improved Iggy's.

"Gosh, I wonder what Iggy and the Gasman are doing now?" Nudge babbled. "Maybe they got the TV working again. I hope they don't feel too bad. It would have — I mean, I guess it's kind of easier for them to be home. But I bet they're not cleaning up or getting wood or doing any of their chores."

I bet they're cursing my name from dawn to dusk. But at least they're safe. Absently, I chose a flickering shape below and focused on it, watching a small blob become people, take on features, clothing, individuality. It was a group of kids, maybe my age, maybe older. Who couldn't be more unlike me.

Well, so *what?* I thought. They were just boring kids, stuck on the ground, doing homework. With bedtimes and a million grown-ups telling them what to do, how to do everything, all the time. Alarm clocks and school and afternoon jobs. Those poor saps. While we were *free, free, free.* Soaring through the air like rockets. Being cradled by breezes. Doing whatever we wanted, whenever we wanted.

Pretty good, huh? I almost convinced myself.

I glanced down again and refocused. Then I scowled. What had, at first glance, looked like just a bunch of boring, earthbound kids schlepping to school together now turned, upon closer examination, into what looked like several big kids surrounding a much smaller kid. Okay, maybe I'm paranoid, *danger everywhere,* but I could swear the bigger kids looked really threatening.

The bigger kids were boys. The smaller kid in the middle was a girl.

Coincidence? I think not.

Don't even get me started about the whole Y chromosome thing. I live with three guys, remember? They're three of the *good* ones, and they're still obnoxious as all get-out.

I made one of my famous snap decisions, the kind that everyone remembers later for being either the stupidest dumb-butt thing they ever saw or else the miraculous saving of the day. I seemed to hear more about the first kind. That's gratitude for you.

I turned to Fang and barely opened my mouth.

"No," he said.

My eyes narrowed. I opened my mouth again.

"No."

"Meet me at the northernmost point of Lake Mead," I said.

"What? What are you talking about?" Nudge asked. "Are we stopping? I'm hungry again."

"Max wants to go be Supergirl, defender of the weak," Fang said, sounding irritated.

"Oh." Nudge looked down, frowning at the ground as if it would all become clear soon.

I had started a wide circle that would take me back toward the girl below. I kept thinking, *What if that girl was in trouble, like Angel, and no one stopped to help her?*

"Oh! Max, remember when you got that little rabbit away from the fox, and we kept it in a carton in the kitchen, and then when it was well you let it go? That was cool." Nudge paused. "Did you see another rabbit?"

"Kind of," I said, my patience starting to wear thin. "It'll take two seconds."

I told Fang, "I'll catch up with you guys before you've

gone forty miles. Just keep on course, and if anything weird happens, I'll meet you at Lake Mead."

Fang stared ahead, the wind whipping through his hair. He hated this, I knew.

Well, you can't please everybody *all* the time.

"Okay," I said briskly. "See you in a few."

20

The thing about Iggy was, well, sometimes he could figure stuff out like a real scientist. He was that supersmart, scary smart.

"Do we have any chlorine?" the Gasman asked Iggy. "It seems to be kind of explosive when mixed with other stuff."

Iggy frowned. "Like what, your socks? No, we don't have chlorine. No swimming pool. What color is this wire?"

The Gasman leaned over and examined the tangled pile of stereo guts spread out on the kitchen table. "It looks like a robot came in here and threw up," he observed. "That wire's yellow."

"Okay. Keep track of the yellow wire. Very important. Do not confuse it with the red one."

The Gasman consulted the schematics he had downloaded off the Internet. This morning Iggy had unfrozen the compressor fan inside the CPU, so the computer now worked without shutting down in hysteria every ten minutes. He had just *fixed* the computer, presto change-o.

"Okey dokey," Gazzy muttered, flipping through pages. "Next step, we need some kind of timing device."

Iggy thought for a moment. Then he smiled. Even his eyes seemed to smile.

"Well, *that's* an evil grin," Gasser said uneasily.

"Go get me Max's alarm clock. The Mickey Mouse one."

21

I landed a bit hard and had to run really fast to keep from doing a total face plant. I was somewhere in Arizona, trotting through scrubby brush behind a deserted warehouse. I pulled my wings in, feeling them fold, hot from exercise, into a tight accordion on either side of my spine. I tied my windbreaker around my neck. *There. Perfectly normal looking.*

When I rounded the corner of the warehouse, I saw that there were three guys, maybe fifteen, sixteen years old. The girl looked younger, maybe twelve or so.

"I told you not to tell anybody about my little situation with Ortiz," one boy was yelling at her. "It was none of your business. I had to teach him a lesson."

The girl bit her lip, looking angry and scared. "By beating him up? He looks like he got hit by a car. And he didn't do anything to you," she said, and I thought, *You go, girl.*

"He mouthed off to me. He exists. He breathes my air," said the guy, and his jerk friends laughed meanly. God, what creeps. *Armed* creeps. One of them was holding a shotgun loosely in the crook of his arm. America, right to bear arms, yada, yada, yada. How old were these yahoos? Did their parents know they had guns?

It gets so tiring, this strong-picking-on-the-weak stuff. It was the story of my life — literally — and it seemed to be a big part of the outside world too. I was sick of it, sick of guys like these, stupid and bullying.

I stepped out from beside the building. The girl saw me, and her eyes flicked in surprise. It was enough. The guys wheeled to look behind them.

Just another stupid girl, they thought, relieved. Their eyes lingered a moment on my scratched face, my black eye, but they didn't keep watching me. Mistake number one.

"So, Ella, what have you got to say for yourself?" the lead guy taunted. "Is there any reason I shouldn't teach you a lesson too?"

"Three guys against one girl. That seems about even," I said, striding up. It was hard to keep the fury off my face. My blood was singing with it.

"Shut up, *chick,*" one of the boys snapped. "You better get out of here if you know what's good for you."

"Can't," I said, walking to stand next to the girl named Ella. She looked at me in alarm. "Actually, I think kicking your stupid butts would be good for me."

They laughed. Mistake number two.

Like the rest of the flock, I'm much stronger than even a grown man — genetic engineering at work. And all of us had been trained in self-defense by Jeb. I had skills. Until yesterday, I'd never had to use them. If I could just get Ella out of here . . .

"Grab Big Mouth," said the head guy, and the other two moved to flank me.

Which made mistake number three. Bam, you're out.

I moved fast, fast, fast. With no warning, I snapped a high kick right into the lead jerk's chest. A blow that would have only knocked Fang's breath away actually seemed to snap a rib on this guy. I heard the crack, and the guy choked, looking shocked, and fell backward.

The remaining guys rushed me at once. I whirled and grabbed the shotgun out of one's hands. Holding its barrel, I swung it in a wide arc against the side of his head. Crack! Stunned, he staggered sideways as a bright red flow of blood streamed from his scalp.

I glanced over and saw Ella still standing there, looking afraid. I hoped not of me.

"Run!" I yelled at her. "Get out of here!" After a moment of hesitation, she turned and ran, leaving a little cloud of red dust behind her.

The third grabbed my arm, and I yanked it loose, then swung and punched him, aiming for his chin but hitting his nose. I winced — oops — feeling his nose break, and there was a slow-motion pause of about a second before it started gushing blood. Jeezum — humans were like eggshells.

The bullyboys were a mess. But still they staggered to their feet, rage and humiliation twisting their ugly faces.

One of them picked up his gun and cocked it, favoring his right arm.

"You're gonna be so sorry," he promised, spitting blood out of his mouth and starting toward me.

"Bet I won't," I said. Then I turned tail and raced for the woods as fast as I could.

22

Of course, if I could have taken off, I'd have been a little speck in the sky by then. But I couldn't let those yo-yos see my wings, and within seconds I was in the woods anyway.

I ran through the underbrush, smacking branches out of my way, glad I was wearing shoes. I had no idea where I was going.

Behind me I could hear a couple of the bozos yelling, swearing, threatening. I wanted to laugh but couldn't spare the time. I was steadily increasing the distance between us.

Then I heard a loud *bang!* from the shotgun, and tree bark exploded around my head. That stupid *gun.*

Are you thinking what I think you're thinking? Are you wondering if I noticed the similarities between this asinine situation and my dream? Well, *yeah.* I'm not an *idiot.* As to what it all meant, well, I'll work on that later.

In the next second, there was another bang, and almost simultaneously a sudden, searing pain in my left shoulder. I gasped and glanced over to see blood blossoming on my sleeve. That idiot had actually hit me!

Then sheer bad luck made me instantly trip over a tree root, fall on my hurt shoulder, and slide crazily down a steep slope, through bushes, underbrush, vines, and rocks. I tried to grab anything, but my left arm couldn't move well, and my right hand scrabbled uselessly.

Finally, I tumbled to a stop at the bottom of an overgrown ravine. Looking up, I saw only green: I was covered by vines and shrubs.

I lay very still, trying to catch my breath, trying to think. Far above me, I heard the wild boys yelling and shooting again. They sounded like elephants crashing through the woods, and I tracked them clearly as they ran right past where I fell.

I felt like an ogre had just beaten me all over with a club. I could barely move my left arm, and it hurt like fire. I tried to stretch out my wing, only to suck my breath in hard as I found out it had been hit too. I couldn't see it well over my shoulder, but my big clue was the screaming pain.

I was scraped all over, had lost my windbreaker, and, if I wasn't mistaken, I was sitting in a patch of poison ivy.

Slowly, I stood up, smothering gasps of pain. I had to get out of here. I checked the sun and started working my way north. I swallowed a groan as I realized that Nudge and Fang were no doubt wondering where the heck I was.

I had messed up big-time. Angel was waiting for me too — if she was still alive. I had let them all down.

On top of it, I was hurt pretty bad and had gun-toting maniacs after me. Crap.

I scowled. It's in my nature to fight for the underdog. Jeb had always told me it was my fatal flaw.

Jeb had been right.

23

"Fang? I'm really hungry, you know?" It had been almost an hour since Max had left them. Nudge still didn't understand exactly what had happened, where Max had gone.

Fang nodded curtly, then motioned with his head. Nudge banked slightly and followed him.

They were coming up on some cliffs, flat on top and made of striated rock. Fang headed toward a shadowy indentation, and Nudge started backpedaling to slow down for a landing. This close, the indentation turned into a broad, shallow cave, and Nudge ducked a bit as she set down inside.

Fang landed almost silently beside her.

The cave went maybe fifteen feet in and was about twenty feet wide, tapering at both ends. The floor was sandy and dry, and Nudge sat down thankfully.

Fang took off his backpack and started handing her food.

"Oh, yes, yes," Nudge said, ripping open a bag of dried fruit.

Fang waved a chocolate bar in front of her, and she squealed happily. "Oh, Fang, where did you find this? You must have been hiding it — you didn't say anything, and all this time you've had *chocolate,* and oh, God, it's so good . . ."

Fang gave her a little smile and sat down. He bit into his chocolate and closed his dark eyes for a few moments, chewing slowly.

"So where's Max?" Nudge asked a few minutes later. "Why'd she go down there? Shouldn't she be back by now? Aren't we supposed to go all the way to Lake Mead? What are we gonna do if she doesn't come back soon —" She stopped when Fang held up his hand.

"Max saw someone in trouble, down below, and went to help," he said in his quiet, deliberate voice. "We'll wait here for her; Lake Mead is right below us."

Nudge worried. Every second counted. So why were they stuck here? What was Max doing that was more important than Angel? She finished her last dried apricot and looked around.

Okay, now that Fang mentioned it, she could see the blue edge of Lake Mead off to her left. Nudge stood up; her head barely touched the ceiling. Their cave had a fairly wide ledge on either side of it, and she walked out on the left ledge to see the lake better.

She froze. "Uh, *Fang?*"

24

Fang came out next to Nudge, then stood perfectly still. The ledge curved upward toward the top of the cliff. Thin, scrubby plants dotted the area, and boulders stuck out of hard-packed clay and rock.

In and among the rocks and plants were large nests, each about two feet across. Most of the nests had large fuzzy fledglings in them, and most of the fledglings had larger rust-colored parents, and most of the parents were staring tensely at Nudge and Fang with cold predators' eyes.

"What are they?" Nudge whispered out the side of her mouth.

"Ferruginous hawks," Fang said softly. "Largest raptor in the States. Sit down, *very slowly*. No sudden movements or we're both bird feed."

Okaaaay, Nudge thought, gradually sinking to her knees. She wanted to turn and run but guessed if she did, she might be attacked. The few talons she could see looked lethal. Not to mention the severe beaks, sharply curved and mean looking.

"Do you think —" she began softly, but Fang motioned for her to be quiet, *very* quiet.

He lowered himself next to her, his eyes on the birds. One of the hawks had a partially dismembered gopher in its mouth. Its fledglings were squawking loudly for it.

After several minutes, Nudge felt like she needed to scream. She hated sitting still, had a million things to ask, didn't know how much longer she could take this inaction.

A small movement caught her eye. Fang was very slowly extending one of his wings.

Every hawk head swiveled in unison, their eyes focusing on the wing like lasers.

"I'm letting them catch my scent." Fang's lips barely moved.

What felt like a year later, the hawks seemed to relax a bit. They were huge, with an almost five-foot wingspan, and looked cold and powerful. On top, their wing feathers were mostly brown with russet streaks, and they were streaked with white below. Not unlike Nudge's own wings, except hers were so much bigger, twice as big.

Some hawks went back to feeding their noisy offspring, others left in search of food, still others returned with dinner.

"Eew," Nudge couldn't help whispering when one hawk brought back a still-wriggling snake. The fledglings were excited to see it and practically climbed over one another trying to get the first bite. "Double eew."

Fang turned his head slowly and grinned at her. Nudge was so surprised that she smiled back.

This *was* pretty cool. She was itchy to leave, wished Max would show up soon, and she wished they had more food, but all the same, it was pretty awesome to sit here in the sun, surrounded by huge, beautiful birds, her own wings stretched out and resting. She guessed it couldn't hurt to do this for a little bit longer.

25

But not that long.

"Angel's *waiting* for us," Nudge said a bit later. "I mean, she's like a little sister, like everyone's little sister."

She brushed some rock dust off her already dusty tan legs and scowled, picking at a scab on her knee. "At night, when we're supposed to be asleep, me and Angel talk and tell jokes and stuff." Her large brown eyes met Fang's. "I mean, am I going to have to sleep in that room alone, whenever we get home? Max has to come back. She wouldn't let Angel go, right?"

"No," said Fang. "She won't let Angel go. Look — you see how that big hawk, the one with the dark stripe on its shoulders — you see how he seems to move one wing faster than the other when he banks? It makes his bank really tight and smooth. We should try it."

Nudge looked at him. That was probably the longest speech she'd ever heard Fang make.

She turned to watch the hawk he'd pointed out. "Yeah, I see what you mean." But she'd barely finished before Fang had stood up, run lightly toward the edge of the cliff, and leaped off. His large, powerful dark wings caught the air and swooped him up. Fang flew closer to where the other hawks were circling in a kind of hawk ballet.

Nudge sighed. She really, really wished Max were here. Was Max hurt? Should they go back? She would ask Fang when he returned.

Just then he swept past her, level with their cave. "Come on!" he called. "Try it! You'll fly better."

Nudge sighed again and brushed some chocolate crumbs off her shirt. Wasn't he worried about Angel? If he was, he probably wouldn't show it, she guessed. But she knew Fang loved Angel — he'd read to her before she learned how to read, and even now he still held her when she was upset about something.

Well, I might as well practice too. Better than sitting around doing nothing. She flung herself off the cliff, unable to keep a bittersweet happiness from flooding her chest. It just felt so — beautiful, to float in the air, to move her wings strongly and feel herself glide freely through space.

She flew alongside Fang, and he demonstrated the move for her. She watched him and imitated it. It worked great.

She flew in huge circles, practicing the move and flying closer to the hawks, who seemed to be tolerating her. As long as she didn't think about Max or Angel, she would be okay.

That evening Nudge lay on her stomach, her wings flat out around her, and watched the parent hawks grooming their young. They were so gentle, so attentive. These fierce, strong birds were carefully smoothing their fledglings' mottled white feathers, feeding them, helping them get out of the nest to practice flying.

A lump came to her throat. She sniffled.

"What?" said Fang.

"These birds," said Nudge, wiping her eyes and feeling stupid. "Like, these dumb hawks have more of a mom than I ever had. The parents are taking care of the little ones. No one ever did that for me. Well, besides Max. But she's not a mom."

"Yeah. I get it." Fang didn't look at her. His voice almost sounded sad.

The sun set, and the hawks settled down in their nests. Finally, the raucous fledglings quieted. When it had been dark for an hour, Fang edged closer to Nudge and held out his left hand in a fist. Nudge looked up at him, then stacked her left fist on top of his. It was something the flock always did together before bedtime.

Except they hadn't done it when they'd fallen asleep in that cabin last night. And now it was just the two of them.

Nudge tapped his fist with her right hand, and he tapped hers.

"Night," she whispered, feeling as if everything she cared about had been ripped away from her. Silently, she curled up against the wall of the cave.

"Night, Nudge," whispered Fang.

26

Oh, man. This was *not* the best day I'd ever had. My shoulder was still bleeding a bit, even though I'd been pressing on it for hours. Every time I jostled it, warm blood oozed through my fingers.

I hadn't run into the gun-carrying clowns again, but I'd heard them off and on. I'd been working my way north in a big arc, trying to weave a confusing trail for whoever might be following me. Every time I heard them, I froze for endless minutes, trying to blend in with the brush.

Then, cramped and stiffening, I would painstakingly start again. In case they brought dogs, I'd splashed through streams at least four times, and let me tell you, trying to keep your balance on moss-covered rocks in icy water with a hurt shoulder is no picnic.

I'd felt around on my shoulder and wing, and as far as I could tell, the shot had just scooped out a trail of flesh and wing but hadn't actually lodged inside. Whatever — my arm and wing felt useless and they hurt awfully.

It was getting late. Angel was somewhere hours away, being subjected to God knows what horror, wondering where I was. I pressed my lips together, trying not to cry. I couldn't fly, couldn't catch up to Fang and Nudge, who were probably furious by now. It wasn't like I could call their cell phones or anything.

This situation totally sucked, and it was 100 percent my own stupid fault, which made it suck even worse.

Then, of course, it started pouring rain.

So now I was slogging my way through wet woods, wet brush, red clay mud, wiping water out of my eyes, getting more chilled and more miserable and more hungry and more insanely *furious* at myself.

I hadn't heard the guys in a long time — they had probably gone home to *get out of the rain.*

A minute later I blinked and wiped my eyes. I squinted. There were lights ahead.

If it was a store or shed, I could wait till everyone left and then hole up for the night. Soon I was only ten yards away, hunching down in the darkness, peering through the wet trees. It was a house.

A figure passed a window, and my eyebrows raised. It was that girl, Ella. This must be her house.

I bit my lip. She probably lived here with her two doting parents and her 1.6 siblings. How nice for her. Anyway, I was glad she had gotten home safe. Despite everything, if I had let those horrible guys beat her up, I never would have forgiven myself.

I shivered hard, feeling the icy rain run down my back. I was about to fall over. What to do here, get a plan . . .

I was still waiting for a brilliant inspiration when the side door of the house opened. Ella came out holding a huge umbrella. A shadow moved at her feet. It was a dog, a low-to-the-ground, fat dog.

"Come on, Magnolia," Ella called. "Make it fast. You don't want to get too wet."

The dog started sniffing around the edge of their yard, snuffling in the weeds, oblivious to the rain. Ella turned and walked up and down, twirling her umbrella, scanning her yard. Her back was to me.

Desperate times call for desperate measures. I don't know who first said that, but they were right on the money. I took a deep breath, then very, very quietly, began to move toward Ella.

27

Okay, two more blood samples and the glucose assay will be done. Then we can do the EEGs.

Why isn't this over? Where are you, Max? Angel thought sadly as the whitecoat approached. The front of Angel's dog crate opened, and a guy knelt down and peered in at her. She pressed herself against the back as hard as she could.

He reached in to grab her hand, where the shunt was, and noticed her face. He turned back to his fellow whitecoats. "What happened to it?"

"It bit Reilly earlier," someone said. "He hit it."

Angel tried to pull herself into a tight little ball. The whole left side of her face throbbed. But she was glad she'd bitten him. She hated him. Hated all of them.

Stupid Reilly. Guy should work in a car wash. If he wrecks this specimen, I'll kill him.

"Doesn't he realize how unique this subject is?" the whitecoat said angrily. "I mean, this is Subject *Eleven*.

Does he know how long we've been looking for it? You tell Reilly not to damage the merchandise."

He reached in and tried to take Angel's hand again.

Angel didn't know what she should do. The plastic shunt on the back of her hand hurt, and she'd cradled it against her chest. All day she'd had nothing to eat or drink, and then they'd made her drink some horrible, sickly sweet orange stuff. They'd taken blood from her arm, but she'd fought them and bit that one guy. So they'd put a shunt in the back of her hand to make taking blood easier. They'd drawn her blood three times already.

Angel felt near tears but clenched her jaw.

Slowly, she uncoiled herself a tiny bit and edged closer to the opening. She stretched her hand toward the lab guy.

"That's it," he said soothingly, and pulled out a needle with a test tube attached. He unclipped the stop on the shunt and pushed the needle in. "This won't hurt. Honest."

Angel turned away, keeping her back to him, that one hand stretched away from her.

It didn't take long, and it didn't hurt. Maybe he was a good whitecoat — like Jeb. And maybe the moon was made out of cream cheese.

28

"Okay," said Iggy. "We're being *very* careful. Hello? Gazzy? We're being *very* careful?"

"Check," said the Gasman, patting the explosive package they called Big Boy.

"Nails?"

The Gasman rattled the jar. "Check."

"Tarp? Cooking oil?"

"Check, check." The Gasman nodded. "We are *geniuses*. Those Erasers'll never know what hit 'em. If only we had time to dig a pit."

"Yeah, and put poison stakes at the bottom," Iggy agreed. "But I think what we've got is good. Now we need to fly out, stay out of sight, and check on how the roads run, and whether the Erasers have made camp anywhere."

"Okay. Then we can seed the roads with the nails and set up the tarp and oil." The Gasman grinned. "We just have to make sure not to get caught."

"Yes. That would be bad," Iggy said with a straight face. "Now, *is it night yet?*"

"Pretty much. I found you some dark clothes." The

Gasman pressed a shirt and pants into Iggy's hands. "And I've got some too. So, you ready to roll?" He hoped Iggy couldn't hear how nervous he was. This was a great plan; they had to do it — but failure would be disastrous. And probably deadly.

"Yeah. I'm bringing Big Boy in case an opportunity arises." Iggy changed his clothes, then put their homemade bomb into a backpack and slung it onto his shoulders. "Don't worry," he said, as if he could see the Gasman's expression. "It can't go off till I set the timer. It's, like, a safety bomb."

The Gasman tried to smile. He cranked open the hall window as wide as it would go and perched on the ledge. His palms were sweating, and his stomach was all fluttery. But he had no choice — this was for Angel. This was to show people what would happen if they messed with his family.

He swallowed hard and launched himself out into the night air. It was amazing, to be able to spread his wings and fly. It was *great.* As he felt the night wind against his face, the Gasman's spirits rose. He felt strong, powerful, and dangerous. Not at all like an eight-year-old mutant freak.

29

"Um, Ella?"

The girl stiffened and jumped back.

I stepped forward a bit, out of the underbrush, so she could see my face. "It's me," I said, feeling even stupider. "The girl from before."

It was getting dark and still raining, and I hoped she could recognize me. The dog trotted over, saw me, and gave a halfhearted woof of warning.

"Oh, *yeah*. Hey, thanks — for helping me," said Ella, squinting at me through the rain. "Are you okay? What are you doing?" She sounded wary and glanced around, like maybe in the time since she'd last seen me I had gone over to the side of evil.

"I'm okay," I said lamely. "Well, actually, I guess I need help." Those words had never left my lips before. Thank God Jeb wasn't here to see me doing something so incredibly boneheaded and weak.

"Oh," said Ella. "Gosh. Okay. Did those guys . . ."

"One of them managed to clip me with some shot, if you can believe that," I said, inching closer.

Ella gasped and put her hand over her mouth. "Oh, no! Why didn't you tell me? You're hurt? Why didn't you go to the hospital? Oh, my gosh, come on in!"

She stepped back to give me room and urged Magnolia, who had lumbered over and started sniffing my wet clothes with interest, away from me.

Guess what. I hesitated. Here was the moment of decision. Until I stepped into that house, I could still turn and run, escape. Once I was in that house, it would be much harder. Call it a little quirk of my personality, but I tend to freak out if I feel trapped anywhere. We all do — the flock, I mean. Living in a cage during your formative years can do that.

But I was honest enough with myself to know that I really couldn't go on like this — wet, cold, starving, and a little wonky from loss of blood. I had to suck it up and accept help. From strangers.

"Are your parents home?" I asked.

"There's just my mom," said Ella. "No dad. Come on, let's get you inside. My mom can help. Magnolia, here, girl." Ella turned and strode toward the house. She clomped up wooden steps, then turned and looked for me. "Can you walk okay?"

"Uh-huh." Slowly, I headed toward Ella's small house, which was glowing with warmth and light. I felt lightheaded and panicky. This could be the last huge mistake in a long line of huge mistakes I had already made today.

I cradled my hurt arm with my good one.

"Oh, my God — is that blood?" Ella said, staring at my pale blue sweatshirt. "Oh, no, come on, we have to get you inside quick!" She shoved the door open with her shoulder, almost tripping on Magnolia, who trotted in quickly. "Mom! Mom! This girl needs help!"

I felt frozen. Stay or run. Stay or run. Stay?

30

"You think that wire will hold?" the Gasman whispered.

Iggy nodded, frowning as he twisted the two cable ends together with pliers. He leaned against a pine tree for leverage, and when the wire was tight, he snapped on a cable clamp and pinched it shut. "That'll hold a bit," he whispered back. "Until a certain Hummer hits it at top speed."

The Gasman nodded grimly. What a night. They had gotten so much done — Max couldn't have done better herself. He hoped Max had already rescued Angel by now. He hoped nothing had gone wrong. If the whitecoats had gotten hold of Angel . . . For just an instant he saw her, white and lifeless, laid on a cold steel slab while whitecoats lectured about her unusual bone structure. He swallowed and shook the dreadful image off. Once more, he glanced around, listening.

"Back home?" Iggy whispered.

"Yeah." Standing up, the Gasman pushed off from the ground, staying close to the trees. He followed Iggy's dark shadow as he braked and headed back west, toward home. From up here, the Gasman couldn't see any of their handiwork — which was a good thing. They didn't want the Erasers' chopper to be able to pick out the tarp or the trip wire until it was too late.

"We covered the ways in and out," he said to Iggy once they were at cruising height. "Oil slick, nails in the road, trip wire. That should do it."

Iggy nodded. "I'm bummed we couldn't use Big Boy," he said. "But I don't want to waste it. We have to actually see them first. I mean, *you* do."

"Maybe tomorrow," the Gasman said encouragingly. "We'll go out and see what havoc we've wreaked."

"Wrought," said Iggy.

"Whatever," said the Gasman, breathing deeply in the cool night air. Wait till Max found out how cool they had been.

31

A dark-haired woman with worried eyes opened the door wider. "What is it, Ella? What's wrong?"

"Mom, this is —" Ella stopped, her hand in midair.

"Max," I said. Why didn't I give a fake name? Because I didn't *think* of it.

"My friend Max. She's the girl I told you about, the one who saved me from José and Dwayne and them. She saved me. But they shot her."

"Oh, no!" exclaimed Ella's mother. "Please, Max, come in. Do you want me to call your parents?"

I stood on the doormat, reluctant to drip rain, and blood, on their floor. "Um . . ."

Then Ella's mom saw my bloodstained sweatshirt, and her eyes flew to my face. My cheek was scratched, one eye was black. The whole situation changed in that instant.

"Let me get my stuff," she said gently. "Take off your shoes and go with Ella to the bathroom."

I sloshed down the hallway in my wet socks. "What stuff is she going to get?" I whispered.

Ella turned on a light and ushered me into an old-fashioned

bathroom with green tiles and a rust ring around the sink drain.

"Her doctor stuff," Ella whispered back. "She's a vet, so she's good with injuries. Even on people."

A vet! I started laughing weakly and had to sit down on the edge of the tub. A vet. Wait till they found out how appropriate that was.

Ella's mom came in with a plastic box of first aid supplies. "Ella, maybe you could get Max some juice or something. She probably needs some sugar and fluids."

"Juice would be *great*," I said with feeling.

Ella nodded and hurried down the hall.

"I take it you don't want me to call your parents?" Ella's mom said softly, starting to cut away the neck of my sweatshirt.

"Uh, no." *Hello, lab? May I speak to a test tube, please?*

"Or the police, either, right?"

"No need to get them involved," I agreed, then I sucked in my breath as her gentle fingers found the wound on my upper arm. "I think the bullet only grazed me."

"Yes, I think you're right, but it's pretty deep and messy. And over here —" I sat frozen, staring straight ahead, as all my senses tensed. I was taking a huge risk here. You have no idea how huge. I had never, ever let someone outside the flock see my wings. But this was one situation I couldn't fix by myself. I *hated* that.

Ella's mom frowned slightly. She finished cutting the neck and then stretched the shirt off, leaving me in my tank top. I sat there like a statue, feeling a chilled coldness inside that had nothing to do with being wet.

"Here." Ella handed me a big glass of orange juice. I practically choked, trying to drink it down as fast as possible. Oh, my God, it was so good.

"What's —" Ella's mom said, her fingers skimming along the edge of my wing where it folded and tucked into an indentation next to my spine, between my shoulder and my waist. She leaned over to see better.

I stared at my wet socks, my toes clenching.

She turned me slightly, and I let her.

"Max." Her dark brown eyes were concerned, tired, and upset, all at once. "Max, what is this?" she asked gently, touching the feathers that were just barely visible.

I swallowed hard, knowing that I had just lost any hope for a normal connection with Ella and her mom. In my mind I reviewed the house layout: a right down the hall, a quick left, and through the front door. It would take only a few seconds. I could do it. I could probably grab my boots on the way out too.

"It's a . . . wing," I whispered. Out of the corner of my eye, I saw Ella frown. "My, um, wing." Silence. "It got hurt too."

I took a deep breath, feeling like I was going to hurl, then slowly and painfully extended my wing just a bit, so Ella's mom could see where I'd been shot.

Their eyes widened. And widened. And widened. Until I began to expect them to just pop out and land on the floor.

"Wha' . . ." Ella began wonderingly.

Her mom leaned over and examined it more closely. Amazingly, she was trying to act casual, like, oh, okay, you have a *wing*. No biggie.

I was practically hyperventilating, feeling light-headed and kind of tunnel-visiony.

"Yeah, your wing got hit too," Ella's mom murmured, extending it ever so gently. "I think the shot nicked a bit of bone." She sat back and looked at me.

I stared at the floor, feeling the weight of her gaze. I could not believe I was in this situation. Fang was going to kill me. And after I was dead, he would kill me again.

And I deserved it.

Ella's mom took a deep breath and let it out. "Okay, Max," she said in a calm, controlled voice. "First, we have to clean the wounds and stop the bleeding. When's the last time you had a tetanus shot?"

I stared up into her eyes. Ella's mom seemed no-nonsense and . . . incredibly caring. About me. I had become a huge crybaby in the last couple days, so I wasn't surprised to feel tears haze my vision.

"Um, never?"

"Okay. I can take care of that too."

32

"Come on, come on," the Gasman breathed. He was holding on to the pine branch so hard that he could barely feel his fingers anymore.

"What's happening?" Iggy demanded impatiently. "Tell me everything."

It was early morning, and the two of them were perched near the top of an old-growth pine overlooking one of the abandoned logging roads. They had cased the situation, and the Gasman had been right: At least two Erasers, maybe more, had set up a rough camp not far from where the helicopter had landed. It seemed clear they were looking for the rest of the flock. It didn't matter whether they wanted to kill them or only kidnap them: Capture was unthinkable.

The Gasman still had nightmares in which he found himself back at the School. He dreamed that whitecoats took blood, injected him with various drugs to see how he reacted, made him run and jump and then swallow radioactive dye so they could study his circulation. Days and endless weeks and years of feeling sick, hurting, vomiting, being exhausted, being stuck in a cage. The Gasman would die before he went back there. Angel would rather have died too, he knew — but she hadn't had a choice.

"The Hummer's *coming*," the Gasman said under his breath.

"On the right road?"

"Uh-huh. And they're driving too fast." The Gasman gave a tight, worried smile.

"They're not practicing safe driving habits. Tsk. What a shame."

"Okay, they're coming up," the Gasman muttered. "Another quarter mile."

"Can you see the tarp?"

"No."

The Gasman watched tensely as the muddied black Humvee sped down the unpaved logging road. "Any second now," he whispered to Iggy, who was practically vibrating with excitement.

"Hope they're wearing their seat belts. *Not!*"

Then it happened.

It was like watching a movie. One second, the boxy black vehicle was tearing along the road, and the next second, it swerved violently to the left with an audible squealing of brakes. It began a slow, graceless series of jerky spins down the road, then gave an unexpected jump toward the trees on one side. It hit the trees at an angle and went airborne, sailing upside down about fifteen feet before landing with a heavy crunching sound.

"Whoa," the Gasman said softly. "That was *incredible.*"

"You have two seconds to give me the picture," Iggy said irritably.

"It hit the oil, all right. It spun, hit the trees, and did a flip," the Gasman told him. "Now it's on its back, like a big, ugly, dead beetle."

"Yes!" Iggy punched the air, making their branch sway. "Signs of life?"

"Uh . . . oh, yeah. Yeah, one of them just punched out a window. Now they're climbing out. They look pretty dang mad. They're walking, so they're not that hurt." The Gasman wanted the Erasers out of the picture, so he wouldn't have to worry about them anymore. At the same time, he wasn't sure how he would feel if they had actually died.

Then he remembered that they had taken Angel.

He decided he was probably okay with them suffering a life-threatening accident.

"Shoot." Iggy sounded disappointed. "Any point in dropping Big Boy on them right now?"

The Gasman shook his head, remembered Iggy couldn't see it, and said, "I don't think so. They're talking on walkie-talkies. Now they're heading straight into the woods. We'd probably cause a huge forest fire or something."

"Hmm." Iggy frowned. "Okay. We need to regroup, come up with Phase Two. How about we hang at the old cabin for a minute?"

"Cool," said the Gasman. "Let's go. We've done enough good for one day."

33

Eighty years ago, loggers had used a makeshift cabin nearby as a base during logging season. Abandoned for the last thirty years, it was practically in ruins. Which made it an especially good clubhouse for the flock.

"So Phase One is complete," said Iggy, sitting in a broken plastic lawn chair. He sniffed the air. "We haven't been here in ages."

"Uh-uh," said the Gasman, glancing around. "In case you're wondering, it's still a dump."

"It's always been a dump," Iggy said. "That's why we like it."

"Man, I can't get over it — that tarp full of oil so totally wiped the Hummer out," the Gasman said. "It was kind of — scary. To really do it."

Iggy opened the backpack and took out Big Boy, running his sensitive fingers over the clock duct-taped to the explosive package.

"We have to eliminate the Erasers," he murmured. "So they can't ever hurt us again."

"So they can't ever take Angel again," the Gasman said, his eyes narrowing. "I say we bomb the chopper."

Iggy nodded and stood up. "Yeah. Listen, let's get out of here, get back home, make more plans."

In the next instant, the faintest vibration of the floorboards made Iggy freeze. The Gasman quickly looked at him, saw Iggy's sightless eyes flick to and fro.

"Did you hear?" the Gasman whispered, and Iggy nodded, holding up his hand. "Maybe a raccoon —"

"Not in the daytime," Iggy barely mouthed back.

A slight scratching on the door made the Gasman's blood turn to ice in his veins. Surely it was just an animal, a squirrel or somethi —

"Little pigs, little pigs, let me come in." The whispered voice, serene and angelic, seemed to float through the cracks in the door like poisonous smoke. It was an Eraser's voice, a voice that could ask you to jump off a cliff and you'd do it.

Heart pounding, the Gasman quickly scanned the room. The door. Two windows, one in the main room and a tiny one in the bathroom. He doubted he could fit through the one in the bathroom, much less Iggy.

The Eraser scratched at the door again, and the hairs on the back of the Gasman's neck stood up. Okay, the window in here, then. He began to edge his way over to it, knowing that Iggy would be able to follow the almost imperceptible sound.

Crash! The door burst open, splintered wood flying through the air like darts.

"Eight o'clock!" the Gasman whispered, telling Iggy where the window was as his brain registered the hulking Eraser filling the doorway. His muscles tensed for the leap through the window — but its light was suddenly blocked by a huge, grinning head.

"Hey, piggy, piggy, piggy," a second Eraser taunted through the dirt-clouded glass.

Years of Max-enforced training kicked in as adrenaline sped through the Gasman's body. Door blocked. Window blocked. They were surrounded, with no clean escape available. It was going to be a fight, he realized, already preparing himself.

More than likely a fight to the death.

34

Nudge woke up four times before she finally rolled over and pried her eyes open.

It was barely dawn. Fang was gone. First Angel, then Max — now Fang.

Gone! Nudge looked around, crawling to the opening of the cave on her hands and knees. There's nothing like panic to really wake you up, get all your senses going. Nudge felt keenly alert, frightened, too many thoughts starting to rush in her brain.

Movement caught her eye, and her head swiveled in line with a loose formation of hawks wheeling through the crisp, white blue sky. They were so beautiful, powerful, graceful, completely one with the sky and the earth and the rough cliffs.

One of them was Fang.

Nudge stood quickly, almost bumping her head on the low ceiling of the cave. Without hesitation, she leaped off the cliff edge, out into the sky. Her wings unfolded and caught the wind like sails, and suddenly she was a small brown boat soaring across an endless blue sea.

She approached the hawks, and after hard, glinting glances at her, they moved so she could join them. Fang was watching her, and Nudge was surprised by his face — how alive he looked, how . . . untight. Fang always looked very tight, somehow, taut, like the string on a bow. Now he looked loose and free and alive.

"Morning," he said.

"I'm hungry," said Nudge.

He nodded. "Town about three minutes away. Follow me." He tilted his body in a new way that led him up and away without moving his wings. It was cool, like a plane. Nudge tried it, but it didn't work as well for her. She would practice.

Below them was a thin two-lane highway, clotted with a last few shops and businesses before the road wound away into the desert. Fang dipped his head: A fast-food place had a large Dumpster out back. Even from up this high, Nudge could see a worker tossing cardboard boxes of stuff into it, getting ready for a new day.

They circled a couple times till they were sure the worker wasn't coming out again, then dropped quickly, like bombs, tucking their wings in tight with just the feather tips guiding their descent. Thirty feet above the Dumpster, they blew their wings out again, braking sharply, then they landed, almost silently, on the metal edge of the Dumpster.

"Nirvana," Fang said, pawing through food that was still good but not sellable. "Burger?"

Nudge thought, then shook her head. "I don't know —

after watching the hawks shredding little animals — oh, but look, here's a couple salads. And some apple pies! Bonus!"

They tightened the drawstrings of their windbreakers around their waists. Then, working fast, they started stuffing food inside their jackets, anything that would travel. Three minutes after they'd landed, they were airborne again, lumpy and smiling.

It was amazing how much better Nudge felt after eating. She sighed and sat cross-legged in the cave entrance, watching the hawks fly.

Fang finished his fifth thin hamburger patty and wiped his fingers on his jeans. "You know, I think the way they swoop and stuff is like a message to the other hawks," he said. "Like they're telling them where there's game or where they'll be or something. I haven't figured it out yet. But I will."

"Oh." Nudge sat back on her heels and spread her wings out, enjoying the feel of the sun warming her feathers. She tried to be quiet and not disturb Fang, but after five minutes she was close to meltdown.

"Fang? We've just got to go find Max," she said. "Or should we go on and try to find Angel?"

Fang pulled his attention away from the hawks with difficulty. "We're going to circle back, look for Max," he said. "She must have — run into something."

Nudge nodded solemnly, unable to define what kind of something would have kept Max from them. She didn't want to think about it.

Fang stood, tall and dark against the weathered sandstone of the rock cliff. He looked down at her, his face calm and patient, his eyes reflecting no light whatsoever. "You ready?"

Nudge jumped to her feet, brushing sand off her butt. "Absolutely. Um, where do you think we should —"

But Fang was already gone, snatched away by the wind, borne upward by air rising from the canyon below.

Nudge took a small running leap off the cliff after him.

"Tarzan!" she yelled. Whatever that was supposed to mean.

35

I woke up warm, dry, bandaged, and safe.

I felt like death.

As always, as soon as I was conscious, I panicked for a second, not knowing where I was. My brain anxiously registered flowered wallpaper. A soft, warm bed that smelled like laundry softener. I looked down. I was wearing a huge T-shirt that had a cartoon character on it, one I didn't know.

I was at Ella's house. I was supposed to be rescuing Angel — if she was even still alive. Fang and Nudge were probably sticking pins in a Max doll by now. I didn't blame them.

Now that I was awake, the pain in my shoulder and wing hit me all over again, a stinging ache that radiated out like a starburst. Ugh. I remembered once I'd dislocated my shoulder, sparring with Fang. It had hurt so bad, and I had staggered around clutching my shoulder and trying not to cry. Jeb had calmed me down, talking to me, taking my mind off it, and then, when I least expected it, he had popped it right back into place. Instantly, all the pain was gone. He'd smiled and stroked my sweaty hair off my forehead and gotten me some lemonade. And I'd thought, *This is what a dad would do. This is better than what a dad would do.*

I still missed Jeb so much it made my throat close.

Suddenly, I froze, because my bedroom door was opening very, very slowly and quietly.

Run! my mind screamed as my hands curled into claws against the sheets. *Fly!*

Ella's brown eyes, curious and eager, peered around the door. She spoke softly over her shoulder. "I think she's awake."

Ella's mom appeared. "Morning, Max. You hungry? Do you like pancakes?"

"And little breakfast sausages?" Ella added. "And fruit and stuff?"

I hoped it only *felt* like I was drooling on my nightshirt. I nodded. They smiled and left, and then I saw the clothes on my bed. My own jeans and socks had been washed, and there was a lavender sweatshirt with large slits newly cut into the back.

Ella's mom was taking care of me, like Jeb had. I didn't know how to act, what to say.

A girl could get used to this.

36

No matter how quickly the Erasers killed them, the Gasman was sure it would feel like forever.

"Up and away," Iggy breathed, inching slightly closer to him.

Up and away? The Gasman frowned. Iggy had to be kidding. *Straight* up?

Crash! The Gasman jumped as the window behind him shattered with a shower of glass and broken wood. An Eraser pushed through the ragged opening with a silent grin.

"Guess what?" the first Eraser asked with a pleasant smile. "We got the little one — they don't need you two alive." They laughed, the sound like deep bells ringing, and then their faces began to change. The Gasman couldn't help grimacing as they morphed, becoming more wolflike, their muzzles extending, their teeth protruding until it looked like they had a mouthful of knives.

"Boys, boys," one almost purred. "Didn't anyone ever tell you? You can run, but you can't hide." His shiny dark hair was becoming thicker, and more hair sprouted grotesquely on his arms and hands. He literally licked his chops and rubbed his huge, hairy hands together, as if he'd learned how to be a bad guy from cartoons.

"Ready?"

Iggy's voice was so faint, his lips so still that the Gasman wasn't sure he'd heard anything. Every second seemed oddly stretched out. His hands closed into fists by his sides. He was ready. Sure.

"This freak's *blind*," one Eraser said, gesturing toward Iggy. "Don't worry, kid. It'll all be over soon, and you won't have to worry about being blind anymore. But it's a shame they didn't give you one of their new eyes — like mine."

The Gasman looked up at him, and a feeling of revulsion rose in his throat as he saw what the Eraser meant. Set deep into one orbital socket was a stainless steel ball. A red laserlike glow made it look as though it was filled with blood. The Eraser grinned and turned his eye to the Gasman. A red dot appeared on the Gasman's shirt and, as he watched, it slowly began to burn a small hole in the fabric.

The Erasers laughed.

"You left before they could fix you up with the latest technology," one said. "Your loss."

Yeah, right, the Gasman thought in disgust.

"How about it, piggies?" the first Eraser asked. "Do you want to try to run? Who knows — you might get lucky. For a little while."

Grinning with anticipation, the Eraser drew closer.

"On three."

Once again, the Gasman wasn't sure if he'd heard Iggy or if he was imagining it.

"One."

The Gasman's toes clenched inside his sneakers.

"Two."

When Iggy shouted, "Three!" the Gasman leaped straight into the air, unfurling his wings with a huge *whoosh.* With a roar of anger, one Eraser grabbed the Gasman's foot and yanked. Above him, Iggy burst through the rotting roof of the cabin, out into the sky. The Gasman broke free of the Eraser's grip.

Then he was pushing through the shattered roof, tucking his wings in tight to get through the hole. Outside, he lost altitude too fast and landed clumsily on a rickety roof beam. He slid sideways, grabbing roof shingles that came off in his hands.

Iggy yelled from twenty feet above him, *"Gasser! Move!"*

Just as he slid over the edge of the roof, the Gasman spread his wings. He pushed down hard with all his strength, then pulled his wings up and pushed them down again. As he surged up to meet Iggy, Iggy threw a package down into the cabin.

"Move, move, move!" Iggy yelled, flapping like crazy. Within seconds, they were a hundred yards away.

Boom! Only it was more like *ba-ba-boooooom!*

The two boys recoiled from the blast, tumbling backward

111

in the air from the shock wave. The Gasman righted himself, eyes wide, as a fireball ten yards in diameter rose from where the cabin had been.

He was speechless.

After the fireball from Big Boy disintegrated, the cabin burned brightly, its old, rotted wood consumed as instantly as kindling. Flames reached for the sky, licking at the green trees nearby, snaking along the ground as brittle brown pine needles caught fire.

God, it was beautiful.

"Well," Iggy said after a long while, "that takes care of *them*."

The Gasman nodded, feeling sick. One dark body had flown upward in the blast, falling back to earth as a glowing coal. The other Eraser had crawled a few feet away from the cabin, a burning silhouette that had collapsed, its outlines blurred by flame.

"Unless they escaped," Iggy added.

Of course Iggy hadn't seen anything. The Gasman cleared his throat. "No," he said. "They're dead." He felt slightly queasy, guilty, and dirty. Then he remembered Angel, how she'd shared the last of the ice cream with him three nights ago. She was so small, and God only knew what horrible things they were doing to her. His jaw hardened.

"Take *that*," he muttered. "That was for my sister, for *Angel*, you scum-sucking jerks."

Then he saw the black Hummer, its hood crumpled, driving fast toward the burning cabin. An Eraser was leaning out the passenger window, looking through binoculars.

"Come on, Iggy," said the Gasman. "Let's get out of here."

37

The bell clanged jarringly, and rough hands pushed Angel forward. She stumbled, catching herself at the last second before falling onto coils of razor wire.

Angel wanted to cry. She'd been doing this all day — it was late afternoon by now.

She was starving and light-headed and every muscle ached — and still they made her run.

It was a maze, Angel knew that.

They had made it in a huge gymlike room in the School's main building. They rang a bell and pushed her forward, and then she had to run as fast as she could to find the exit. Each time, the maze was different, the exit in a different place. If she slowed down, she got an electric shock so strong it scrambled her brain, or red-hot wires under her feet burned her. So, eyes blurry with tears, Angel ran forward blindly, taking this turn and that until she finally stumbled out the exit.

Then she would get a sip of water and a five-minute rest while they redid the maze.

Angel sniffled, trying to keep quiet. She hated this! If

only she knew beforehand — if only she *knew,* she could run through fast and not get shocked or burned.

Angel sat up, a tingle of excitement running down her spine. She closed her eyes and tried to listen to what the whitecoats were thinking.

One of them wanted to let an Eraser loose in the maze, have it fight with her, see how strong she really was. One of them thought they should increase the heated wires so she always had to run on them, whether she was slowing down or not. Then he could study the effect of stress on her adrenaline levels.

Angel wanted them all to burn in h-e-double toothpicks forever.

One of them was designing the next maze, the creep.

Angel concentrated, trying to look as though she was resting. Someone gave her another sip of water, and she sucked it down fast. She could see the rough plan of the maze! It was in her mind because it was in the whitecoat's mind. Deliberately, Angel breathed in and out, looking spent, but she felt a new surge of possibility.

She got it. She knew what the next maze would look like. Blinking tiredly, Angel sat up, keeping her eyes unfocused. In her mind, she was reviewing the maze's layout: a quick right, then another right, then a left, skip the next three rights and take the fourth one . . . and so on, till she saw the exit.

She could see all the traps, the dead ends, the paths that led nowhere.

She could hardly wait to blow their minds. This would be fun!

A whitecoat grabbed her, made her stand in front of the new maze's entrance.

The bell clanged.

Someone pushed her.

Angel took off. Running as fast as she could in case all the wires were hot, she took a quick right, another right, then a left, and so on. She raced through with record speed, with no hesitation. She didn't get shocked once and never felt a hot wire under her feet.

She burst out of the maze's exit, then collapsed onto the cool wooden floor.

Time passed.

Words floated to her: *Amazing. Cognitive ability. Interpretive skills. Creative problem solving. Dissect her brain. Preserve her organs. Extract her DNA.*

A voice said, "No, no, we can't dissect her brain just yet." The speaker laughed, as if it were funny. His voice sounded . . . like she'd heard it in a fairy tale or something, like at night, or at home, or with Max. . . .

Angel blinked and swam toward consciousness. She made the mistake of looking up. An older man was there. He wore wire-rimmed glasses and was smiling at her. She got no thoughts from him whatsoever. He looked . . .

"Hello, Angel," said Jeb Batchelder kindly. "I haven't seen you in a long time. I missed you, kiddo."

38

Nudge didn't know exactly what Fang expected to see. Max, flying toward them? Max, standing on the ground below, waving her arms to get their attention? Max's body, crumpled — Nudge shut that thought down. She would just wait. Fang was older and really smart; Max trusted him. Nudge trusted him too.

How far back had Max separated from them? Nudge couldn't remember. She and Fang had been flying in ever-widening circles for hours. How did they know Max hadn't passed them somehow and was waiting for them back at Lake Mead?

"Fang? Do you remember where we left Max?"

"Yes."

"Are we going to go there?"

Pause. "Not if we can help it."

"But why? Maybe Max is hurt and needs help. Maybe we need to save her before we go save Angel." It was hard, keeping these missions separate. First Angel, now Max, then Angel again.

Fang banked to the left, tightening the angle as they'd

seen the hawks do. Nudge followed him. Below them, the ground looked parched, with only occasional roads, cactuses, brush.

"I don't think Max would have gotten hurt all by herself," Fang said slowly. "She's not going to fly into a tree or crash-land. So if she's late because she's hurt, it probably means that someone, a person, hurt her. Which means that someone knows about her. We don't want that someone to know about us too. Which they would if we went to where Max is."

Nudge's jaw dropped.

"And if Max is late because she's busy, then our going to her won't speed things up — she'll come when she's good and ready. So for right now, we do a general look-see. But we're not going all the way back."

Nudge heard Max's voice in her head: *Think before you speak.* So she shut her mouth and thought. She had no idea how Fang could *not* get Max, even if it meant they might get captured or hurt themselves. They *all* might get captured or hurt saving Angel, right? Why was Max different from Angel? Max was more important than Angel, Nudge thought, feeling guilty. Max took care of them, helped run their whole lives.

She snuck a look at Fang. Fang was good, if not very warm or huggy. He was strong and handsome and capable. But would he stick around to take care of everyone if there were no Max? Or would he take off and go live by himself somewhere and not be bothered with them? Nudge didn't know what Fang was really thinking.

Suddenly, Nudge was brushing tears out of her eyes, swallowing down the lump in her throat, feeling her nose clog up. Oh, God. She couldn't bear it without Max. Blinking, she tried to clear her vision, tried to think about something else. She saw a white truck down below and focused on it, forcing herself to wonder what it was carrying, where it was coming from. Like any of it mattered.

She drew in deep breaths and held them, refusing to cry in front of Fang. She might have to start being very strong, very soon. She might as well practice now.

The truck headed toward an intersection that had signs marking a junction. Nudge blinked and looked as the signs became clear and she could read them. One said, California Welcome Center, 18 miles. One said, Las Vegas, North, 98 miles. One said, Tipisco, 3 miles.

Tipisco! Tipisco, Arizona! Where Nudge was from! Where her parents had been! Oh, God — could she still find her parents? Would they want her back? Had they missed her so much all these years?

"Fang!" she shouted, already beginning the descent. "It's Tipisco, down below! I'm going there!"

"No way, Nudge," Fang said, flying closer to her. "Don't get sidetracked now. Stay with me."

"No!" said Nudge, feeling daring and desperate and brave. She hunched her shoulders and tucked her head down, feeling herself lose altitude. "I have to go find my parents! If Max is gone, I'm going to need someone."

Fang's dark eyes widened in surprise. "What? Nudge, you're crazy. Come on, let's talk about it. Let's find a place, take a break."

"No!" said Nudge, tears coming to her eyes again. "I'm going down — and you can't stop me!"

39

"We're pretty safe, unless the Erasers catch our scent," the Gasman whispered to Iggy. The two of them were tucked inside a narrow fissure in the side of a cliff, up high. Scraggly bushes obscured the opening. The Erasers would have to rock climb to get them, or use the chopper.

Iggy kicked back and rested his hands on his knees. "Well, this is a total suckfest," he said grumpily. "I thought with those two Erasers taking dirt naps, we'd be free and clear, at least for a while. They must have sent for backup even before they attacked the cabin."

The Gasman ground dust between his fingertips. "At least we took two of them out." He wondered if Iggy felt as weird and bad about it as he did. He couldn't tell.

"Yeah, but what now? We're kinda all dressed up with no place to go," Iggy said. "There's no way we can go home — they're probably everywhere. What are we supposed to do with ourselves? And what if Max and the others come back just to fly into an ambush?"

"I don't know," the Gasman said in frustration. "I

hadn't thought beyond just blowing them the heck up. Maybe *you* should come up with a plan."

The two boys sat in the semidarkness of the fissure, breathing the stale air. The Gasman's stomach rumbled.

"Tell me about it," Iggy said, resting his head on his knees.

"Okay, okay," the Gasman said suddenly. "I have an idea. It's risky, and Max will kill us when she finds out."

Iggy raised his head. "Sounds like my kind of idea."

40

Never in my fourteen looong years have I felt the slightest bit normal — except for my day with Ella and her mom, Dr. Martinez.

First, we ate a real breakfast together, around the kitchen table. On plates, with forks and knives and napkins. Instead of, like, a hot dog stuck on a barbecue fork, burned black over an open flame, then eaten right off the fork. Or cereal with no milk. Or peanut butter off a knife. Beanie weenies from the can.

Then Ella had to go to school. I was worried about the jerks from before, but she said her teacher was good at keeping kids in line, and so was the school bus driver. A real school bus! Like on TV shows.

So it was me and Dr. Martinez. "So, Max," she said as she unloaded the dishwasher.

I tensed.

"Do you want to talk about . . . anything?"

I looked at her. Her face was tan and kind, her eyes warm and understanding. But I knew if I started talking, I would never stop. I would break down and start crying.

I would freak out. Then I wouldn't be Max anymore, wouldn't be able to function, take care of the others, be the alpha girl. To save Angel. If it wasn't already too late.

"Not really," I said.

She nodded and started stacking clean plates. I fantasized about actually being friends with Ella and her mom long after I left here and went home. I could come back and visit sometimes. . . . Yeah, and we could have picnics, exchange Christmas cards. . . . I'm so *sure.* I was totally losing my grip on reality. I had to get out of here.

Dr. Martinez put away the clean plates and loaded the dirty ones into the dishwasher. "Do you have a last name?"

I thought. Since I didn't have an "official" identity, there wasn't anything she could do with the information. I rubbed my temples — a headache had been creeping up on me since breakfast.

"Yeah," I said finally. I shrugged. "I gave it to myself."

On my eleventh birthday (which was also a day I picked for myself), I had asked Jeb about a last name. I guess I was hoping he would say, "Your name is Batchelder, like me." But he hadn't. He'd said, "You should choose one yourself."

So I'd thought about it, thought about how I could fly and who I was.

"My last name is Ride," I told Ella's mom. "Like Sally Ride, the astronaut. Maximum Ride."

She nodded. "That's a good name. Are there others like you?" she asked.

I pressed my lips together and looked away. My head was throbbing. I *wanted* to tell her — that was the awful part. Something inside me wanted to blurt out everything. But I couldn't. Not after years of Jeb telling me I couldn't trust anybody, ever.

"Do you need help?"

My eyes flicked back to her face.

"Max — with your wings — can you actually fly?"

"Well, *yeah,*" I was startled into saying. That's me: mouth-like-a-steel-trap Maximum. Yep, you have to use all your tricks to get *me* to talk. Jeez. That's what I get for sleeping on a soft bed and eating homey food.

"Really? You can really fly?" She looked fascinated, alarmed, and a little envious.

I nodded. "My bones are . . . thin," I began, hating myself. *Shut up, Max!* "Thin and light. I have extra muscles. My lungs are bigger. And my heart. More efficient. But I need to eat a lot. It's hard." Abruptly, I clammed up, a furious blush heating my cheeks. That, folks, was the most I had ever said to a non–flock member. But when I spill the beans, I spill big! I might as well have hired a skywriting plane to scrawl, "I'm a mutant freak!" in huge letters across the sky.

"How did this happen?" Ella's mom asked softly.

My eyes shut of their own volition. If I'd been alone I would have put my hands over my ears and hunkered down into a little ball on the floor. Fractured images, memories, fear, pain, all came crashing together inside my brain. You think being a regular teenager with growing pains is hard? Try doing it with DNA that's not your own, not even from a *mammal*.

"I don't remember," I told her. It was a lie.

41

Dr. Martinez looked distressed. "Max, are you sure I can't help in some way?"

I shook my head, irritated at myself, irritated at her for bringing all this up. "Nah. It's all over, anyway. Done. But — I have to get out of here. Some friends are waiting for me. It's really important."

"How will you get to them? Can I give you a ride?"

"No," I said, frowning and rubbing my hurt shoulder. "I need to, um, fly there. But I don't think I can fly yet."

Dr. Martinez creased her forehead, thinking. "It would be dangerous for you to strain your injury before it's healed. I couldn't tell the extent of it. But I could give you a better idea if we had an X-ray."

I looked at her solemnly. "Do you have X-ray vision?"

She laughed, startled, and I couldn't help grinning too. God, Ella had this *all the time*. A real mom.

"No. Not all of us have superhuman powers," she said teasingly. "But some of us have access to X-ray machines."

Dr. Martinez shared a vet practice with another doctor. Today was her day off, but she was sure no one would think it was weird for us to show up at the office. She gave me a windbreaker to wear, but I was still pretty freaked about seeing other people up close.

"Hi, guys," Dr. Martinez said as we walked into the office. "This is a friend of Ella's. She's doing a report on being a vet, and I told her I'd give her a quick tour."

The three people behind the counter smiled and nodded as if this was totally believable. Maybe it was. How would I know?

Two seconds after I walked in, I froze in the doorway, feeling the blood rush out of my face and a wash of terror sweep over me.

There was a man there.

In a white coat.

Dr. Martinez glanced back. "Max?"

I stared at her mutely. She gently took my arm and led me off into an exam room. "Yes, in here is where we see our patients," she said cheerfully as she shut the door behind us. Then she turned and lowered her voice. "Max, what's wrong? What's the matter?"

I forced myself to take several slow, deep breaths, to uncoil the fists at my sides. "It's the smell," I whispered, embarrassed. "The chemical smell, like a lab. The guy in the white coat. I have to get out of here, okay? Can we just go now, really fast?" I looked for an exit, a window.

Her hand rubbed my back. "I can promise that you're safe here. Can you stay just long enough for me to get a quick X-ray, and then we'll leave right away?"

I tried to swallow, but my mouth was dry. My heart was pounding so hard it made a rushing sound in my ears.

"Please, Max."

I forced myself to nod. Dr. Martinez checked to make sure I wasn't wearing jewelry — as if — then carefully positioned me on a table. A machine hovered over me. I felt like my nerves were about to snap.

She stepped out of the room, I heard a tiny *buzz*, and it was all over.

Two minutes later she showed me a large dark sheet with my shoulder bones, arm, and part of my wing showing in shades of white. She stuck it up on a glass box on the wall and turned on its light. The picture jumped out brightly.

"Look," she said, tracing my shoulder blade with her finger. "This bone is fine. It's all muscle damage — you can see the torn tissue here and here."

I nodded.

"And your wing bones," she said, unconsciously lowering her voice, "all seem fine. Which is good. Unfortunately, muscle damage usually takes longer to heal than bones do. Though your rate of regeneration seems weirdly fast, I must say."

She frowned at the X-ray, tapping it with her finger. "Your bones are so fine and light," she murmured, as if talking to herself. "They're beautiful. And then . . . huh. What's this thing?"

She was pointing to a bright white square, maybe half

an inch wide, that sat smack-dab in the middle of my fore-arm. "That's not jewelry, is it?" She glanced down at me. "Is it the zipper of the windbreaker?"

"No — I took it off."

Dr. Martinez leaned closer to the picture, squinting her eyes. "It's a — it looks like a . . ." Her voice trailed off.

"What?" I said, unnerved by the expression on her face.

"It's a microchip," she said hesitantly. "We put something similar into animals. To identify them in case they're lost. Yours looks like a, like ones we use on really expensive pets, show dogs and such. They have a tracer in them in case they're stolen. They can be tracked, wherever they are."

42

The look of comprehending horror that rose in my face alarmed Dr. Martinez.

"I'm not saying that's what it is," she said quickly. "It's just what it looks like."

"Take it out," I said hoarsely. I held out my arm and pushed up my sleeve. "Please. Take it out right now."

She looked at the X-ray again, studying it for several minutes while I tried not to jump out of my skin.

"I'm sorry, Max," she said at last. "I don't think it can be surgically removed. It looks like it was implanted a long time ago, when your arm was much smaller. Now your muscles and nerves, blood vessels, have grown around it so completely that I think if we tried to take it out, you could possibly lose the use of your hand."

You'd think I'd get used to the ongoing nightmare that was my life, but I was actually pathetically surprised that those demonoids from the School could continue to wreak havoc on me from so far away, so long ago.

But why was I surprised? I asked myself bitterly. They had done just that two days ago, when they'd kidnapped

Angel. An image of her popped into my mind, her sweet, small face smiling up at me, love shining out. I swallowed hard and took a deep breath.

Right then, we became aware of voices in the waiting room, men's voices, smooth and charming, asking questions.

I froze again, doing my deer-in-the-headlights imitation.

Dr. Martinez looked at me and listened to the voices. "I'm sure this is nothing, Max," she said calmly. "But why don't you step in here for a minute?"

In the hall was a small door that led to their medicine storage closet. Several long white coats hung inside, and I slid in behind them, flattening myself against the wall.

And yes, I get the irony, thanks.

Dr. Martinez turned off the light and closed the door. Barely twenty seconds later, I heard the voices in the examining room where I had been.

"What's going on here?" Dr. Martinez said sharply, sounding outraged. "This is a doctor's office!"

"Sorry, ma'am," one voice said, sounding as if it were made of honey. My heart began to pound.

"Doctor!" she snapped.

"Sorry, Doctor," another voice said. It was soothing, calming, placating. "Forgive us for interrupting. There's nothing to be concerned about. We're with local law enforcement."

"We're looking for anything unusual," said the first voice. "Just a precaution. I'm afraid I can't tell you more than that." Implying that it was all top-secret government stuff. Maybe I was.

There was a pause. Was Dr. Martinez being drawn in by their voices? She wouldn't be the first one. Oh, God . . .

I suddenly remembered my X-ray up on the light box, and I clapped my hand over my mouth. My stomach tightened. In the next minute I could be fighting for my life. It was too dark to look for possible weapons. *Think, think . . .*

"Unusual like what?" Dr. Martinez said acidly. "A double rainbow? Gasoline for less than a buck fifty? Sugar-free soda that actually tastes good?"

I couldn't help grinning. She was just so great. And she seemed immune to Erasers, which was really weird.

"No," said the second voice after a moment. "Unusual *people,* for instance. Strangers in the neighborhood. Children or teenagers that you don't know or who look suspicious. Or unusual animals, even."

"I'm a veterinary surgeon," said Dr. Martinez in a chilling voice. "To tell you the truth, I usually don't look at my patients' owners much. And I haven't seen any strangers around. As for unusual *animals,* last week I treated a cow that had a bicornuate uterus. She had a healthy calf in each side. Does that help?"

Silence. I would hate to be on the receiving end of her anger.

"Um . . ." said the first voice.

"If you gentlemen will excuse me, I have a business to

run." Icicles dripped off her words. "The way out is through that door."

"If you do see or hear of anything unusual, here's a number for you to call. Thanks for your time. Sorry to disturb you."

Heavy footsteps faded from my hearing. A minute later I felt the front door slam shut.

"If you see those two guys again, call the cops," Dr. Martinez said to the receptionist.

She came and let me out of the closet, looking at my face solemnly.

"Those guys were bad news," she said, "am I right?"

I nodded. "I better leave right now."

She shook her head. "Tomorrow morning is soon enough. One more night of rest. Promise me."

I opened my mouth to argue, but what came out was "Okay. I promise."

43

"Nudge, for the last time, give this up. This is a bad idea," said Fang. "A *terrible* idea."

Privately, Nudge was surprised that Fang was still with her. Fang had threatened to leave her several times, but when he saw she really wouldn't budge, he'd retreated into angry silence.

Now they were at the edge of a trailer home neighborhood. Nudge had remembered an address, and Tipisco was so small that it wasn't hard to get around and find it. She didn't know what she had expected, but somehow this wasn't it.

The trailer park was divided into meandering rows, most marked by rickety wooden signs with names like Roadrunner Lane or Seguro Street on them.

"Come on," Fang said softly. "I see Chaparral Court."

They snaked their way through the chokecherry bushes, gnarled junipers, abandoned appliances, and car skeletons that surrounded the neighborhood. No white picket fences anywhere.

Nudge's quick eyes spotted an address, 4625, on the

last mobile home of the line. She swallowed. Her parents could be *right there*. She pushed aside some spray paint cans, and she and Fang crouched beside an abandoned, graffitied car.

"What if they moved?" Fang asked for the nth time. "What if you misunderstood what you read and these people aren't related to you at all?" Then, with horrible gentleness, he said, "Nudge, even if you weren't a test-tube baby — which you probably were — what if there was a reason they gave you up? They might not want you back."

"Do you think I haven't thought of that?" she whispered with uncharacteristic anger. "I know that! But I have to try. I mean, if there's the slightest chance — wouldn't you try?"

"I don't know," Fang said after a pause.

"That's because you don't need anything or anybody," Nudge said, turning back to stare at the mobile home. "But I'm not like that. I need people."

Fang was silent.

They were fairly out of sight between the car and some small pinyon trees. Nudge felt so nervous she was practically shaking.

Beside her, Fang tensed, and then Nudge heard a door opening. She held her breath as a woman came out of the mobile home. Nudge quickly looked at her own arm to see if their skin tones matched. Kind of. It was hard to tell. The woman came down into the front yard, which was covered in brown pine needles, and sat down in a cheap lawn chair in the shade.

Her hair was wet and in curlers, and there was a towel draped around her shoulders. She leaned back, lit a cigarette, and popped the top on a can of soda.

"Coke. It's not just for breakfast anymore," Fang whispered, and Nudge elbowed him.

Hmm. Nudge sat back on her heels. It was weird. Part of her hoped that *wasn't* her mom. It would have been better if she'd been, like, setting a tray of cookies on the windowsill to cool or gardening or something. Something mommish. But part of her still hoped it was her mom, because, frankly, *some*one, *any*one, was better than no one.

Nudge just needed to get up, stroll over there, and say, "Um, did you lose a daughter named Monique, about ten, eleven years ago?" Yep, that's all she had to say. And then the woman would say —

"Looking for something, freaks? Guess you found it."

There was no mistaking that beautiful, melodic Eraser laugh, right behind them.

44

Nudge jackknifed to her feet. There were three of them, and they were already beginning to morph. They started off looking like male models, but then their freaky muzzles elongated, fangs erupted from bloodred gums, ragged claws grew from their fingertips.

"Ari," Fang said evenly.

Nudge frowned and looked at the leader. Her eyes widened. "Ari!" she said. "You were just a little kid."

He smiled, flexing his clawed hands. "And now I'm a great big grown-up Eraser," he said. He snapped his teeth together playfully, making strong clicking sounds. "And you're a little brown piglet. Yum."

"What did they do to you?" Nudge asked quietly. "I'm sorry, Ari."

He frowned, his hairy brow lowering. "Save your pity for yourself. I'm exactly who I want to be. And I've got some news for you." He rolled up his sleeves to reveal heavily corded, muscled, hairy arms. "Your hideout in the mountains is nothing but ashes. Your pals keep having unfortunate accidents. You two are the last ones alive — and now we've got you."

This struck the Erasers as funny, and they chuckled, shoulders shaking, while Nudge's brain reeled. Last two alive? The others were dead? Their house had burned down?

She began to cry and commanded herself to stop but couldn't. Then she was weeping like a baby.

She glanced anxiously at Fang, but he was watching Ari, his jaw tight, his hands coiled into fists.

"Pinwheel," he muttered out of the side of his mouth.

Ari frowned, obviously wondering what *pinwheel* meant, his large, beautiful eyes narrowing.

"Cholla first," Nudge muttered. She couldn't believe she was being so brave, almost like Fang. *The rest of the flock was dead? It couldn't be! It just couldn't!*

"Count of three," Fang said evenly. Which meant *count of one*.

Ari leaned over, lightning fast, and cuffed Fang's shoulder. "Shut up!"

"One," Fang said, regaining his balance, and Nudge instantly lunged forward, shoving the second Eraser in the chest as hard as she could. Taken off guard, he staggered backward, right into the sharp spines of a cholla cactus. Cursing, the Eraser waved his arms but landed smack on top of its three-inch needles, shrieking like a train wreck in the making. A lovely, musical train wreck.

In the next second, Nudge launched herself into the air sideways, praying that Fang would catch her.

He did, grabbing her arms and swinging her, following her momentum. Her feet kicked outward, smashing Ari in the side of the neck, almost knocking him over, and leaving him choking and gagging.

Then Fang swung Nudge as hard as he could, spinning her through the air as she snapped out her wings and beat them so fast that she stayed airborne.

"You're gonna die, mutant," Ari snarled, leaping for Fang as he pushed off the ground. He grabbed Fang's leg, and they both fell heavily. Then Ari was sitting on Fang's chest, punching him. Nudge gasped and put her hand over her mouth as she saw blood erupt from Fang's nose. The second Eraser kicked at Fang's chest, hard, over and over, *thunk, thunk.*

Nudge was freaking — this was a disaster. The people in the trailer park were bound to notice her, hovering in front of the trees. Fang took another hit, his head jerking sideways, and then he spit a stream of bloody saliva right into Ari's face. Ari roared and brought both hands down onto Fang's chest with enough force to snap his ribs. Nudge heard Fang's breath leave him with a *whoosh.*

What to do? If she went down to the ground she would be dead meat, and so would Fang. If only she could —

Then she remembered the cans of spray paint on the ground. Maybe they were empty. *Maybe not.*

In an instant, she had dropped down, grabbed up the

nearest can, and leaped back into the air, out of reach. She shook the can hard, then dropped a few feet and aimed it right at Ari's face. After a heart-stopping wheeze, green paint arced through the air. Ari screamed and jumped to his feet, his clawed hands swiping at his eyes.

Fang leaped up and took off faster than she'd ever seen him move. Nudge managed to get another Eraser in the face, and then the paint ran out. Nudge threw it hard at Ari's head, where it bounced off his healthy, thick, *green* hair.

Then she and Fang were in the air, well above the Erasers. Ari was still standing, but his pal was on the ground, swearing and trying to wipe paint out of his eyes. The one who'd finally gotten off the cactus was way scratched up. Between the red blood and green paint, they looked kind of Christmassy.

"You're *dead,* freaks," Ari snarled, his eyes streaming with tears, his long yellow teeth seeming too large for his mouth.

"Oh, like you're not a freak *yourself,*" Nudge said meanly. "Try looking in a mirror, dog boy!"

Ari fumbled in his jacket, then pulled out a gun. Nudge and Fang rocketed out of there as fast as they could. A bullet whistled right past Nudge's ear. She'd been *that* close to being deaf and dead.

When they were safely away, Nudge said breathlessly, "I'm sorry, Fang. It was my fault you got hurt."

Fang spit more blood out and watched it fall a long,

JAMES PATTERSON

long way to the ground. "It wasn't your fault," he said. "You're just a kid."

"Let's go home," she said.

"They said it burned down," Fang answered, wiping blood from his lip.

"No, I mean the home with the hawks," said Nudge.

45

Angel stared and stared and stared at Jeb Batchelder.

She knew who he was. She had been only four years old the last time she'd seen him, but still, she knew his face, his smile. She remembered Jeb tying her shoes, playing Old Maid with her, making popcorn. She remembered hurting herself and Jeb picking her up to hold her tight. Max had filled in for her how good Jeb had been, how he'd saved them from the bad people at the School. How he'd disappeared and they thought he was dead.

But he was alive! And he was here! He had come *back* to save her again! Hope filled her like warm light. Angel almost jumped up to run to his arms.

Wait. Think. There was something wrong with this picture.

She couldn't get a single thought from his head — it was a gray blank. That had never happened before. Also, he was wearing a *white coat.* He smelled all antisepticky. The fact that he was here *at all.* Her brain felt simultaneously hyper and sluggish, and she blinked several times, trying to figure this out, as if it were a two-minute mystery.

Jeb knelt on the wooden floor in front of her. The white-coats who'd been running the maze melted into the background. Jeb reached back, then held something out to her.

Angel looked at it blankly.

It was a tray of food, lots of delish-looking food, hot and steaming. It smelled so good Angel felt a whimper of longing rise in her throat.

She stared at the tray, her brain crackling with input, and she had a bunch of thoughts all at once.

One, Jeb looked like he was on *their* side now. An enemy of the flock, like all the other whitecoats at the School.

Two, wait till Max found out about this. Max would be, well, she'd be so mad and so hurt and so upset that Angel couldn't even imagine it. She didn't *want* to imagine it. She didn't want Max to ever feel that way.

"Angel, aren't you hungry? You haven't been getting very much to eat, have you?" Jeb looked concerned. "When they told me what they'd been feeding you — well, they misunderstood, sweetheart. They didn't know about your appetite."

He laughed a little, shaking his head. "I remember once we were having hot dogs for lunch. Everyone else had two hot dogs each. But you — you ate four hot dogs by yourself." He laughed again, looking at her as if he thought she was amazing. "You were three years old. Four hot dogs!"

He leaned forward, gently pushing the food tray nearer so it was right beneath Angel's nose.

"The thing is, Angel, with your metabolism, and how old

144

you are now, you should be getting about three thousand calories a day. I bet you haven't been hitting a thousand." He shook his head again. "That's going to change now that I'm here. I'll make sure they treat you right, okay?"

Angel narrowed her eyes. This was a trap. This was exactly the kind of thing Max had warned them all about. Only Max had never guessed it would come from Jeb.

Without saying a word, Angel sat up, crossing her arms over her chest and staring at him the way Max stared at Fang when they were having an argument and she was going to win. Angel made herself not look at the food, not even smell the food. She was so freaked at seeing Jeb here that her stomach was all in knots anyway. The fact that she couldn't pick up any of his thoughts made him seem weird and dead to her.

Jeb smiled ruefully and patted Angel's knee. "It's okay, Angel. Go ahead and eat. You need to. I want you to feel better."

She tried not to even blink, not to show how upset she was.

Sighing, Jeb unrolled the white paper napkin, took out a fork, and placed the fork right into the food on the plate. All she would have to do is reach down . . . and she was doomed?

"I know this is all confusing, Angel," Jeb said gently. "I can't explain everything now. It will all become clear soon, though, and then you'll understand."

"Suurrre." Angel put every bit of pain at her betrayal into that one word.

"The thing is, Angel," Jeb went on earnestly, "life itself is a test. It's all a test. Sometimes you just have to get through it, and then later on everything makes more sense. You'll see. Now, go ahead and eat. I promise it's okay. I *promise.*"

Like she would believe any of his promises.

"I hate you," she said.

Jeb didn't look surprised. Maybe a bit sad. "That's okay too, sweetheart. That's perfectly okay."

46

"I. Am. In. Heaven," I said, inhaling deeply.

Dr. Martinez laughed. "Watched cookies never brown," she teased me.

To make my Mayberry holiday complete, the three of us had actually made chocolate chip cookies — from *scratch* — after dinner.

I ate enough raw cookie dough to make myself sick, and then I got high off the fumes of gently baking cookies. I could see the chocolate chips melting through the oven window.

Note to self: Show Nudge and Angel how to make choc-chip cookies.

If I ever saw Angel again.

Ella's mom took the first cookie sheet out of the oven and slid in the second. I could hardly wait for the cookies to cool and, seizing one, took a bite, almost burning my tongue.

Incoherent murmurings of pleasure escaped my lips as I chewed slowly, savoring every bite. Ella and her mom watched me, identical smiles lighting their faces.

"You'd think you'd never tasted homemade cookies before," Ella said.

"Haven't," I mumbled, swallowing. It was the best thing I had ever tasted in my entire life. It tasted like home.

"Well, have another," said Dr. Martinez.

"I have to take off tomorrow," I told Ella that night when we were getting ready for bed.

"No!" she said, distressed. "I love having you here. You're like a cousin. Or my sister."

Funny how something like that can make you feel worse. "People are depending on me — it's really important."

"Will you come back to visit?" she asked. *"Ever?"*

I looked at her helplessly. It was the first time I had ever connected with a nonflock human being — besides Jeb.

It had been really cool. The best.

Plus her mom was *so* awesome. She was strict about some things — don't leave your socks lying around — but so not strict about other things, like calling the cops about my bullet wound. Unlike any other parent I'd ever heard of, she didn't press for details, didn't lecture, and believed what I said. She actually accepted me. Like she accepted Ella, for who she was.

It was enough to give me a psychotic break — if I let myself dwell on it.

"Probably not," I said, hating the hurt look on Ella's face. "I just — don't think I'll be able to. If I ever could, I would, but —"

I turned away and started brushing my teeth. Jeb had always said to think with your brain, not your emotions. He'd been right, as usual. So I put all my feelings in a box and locked it.

47

Nudge still couldn't accept that Max and the others were dead. It was impossible — she couldn't deal with it — so she forced herself to think other thoughts.

Nudge guessed it was kind of sad that, right now, this scraped-out shallow ledge in the middle of a desert cliff actually felt cozy and comfortable to her. She lay on her back, feet up against the wall, bruised legs out straight, examining the strata of colors — cream, tan, pink, peach — in the solid rock overhead. The sun out there was hot, but it was cool in here, and breezy.

It just goes to show you, she thought. You think you need all your stuff, your favorite cup, your best blanket, soap, your *parents* — and then you realize that all you really need is to be where the Erasers can't get you.

She couldn't get over Ari. He'd been a little kid the last time she'd seen him. She remembered how he'd seemed to get on Max's nerves, always following her around. Now he was a full-grown Eraser, the worst of them all. How could that have happened in only four years?

Half an hour ago, she and Fang had heard the very

distant *chop-chop* of a helicopter. They'd pulled as far back into the cave as they could, flattening themselves against the cool back wall. After twenty minutes of silence, Fang had decided it was safe and gone to look for food. She hoped he came back soon.

Their house was burned to cinders. Every one of her friends except Fang was dead. She and Fang were really on their own — maybe forever.

Fang flapped up the side of the cliff, landing almost silently on their ledge. Nudge felt a warm flow of relief.

"Can I interest you in a bit of raw desert rat?" he asked, patting his windbreaker pocket.

"Oh, no!" Nudge said, horrified.

He shrugged off his windbreaker and brushed some dust off his black T-shirt. Popping something in his mouth, he chewed and swallowed loudly. "Can't get fresher," he said cajolingly.

"Ugh!" Nudge shuddered and turned away from him. Rat! Flying like the hawks was one thing; eating like them was *not* going to happen.

"Okay, then," said Fang. "How about some kabobs? You get the vegetables."

Whirling, Nudge saw Fang unfolding a foil packet. Instantly, the smoky, meaty smell of cooked beef and vegetables filled her nose.

"Kabobs!" she said, hurrying to sit by Fang. "Where did you get them? You didn't have time to go all the way to town. Oh, my gosh, they're still hot."

"Let's just say some campers are going to be a little surprised," Fang said drily, pushing the meat off into one pile, the onions and peppers into another.

Nudge took a bite of grilled pepper. It was warm, smoky, tender — utter heaven.

"Now, *this* is food," she said, closing her eyes.

"So I guess we have to decide whether to keep looking for Max or go try to save Angel," said Fang, eating the chunks of beef.

"But the Erasers said everyone else was dead. Doesn't that mean Angel and Max too?" Nudge asked, feeling a sad weight settle on her again.

"No way to tell," Fang said. "The thing is, if Max isn't here, is it because she's dead? How would they have found her? Angel . . ." He paused. "Well, we *knew* they had Angel. That's probably all over by now."

Nudge held her head in her hands. "I can't think about it."

"I know. But what are your —" He stopped, squinting, looking off into the distance.

Shading her eyes, Nudge looked out too. Way far off, she could barely make out two dark splotches. Well, so what? Just more hawks.

She sat back and slowly ate her last chunk of onion, then licked the foil they'd been wrapped in. Fang had to come up with a plan — that was all there was to it.

But Fang kept looking out at the sky.

Nudge frowned. The two dark splotches were bigger

now, closer. They must be mighty big hawks. Maybe they were eagles!

Suddenly, Fang stood and fished in his pocket for his small metal mirror. Holding out his hand, he caught the last bits of sunset in the mirror, flashing their reflection outward.

He flashed it, then stopped, flashed, then stopped.

The hawks became larger, closer. Now they were definitely spiraling downward in their direction.

Please don't let them be flying Erasers, Nudge thought in sudden panic. She'd realized they were too big, too awkward to be real raptors.

Then her mouth dropped open. Half a minute later, Iggy and the Gasman landed clumsily on the ledge, knocking rocks and dust everywhere. Nudge just stared at them, so happy she could hardly believe it.

"You aren't *dead,*" she said.

"No. You aren't dead either," said Iggy irritably. "How about just 'hello'?"

"Hi, guys," said the Gasman, brushing dust out of his hair. "We couldn't stay home — there's Erasers all over the mountain. So we decided to come here. Anybody have a problem with that?"

48

The next morning I pulled on my new sweatshirt. I'd tried out my wing. It worked, though it was incredibly stiff and sore.

I was relieved to go, to get back in the air. I knew Fang and Nudge were going to kill me. I knew I had let Angel down. But there was no way I could have *not* done what I did. I wouldn't be Max.

To tell you the truth, not being Max sometimes had its appeal.

Dr. Martinez pushed a small backpack at me. "It's an old one — I don't use it," she said quickly, knowing I wanted to refuse any more help. "Please take it."

"Well, since you said 'please,'" I muttered, and she laughed.

Ella was watching the ground, her shoulders hunched. I tried not to look at her either.

"If you ever need anything, anything at all, please call us," said Ella's mom. "I put my phone numbers inside the pack."

I nodded, even though I knew I would never use the numbers. I had no idea what to say. But I had to try.

"You guys helped me," I said stiffly, "and you didn't even

know me. It would have been bad if you hadn't." How's that for eloquent, eh? I sounded like freaking *Tarzan*.

"You helped *me*," Ella pointed out. "And you didn't even know me. You got hurt because of me."

I shrugged in that endearing way I have. "Anyway — thanks. Thanks for everything. I really appreciate it."

"You're welcome," said Ella's mom, smiling kindly. "We were glad to do it. And good luck — with whatever happens."

I nodded, and then — get this — they both hugged me at once, like a Max sandwich. Once again, I felt the horror of tears starting in my eyes, and I blinked them back quickly. But I let them hug me, and sort of patted Ella's elbow, which was all I could reach. I won't lie to you — it felt really good. And really awful at the same time. Because what's worse than knowing you want something, besides knowing you can never have it?

I disengaged myself gently and opened the door. Outside, it was sunny and warm. I gave a little half-wave, hoping it was jaunty, then headed out into the yard. I'd decided to give them a sort-of present. I felt they deserved it.

Would they think I looked goofy? What did we — the flock — look like to outsiders? I had no idea, and I didn't have time to start caring.

I adjusted my sweatshirt and the backpack. I turned. Ella and her mom were watching me with wide, curious eyes.

I ran a few steps and leaped upward, unfurling my wings, feeling them fill with air, wincing slightly as my damaged muscles pulled and strained. Fully extended, my wings were thirteen feet across, speckled brown and splotched with white.

A hard downstroke, *ouch*, then upward, *ouch*, then down. The familiar rhythm. Ella's face was awed and delighted, her hands clasped together. Dr. Martinez was wiping her eyes, her smile wobbly.

A minute later, I was way high, looking down on Ella's little house, at the two small figures waving hard up at me. I waved back, then banked, feeling the familiar joy of flying, the freedom, the speed. I soared off toward the horizon, heading northwest, on my way to meet Nudge and Fang, who I hoped would miraculously still be where I'd told them to be.

Thanks, Ella, I thought, refusing to feel sad. *Thank you both, for everything.*

Angel, I'm on my way at last.

PART 3

SCHOOL — WHAT COULD BE SCARIER THAN THAT?

49

After about half an hour, I felt like I'd worked most of the kinks out of my muscles. I knew tomorrow I'd be horribly sore, but right now I felt okay, and right now was what mattered. I flew hard and fast, coasting on air currents whenever I could.

This time, I didn't look down.

An hour later, I was approaching the meeting place, praying that Nudge and Fang had waited for me.

I was two days late, and I wouldn't blame them for giving up on me, but I didn't want to think about the possibility that they had decided to rescue Angel on their own.

When I got close to the meeting place, I started circling big, losing altitude slowly while examining the ground, the cliffs, the shadows. Nothing.

I flew the length of a canyon, looking for signs, but was disappointed again. Panic made my throat tighten. I'd been so *stupid*.

Oh, God, what if they had never made it here? What if —

A shadow fell across me, and I glanced up, thinking,

helicopter! But it wasn't — just a scattered flock of hawks above me, wheeling through the sky.

I frowned and angled myself upward. Several of the hawks were oddly large and misshapen. But they were flying right along with the others and seemed part of their flock. I squinted and focused, all the time gaining altitude.

My heart swelled — there were four way-too-big hawks, all right. Except hawks usually weren't quite as awkward as these four. And hawks didn't usually wear sneakers.

They had waited for me, all right, and they were safe. Relief and joy flooded through my body and soul. Now we would go find Angel, and then the flock would be whole again.

And yes, I did say *soul.*

50

They spotted me, and bright, goofy smiles lit the faces of the Gasman and Nudge.

Iggy of course didn't see me at all, and Fang wasn't a big smiler. He caught my eye and motioned with his head, over toward a cliff. It had been only two days since I'd seen him, but he seemed to be flying with a new grace and power, his fourteen-foot wingspan glinting darkly in the sun. As we got closer, Nudge squealed happily, brushing her wing against mine. "Max! Max! I can't believe it! *Can* I believe it?"

Fang landed first, almost disappearing into nothing. It was only when I was about twenty feet from the cliff that I saw he had tucked into a shallow ledge scraped out of the cliff face. It was an excellent waiting place.

One after another, we flew in and landed, scurrying toward the back of the cave so others could come in after us. We were together. We five were safe, at least.

"Max!" Nudge cried, rushing over to hug me. Her thin arms gripped me tight, and I hugged her back, scratching her wings where they joined her shoulders, the way she liked. "We were so worried — I didn't know what had happened to you, and we didn't know what to do, and Fang said we were going to eat rats, and —"

"Okay, okay. Everything's okay," I told her. I met Fang's eyes over her shoulder and mouthed *Rats?* silently. A flicker of a grin crossed his lips and then was gone. I looked down into Nudge's big brown eyes. "I'm just so glad to see you safe," I told her. I turned to the Gasman and Iggy. "What are *you two* doing here? Why didn't you stay home?"

"We couldn't," the Gasman began earnestly. "There were Erasers all over the mountain. They were hunting for us. We'd be dog meat by now."

"When did they start hunting for you?" I asked, startled. "Right after we left?"

"No," said the Gasman slowly. He slanted a glance at Iggy, who was standing impassively, brushing dust he couldn't see off his dark pants.

"What?" I said, suspicion starting to rise in me. "When did they start coming after you?"

"Was it — was it after the oil-slick Hummer crash?" the Gasman asked Iggy tentatively.

My eyes widened. *Oil-slick Hummer crash?*

Iggy rubbed his chin, thinking.

"Or maybe it was more — after the bomb," the Gasman said in a low voice, looking down.

"I think it was the bomb," Iggy agreed. "That definitely seemed to tick them off."

"Bomb?" I asked incredulously. *"Bomb?* You guys set off a *bomb?* Didn't that tell the Erasers exactly where you were? You should have stayed hidden!"

"They already knew where we were," the Gasman explained. "They'd seen all of us — they knew we were in the area."

"It was just a matter of time," Iggy agreed.

I didn't know what to say. To tell you the truth, I hadn't actually considered the fact that the Erasers might find our house. I opened my mouth and closed it again, at a loss. Maybe in about twenty years I would get the hang of dealing with boys. And maybe not.

"Well, I'm glad you're safe," I said lamely, and heard Fang trying to smother his laughter. I ignored him. "You were right to come here. Smart thinking. Excellent."

I hugged the Gasman, then Iggy, who was almost five inches taller than I am, I realized. I hugged Nudge again, and she clung to me as I stroked her hair. "It's okay, sweetie," I said softly.

Finally, she let me go and I reached out to hug Fang. Fang is not the huggiest person in the world — he turns into an unbending statue, and you just have to do the best you can. Which I did.

Then I held my left hand out in a fist, and the other four instantly stacked their left fists on top of it. We each tapped the other's hands twice, then threw our arms up in the air.

"To Angel!" I yelled, and their voices echoed mine.

"To Angel! To Angel!"

Then, one by one, we fell off the side of the cliff, opened our wings, and headed for the hated, dreaded School.

51

"Okay," I said, once we were high, flying with a steady rhythm. "How about some quick reports?"

"I tried to find my mom," Nudge said with no warning.

"Whaaat?" My eyes went as wide as they could go. "Your *mom?*"

Nudge shrugged. "I made Fang go down to Tipisco while we were waiting for you. We found the right address. I saw a woman, and she was my kind of color, but I wasn't sure. Then the Erasers, including that dirtbag Ari, showed up, so we kicked butt and left."

It took me a minute to digest this. "So you didn't talk to her? Umm, your mom?"

"No." Nudge carefully examined her fingernails, keeping her wings moving steadily.

"Did she look nice?" I was consumed with curiosity. Parents were something we all obsessed about, talked about constantly, cried about — if truth be told.

"I'll tell you about it later," Nudge said offhandedly, so I knew it had gone badly.

I narrowed my eyes at Gazzy and Iggy. "We know what

you've been up to," I said. Gazzy gave me his sweet, abashed smile. That kid.

Time for news of my own.

"I think I have a tracer chip implanted in me," I said baldly, feeling a coaster current in my face. I angled my wings and glided. "I'm not positive, but it showed up on an X-ray, and that's what it looked like."

Jaws dropped. Everyone stared at me in horror.

"You had an X-ray?" Fang looked incredulous.

I nodded. "Details later. If I do have this chip, it explains all the Erasers everywhere — but not why it's taken them four years to hunt us down. And I don't know if any of you have one," I added, seeing the question on Iggy's face.

Everyone was quiet, flying with their thoughts and fears.

Then, "Max? Do you think there's still a chance?" The Gasman was forcing himself to be strong. Another reason I like that kid.

"I don't know. I hope so," I said honestly. Honesty is always good, except when it's better to lie. Like to protect them. "I know I've delayed us by two days. I'm really sorry about that. I just did what I felt I had to do. But we've come this far — there's no turning back. We're going after Angel, no matter what."

There were a few moments of silence, as if we were all gathering our courage again. I know I was, trying to pull my strength into a tight, hard ball that would carry me through the rest of the day, as we headed back to our worst nightmare.

Anybody's worst nightmare, believe me.

52

I don't think I've mentioned this, but all of us in the flock have an inborn sense of direction. I don't know how it works. We just always know which way we're going. So we rocketed west-northwest for a good two hours. Many of the hawks whose cliff Fang and Nudge had shared stayed with us, flying in loose formation. Our new best pals.

"We learned some stuff from the hawks," Fang said, seeing me watch them. "Some banking moves, how they communicate, stuff like that."

"They're really cool," Nudge added, flying closer to me. "They, like, use the tips of their feathers to help aim them, and we tried it, and it was amazing. A little thing like that makes such a difference. Like, I practically didn't even know I could move those feathers."

"Can you teach us what you learned?" I asked.

"Yeah, sure," said Fang.

We ate our last granola bars in midair. We flew over desert, mountains, rivers, scrubby plains. I only looked down when I had to, and forced myself not to think about Ella or her mom, who I missed like a real mom.

I watched the hawks, imitating their moves, banking, tailing, soaring, diving — all the things they were doing, minus the dead rodents. I was exhilarated to be included among those fierce, awesome birds. When they split away from us at the edge of their territory, I was sad to see them go.

Just as I was starting to feel shaky from lack of sugar, our markers came into view. Signaling to the others, I headed downward, aiming for a small wood on the backside of a foothill.

It was a pretty unpopulated area, and I couldn't see much activity, except for a strip mall about a mile away.

We landed and looked around. I rubbed my aching shoulder. "Okay, we need food. And a street map wouldn't be the worst idea in the world."

"The School isn't going to show up on any map," Fang said.

"I know. But we know pretty much where it is — there'll be a blank space on the map, but it would still help us to find roads to get there," I said.

Fifteen minutes of hiking brought us to the back of the strip mall. It was a decent-sized place, with a dollar store, gas station, a freestanding bank machine, dry cleaner, and a beauty salon. No food, except at the gas station store.

"Need to get your hair done?" Fang asked, and I elbowed him. Like I'd ever had my hair done in my life. Mostly I whacked it shorter with the kitchen scissors when it got too annoying.

"Well, what now?" the Gasman asked. "Should we keep going?"

"Let me think," I muttered, looking the mall up and down. Hitchhiking was out of the question — we'd end up murdered in a ditch or something. It was at least ten miles to the School. We could fly it, but I didn't want to approach from the air. So we'd have to walk, but it would take a while, and we were already hungry.

"Okay," I said finally. "Looks like we'll have to —"

I was interrupted by the squeal of a car pulling in. Without speaking, we drew back into a clump of bushes by the side of the building. A fancy gray car with a silver hood ornament roared up by the little bank machine.

The window opened, and loud music spilled out. A slick-looking guy leaned toward the machine, a cell phone up to his ear.

"Shut up, you idiot!" he was saying. "If you hadn't lost your card, I wouldn't need cash!"

The man stuck his arm out and pushed his card into the machine. Quickly, he punched in his code, then waited. "That's what I get for trusting you with anything!" he snapped into the phone. "You can't handle getting dressed in the morning!"

"Jerk," Nudge whispered next to me. I nodded.

Like magic, the machine spit some green bills through a slit, and the man snatched them and started counting. The next moment, a big black pickup truck screeched into the parking lot, way close to the fancy car. Its rear tires spun and spit rocks, and we could hear little pinging noises as they hit the cushmobile.

We shrank back farther into the woods. Goose bumps rose on my arms, and my breath caught in my throat. Erasers? The chip I had. Should I run now, getting the Erasers to follow me and leave the flock alone?

"He's going to go ballistic," Fang predicted quietly.

Veins practically popping out of his neck, the jerk leaned out his window and yelled a bunch of swear words, including a new one I tucked away in my brain for future use, if necessary.

The darkened window of the pickup rolled down, and I inhaled silently.

"What'd you say, dipstick?" Ari asked with a creepy smile.

53

I swallowed hard, my muscles tightening. I put my hand on Gazzy's shoulder. "Shhh. Shhhh."

The jerk in the gray car's eyes bugged out, and the next thing we knew, he had stomped on his gas pedal. His car leaped forward.

Ari laughed like a maniac, and the black pickup peeled out too, spraying gravel. Five heartbeats later, we could barely hear the roar of the two engines racing down the road.

"He gets around," said Fang quietly.

"Was Ari's hair *green?*" I asked, confused.

"Yep," Nudge said, unusually brief.

The five of us looked at one another — well, not Iggy, so much — then at the ATM.

It was beeping quietly. We glanced around. There were people inside the stores, but the machine faced away from them. Without saying a word, we dropped low and slipped across the parking lot.

None of us had ever used one of these. For some strange reason, the mad scientists at the School had neglected to set up bank accounts and trust funds for us.

Fortunately, the machine was designed to be used by idiots.

Do you want another transaction? it asked in orange letters.

"Get cash," Fang advised unnecessarily.

"You think?" I said snidely.

"Hurry," the Gasman said.

I hit the withdrawal button.

Please enter the amount you wish to withdraw.

I hesitated. "Sixty dollars?" That would buy a lot of food, right?

"He was a total jerk," said Fang. "Take him for all he's got."

I grinned. "You are *evil.* I like that." I worked my way through the account balances, and we all stared and whistled.

"Oh, yeah, oh, yeah," Nudge sang, doing a little dance. "We're ri-ich, we're gonna buy a ca-ar, oh, yeah."

You might not know this, but ATMs have a built-in limit of how much dough they're willing to give you at one time. So our plans to buy our own country crumbled. However, it was willing to give me two hundred bucks.

Once we punched in our access code again, for security purposes.

"Oh, no," I groaned. "Did anyone see it?"

"I *heard* it," said Iggy slowly.

"I think if we put in the wrong code more than twice, the whole thing shuts down and swallows the card," said Fang.

"Can you do it?" I asked Iggy.

"Um, I'll try . . ." Iggy hesitantly put his hand over the keypad. His sensitive fingers oriented themselves to the keys.

"It's okay, Ig," said Fang. "Just give it your best shot." Sometimes the Fangster is incredibly supportive, just not with me.

Iggy punched in five numbers, and we all held our breath.

ACCESS DENIED. PLEASE CHECK YOUR PIN AND TRY AGAIN.

"Try again," I said tensely. "You've got the best ears on the planet."

Once again, Iggy's pale hand hovered over the keyboard. He concentrated and punched in five numbers.

Nothing. My heart sank down into my stomach.

Then the machine started whirring, and soon a stack of twenties shot out.

"Yes!" said Fang, punching the air. "Freaks rule."

"Grab it and go!" I said as Nudge began pulling out bills and stuffing them into her pockets. We were turning to run when the machine beeped again.

THANK YOU FOR YOUR BUSINESS. PLEASE TAKE YOUR CARD.

"Okay, thank *you*," I said, grabbing the card. Then we ran back to the woods. Well, we ran *and* flew.

54

For some reason, I didn't feel too bad about taking that guy's money. Maybe because he seemed like such a jerk. We were like his karma getting back at him.

I don't know. I do know that I wouldn't have stolen even a jar of peanut butter from Ella and her mom. *Never. Nothing.*

"Too bad we couldn't get more," Fang said, counting the money.

"Let's go back to the gas station and buy a bunch of food," Nudge urged.

I shook my head. "People there may have already seen us. We've got to get out of here."

While we'd hidden in the woods, a red van had pulled up behind one of the stores. A young guy had unloaded some stuff from the back of it, then headed inside. Before the door swung shut, we saw him punch a time card.

So he was at work for at least a couple hours, till his first break.

And there was his van, just sitting there.

Fang and I looked at each other.

"Money from a jerk is one thing," I said. "A car from just a guy is something else."

"We'd only need to borrow it for a few hours," Fang said. "We could leave him some money as a rental fee."

"Are we stealing that car?" the Gasman asked. "Let's."

I frowned. "No. We're sort of *thinking* about *borrowing* it." On the one hand, I really didn't want to become a teenage criminal. On the other hand, every minute that ticked by was another minute closer to Angel's being the number one dissection lesson for a bunch of rabid geneticists.

"That's like Grand Theft Auto," the Gasman said helpfully. "I saw it on TV. It's popular with kids."

"Better 'borrow' it soon," advised Iggy. "I hear a chopper."

I made an executive decision. And yeah, I know — *my* karma's going to come back and get *me,* too.

In movies, people always "borrow" cars by yanking some wires out from under the dash and connecting them. But the real way it works involves a screwdriver and the starter thingy, under the hood. My personal ethics prevent me from giving you more information. That'd be just what I need: a rash of car thefts across America, committed by dedicated readers.

I don't think so.

Anyway, I did the engine thing while Iggy sat in the driver's seat, pressing the gas. The motor grumbled into life, I slammed the hood, and we jumped into the van. My heart was pounding at about two hundred beats a minute.

Then I just stared at the controls.

"Oh, my God," said Fang. "None of us has ever driven."

It wasn't like him to have missed this important detail.

"I've seen people drive on TV," I said, trying to sound confident. "How hard could it be?" I knew about the whole neutral, park, drive thing, so I put it into *D*.

"Okay, guys," I said. "Here goes nothing."

55

You might not know this, but cars have a separate parking brake, not just the foot pedal one. That brake is often not immediately obvious to the naked eye.

Attempting to drive a car before you find and release the parking brake is like trying to drag a Saint Bernard into a bathtub. But enough on that.

"Okay, okay, we're doing okay," I said twenty minutes later, after I finally found and released the parking brake. I felt like I was at the helm of a huge, clumsy runaway elephant.

I was sweating and about to jump out of my skin with anxiety about driving, but I tried to look way confident and calm. "I mean, it's not as good as flying, but it beats the heck out of walking!"

I smiled bravely over at Fang to see him giving me a steady look. "What?"

"Could you take it easy on the hairpin turns?" he said.

"I'm getting better," I said. "I just had to practice."

"I didn't know a van could go up on two wheels like that," Nudge said. "For so *long*."

"I don't want to barf in a borrowed car," the Gasman said.

I pressed my lips together and focused on the road. In-grates. "We need to turn east in about five hundred yards," I muttered, peering out the van window.

A half mile later, I pulled over and rested my head against the steering wheel. "Where the heck is the *road?*" I bellowed in frustration. "There's no freaking *road* there!"

"You're going by your own directional senses," Fang pointed out.

"And there can't be roads everywhere you *feel* like there should be a road," Iggy added reasonably.

I wanted to smack them both.

Sighing, I pulled out onto the turnoff-less road and did a U-ey.

"I'll just have to take a less efficient route," I said. I hated the sense of time ticking by, of not knowing whether Angel was still alive. And worse, I hated knowing I was getting closer and closer to the School, where everything bad that had ever happened to us had taken place. It felt like I was driving toward certain death, and it was hard to make myself do that.

"Argh!" After yet another unexpected turn that led us away from where we should have been going, I pulled over again and punched the steering wheel several times. Every one of my muscles was tense from driving and worry. I had a bad headache. Lately, I'd been having a lot of headaches. Gee, I wonder why?

"It's okay, Max," the Gasman said anxiously.

"Is she hitting the steering wheel?" Iggy asked.

"Look," said Fang, pointing to a sign. "There's a town up ahead. Let's go there, get something to eat, and find an actual map. 'Cause this wandering thing ain't workin'.'"

Bennett was a small, almost cute town. I sat up tall in the driver's seat and frowned, trying to look older. There were several places to eat. I turned into a parking lot slowly and then oh-so-carefully edged the van toward the back of the lot, away from everyone else.

I turned off the engine, and Nudge and Gazzy sprang for the door. "We're alive!" yelled the Gasman.

"Wait!" I told them. "Look, we're really close to the School. This might *feel* like the middle of nowhere, but really, Erasers could be anywhere and any*one*. You know that. So we have to be careful."

"We have to eat," Nudge said, trying not to whine. It was hard on her — she seemed to burn through calories faster than anyone, except maybe the Gasman.

"I know, Nudge," I said gently. "We're going to. I'm just saying be really careful. Be on guard, be ready to run, okay? *Anybody we see could be an Eraser.*"

They nodded. I flipped down the visor so I could check myself in the mirror, and something small and heavy dropped into my lap.

I froze, my breath stuck in my throat. *What —?*

Gingerly, I looked down. It wasn't a grenade. It was a key ring. One key was for this van. I looked at it blankly.

"Well, that'll simplify things," Fang said.

56

"I want my room to smell just like this." Iggy inhaled deeply as the scents of flame-broiled burgers and hot french fries wafted around us.

"It would be an improvement," I agreed, reading the menu board. My stomach felt like it was trying to digest itself. I was shaky with tension and adrenaline, and felt like I was going to come apart at the seams.

The fast-food restaurant was crowded and jarringly noisy. All of us felt nervous when we were around regular people. We shuffled into line, trying to be inconspicuous. As far as I could tell, no one here was an Eraser.

But of course Erasers looked pretty normal — until they started morphing and tried to bite your freaking head off.

"I don't eat meat anymore," Nudge announced. At my uncomprehending stare, she said, "Not after seeing the hawks go through rabbits and snakes and other birds. It's just icky."

Fang stepped up and ordered three double cheeseburgers, a chocolate shake, a soda with caffeine *and* sugar, three fries, three apple pies.

"Feeding a crowd?" the woman behind the counter asked.

"Yes, ma'am," Fang said sweetly.

Yeah, him and all his split personalities, I thought. I turned back to Nudge.

"Okay," I said, reaching *deep* into my well of leaderly patience. "But you still need lots of protein."

Iggy ordered the same thing as Fang, and I paid for him. Fang waited for him to get his food and unobtrusively led him to the most private booth.

"Um, let's see," I said, stepping up. "Could I have two fried-chicken sandwiches, two double cheeseburgers, four fries, six apple pies, two vanilla shakes, one strawberry shake, and then two triple cheeseburgers, only hold the hamburger?"

"You mean, just cheese on the bun? No meat?"

"Yes. That would be great." I looked over at Nudge, who nodded.

I was about to faint from hunger, and smelling all the food was killing me. Standing beside me, the Gasman was shifting from foot to foot, looking eager. It seemed like a lifetime before we got our three loaded trays, paid, and joined Fang and Iggy in the back.

Another glance around showed happy families, kids blowing straw wrappers, women talking together, teens hanging out. I sat down warily, and Nudge slid in next to me. The Gasman squeezed in next to her.

Am I tough? Am I strong? Am I hard-core? Absolutely.

Did I whimper with pathetic delight when I sank my teeth into my hot fried-chicken sandwich? You betcha.

Nudge was tearing into her cheese bun things, Fang was on his second burger, Iggy could hardly breathe through all the food in his mouth, and the Gasman was wolfing fries by the fistful. We probably looked like starving orphan children. Hey! We *were* starving orphan children. For several minutes all you could hear were disgusting chomping noises. I had a sudden flashback to the fun, civilized meals with Ella and her mom, where we used napkins and good manners and talked about normal things.

Great. Now I was choking up and having trouble swallowing.

I'm not sure when it happened, but slowly I became aware that my neck muscles were tensing. I glanced at Fang, who was looking at me sideways while he ate his french fries. *I knew that look.*

Acting *trés* casual, I glanced around again. The couple of families who'd been sitting close by were gone. Now it looked as if a bunch of male models had suddenly gotten the munchies. They were surrounding us, *tables of them.*

All good-looking, thick-haired guys with big, pretty eyes and the voices of angels.

Oh, man. My stomach dropped like a wheelbarrow full of lead.

57

I gave Fang an almost imperceptible nod and glanced back at the fire exit door behind him. He blinked to show he understood. Then he tapped Iggy's hand.

"Nudge," I said under my breath. "Gazzy. Don't look up. In three seconds, jump over Fang and out that exit door."

Giving no sign they had heard me, Nudge and Iggy kept chewing. Nudge casually took a sip of her shake. Then, in a burst, she leaped up, sprang off our table, and practically crashed through the fire door. The Gasman was practically glued to her back.

I was so proud of them.

The alarm started clanging, but I was right behind them — and Fang and Iggy were on my heels. We made it to the van before the Erasers were out the door.

Inside, I jammed the key into the ignition and cranked the engine. Erasers were swarming into the parking lot, already starting to become wolflike.

I stomped on the gas and reversed fast, crying out when we felt the thunk of an Eraser being hit. Then I yanked the gear stick into *D* and we roared over the curb, right through the shrubs that lined the parking lot. The tires squealed as I careened out into traffic, causing a bunch of angry honking from other cars.

I cut right through a gas station on the corner, narrowly avoiding hitting several cars. On the other side, I roared back into traffic.

"Max!" Nudge screamed, but I had seen the semitrailer too, and swerved out of its way at the last second. Behind me, I heard the crunch of metal as the truck scraped a car. Then I was weaving in and out of traffic, wishing I knew how to drive better, wishing we had stolen something besides a van.

"It's so bulky!" I cried in frustration as we teetered on two wheels again just turning a corner. Okay, turning fast. But still.

"It's a *van*," Fang said, as though blaming me for not stealing a race car.

We sped out of town — I had to get away from all this traffic. My adrenaline was pumping, my arms felt like corded cables on the steering wheel. *We had to ditch this van.*

"I'm gonna stop!" I yelled over the noise of the engine. "Jump out and get into the air as fast as you can!"

"Okay!" the flock yelled back.

A glance in the rearview mirror showed three black cars following us, catching up to us. They were going a lot faster than we were. I had to buy time.

Gritting my teeth, I swung off road suddenly, right into a field of corn. We plowed through the dry stalks, wincing as they smacked the windshield. I tried to zigzag as best I could, and then a bit of light up ahead made me hopeful for a road.

I didn't see anything in the rearview mirror, and the sound of crunching cornstalks was too loud for me to hear other engines. Had we lost them? And yes, here was a road! Excellent!

The van tumbled heavily out onto the road, with bone-jolting bumps. As soon as the front tires hit asphalt, I gunned the motor again —

Just as a sedan leaped out in front of us.

I hit it head-on at sixty miles an hour.

58

Note to self: Disable the air bags on the next car you steal.

The thing about airbags is that when you hit something at fifty or sixty miles an hour, they inflate with enough raw force to slam you back against your seat like a rag doll, possibly breaking your face. Which is what this one had done to me, I concluded, trying to stem the gush of blood from my nose.

"Report," I called weakly.

"Okay here," Fang said next to me. His neck was scraped raw by the seat belt, which had almost decapitated him.

"Okay here," Nudge said from the backseat, sounding young and scared. I craned around to see her. She was pale, except where her forehead was bruised from hitting Fang's seat. Her eyes widened with shock when she saw my bloody face.

"It's just my nose," I quickly assured her. "Head wounds always bleed a lot. Look, it's already stopping." A lie.

"I feel like, like pudding," Iggy groaned. "Pudding with nerve endings. Pudding in great pain."

"I feel sick," the Gasman said, his face white, lips pale and bloodless.

Crash!

All around us, windows smashed, and we jumped and threw our arms over our faces. I saw a gun hammering at the glass, then hairy hands with ragged claws popped the doors open.

There was no time even to get a good kick in — Fang and I were hauled out of the van and thrown to the ground.

"Run!" I bawled, then hissed in a breath as my nose took another jarring blow.

I glanced up in time to see the rear doors of the van open and Iggy and the Gasman shoot into the air. A rush of pure joy made me beam, then gag as fresh blood ran into my mouth.

I spit it out as the Erasers roared with fury and started shooting at the boys. But Iggy and Gazzy continued to soar into the air. *Yes, yes, yes!*

A kicking and shrieking Nudge was yanked from the back of the van and tossed down next to me. Tears were in her eyes, and I reached out to hold her.

An Eraser kicked me hard with his hand-sewn Italian boot. *Ow!*

"Tag. You're it," Ari cracked, and the others laughed, almost dancing with monstrous excitement and glee.

"It's almost like you don't *want* to go back to School,"

he went on, showing his razor-sharp yellow teeth, dripping Eraser drool on me.

There were five Erasers and three of us. I'm weirdly, incredibly strong for my size, but Ari outweighed me by about 160 pounds, and he kept his booted foot pressed hard against my forehead. I wanted a shot at him — just one lethal, brain-splattering shot.

I met Fang's eyes, which were dark and expressionless, and then Nudge's. I tried to give her a reassuring smile, but since my face was one big gore-fest, it didn't have the cheering effect I'd hoped for.

Then we all heard the horrible *whup, whup* of a chopper headed our way, and the Erasers started to shout and wave their arms.

"What a touching scene," Ari called down at me. "We're all going home. Just like old times."

59

Angel was alive. As long as she was, I could deal with just about anything else.

I knew she was alive because I could see her in the pitiful cage next to mine. If we pushed our fingers through our bars as hard as we could, we were an inch away from actually touching each other.

"At least they gave you a *big* crate," she said in a small, raspy voice. "I'm in a *medium*."

My throat closed up. That she was still trying to be brave just rocked my world. I felt ashamed for taking so long to get here, ashamed for letting the Erasers catch us, ashamed for being a failure, even as a freak.

"It's not your fault," she said, reading my thoughts. She looked just terrible. Her eyes were hollow and smudged with huge purple shadows. One whole side of her face was a bruise going yellow and green at the edges. Angel looked thin and dry, like a leaf, her bones as delicate as stems. Her feathers were limp and dirty.

Across the aisle from us, Nudge and Fang were in crates of their own. Nudge looked really shaky, trying to get her fear under control but losing the fight. Fang sat with his hands clasped around his knees, not moving. He'd smiled at Angel when he'd first seen her, but mostly he looked cool, removed, distant. He was retreating into himself, the only place left to retreat to.

"I'm sorry, Max," Angel whispered, her eyes troubled. "This is all my fault."

"Don't be dumb," I told her, sounding Elmer Fuddish because of my clogged and broken nose. "It could happen to any of us. And it's *my* fault that Fang, Nudge, and I got caught."

All around me, the smells of cold metal and antiseptic were awakening horrible memories I had buried deep a long time ago. Flashes of light, pain, and fear kept popping inside my head, making me feel a little crazy. My nose had finally stopped bleeding, but it hurt. My headache was back — big-time — and I was seeing flashes of the strangest images. What was *that* all about?

"Max, there's something I have to tell you." Angel started to cry.

"Shh," I said soothingly. "It can wait. Just rest. Try to feel better."

"No, Max, it's really important —"

A door opened, and loud footsteps sounded on the linoleum tile. Angel's eyes were panicked in her bruised little face. Fury ignited in me that *anything, anyone,* could make a little girl so afraid.

I coiled my muscles, narrowing my eyes and putting on

my fiercest look. They were going to be sorry they ever picked Angel to mess with. They were going to be sorry they'd ever been *born*.

My hands clenched into fists. I crouched in my crate, ready to spring at whoever opened it so I could rip their lungs out. I'd start with Ari, the creep of creeps.

Angel was hunched over now, crying silently, and inside I started freaking, wondering what on earth they had done to her. I felt totally wired on adrenaline, just *nuts*.

A pair of legs stopped right in front of my crate. I could see the edges of a white lab coat brushing the knees.

He bent down and looked into my crate with a gentle, rueful expression.

My heart almost stopped, and I fell backward off my heels.

"Maximum Ride," said Jeb Batchelder. "Oh, I've missed you so much."

60

I'm hallucinating, I thought dazedly. *I'm having an out-of-body experience.*

Everything else in my vision faded away. I could see only Jeb, smiling at me through the bars of my dog crate.

Jeb had been the only parentlike person I'd ever had. He had kidnapped the six of us four years ago, stolen us away from this freak show and hidden us in the mountains in our house. He'd helped us learn how to fly — none of us had ever been allowed enough space to try before. He'd fed us, clothed us, and taught us survival skills, how to fight, how to read. He'd told jokes and read stories and let us play video games. He'd made us dinner and tucked us in at night. Whenever I'd felt afraid, I'd remind myself that Jeb was there and that he would protect us, and then I'd always feel better.

Two years ago, he'd disappeared.

We'd always *known* he'd been killed. We'd *known* that he would have died rather than disclose our location. That he died trying to protect us. That kind of thing.

For the last two years, we'd all missed Jeb so much, with

a horrible, aching, wailing pain that just wouldn't stop. You know — like if your dad or mom died. It had been so awful in the beginning, when he hadn't come home, and then when we'd had to accept that he never would.

Dead or alive, he'd been my hero. Every day. For the last four years.

Now my eyes were telling me that he was one of *them*. That maybe he'd been one of them all along. That everything I'd ever known or felt about him had been a rotten, stinking lie.

Now Angel's words, her fear, her tears, made horrible sense. She'd known.

I was dying to look at her, at Fang or Nudge, to see their reactions.

I just wouldn't give him that satisfaction.

Like a door slamming shut, everything in me that had loved and trusted Jeb closed down. In its place rose new feelings that were so powerful and full of hate that they scared me.

Which is saying something.

"I know you're surprised," he said with a smile. "Come on. I need to talk to you."

He unlatched my dog door and held it open. In a nanosecond, I had a plan of action: not to act. Just to listen and watch. To absorb everything and give out nothing.

Okay, as a plan, it wasn't the blueprint of Westminster Abbey, but it was a start.

Slowly, I climbed out of my crate. My muscles groaned

when I stood up. I didn't look at any of the flock when I passed, but I put my right hand behind my back, two fingers together.

It was our sign that said "Wait."

Jeb had taught it to us.

61

Jeb and I walked past a bank of computers, out of sight of the others. A door in the far wall led into a smaller, less lablike room furnished with couches, a table and chairs, a sink, microwave.

"Sit down, Max, please," he said, gesturing to a chair. "I'll get us some hot chocolate." He said it casually, knowing it was my favorite, as if we were in the kitchen back home.

"Max, I have to tell you — I'm so proud of you," he said, putting mugs in the microwave. "I just can't believe how well you've done. No, I *can* believe it — I knew you could do it. But seeing you so healthy, so powerful, such a good leader, well, it just makes me so proud."

The microwave beeped, and he set a steaming mug on the table in front of me. We were in a top-secret facility in the middle of Death Valley, officially called "freaking nowhere" on any map, and yet he managed to produce marshmallows, plopping two into my cup.

I looked at him steadily, ignoring the hot chocolate, which was making my stomach growl.

He paused as if to give me time to reply, then sat down

across from me at the table. It *was* Jeb — my brain finally accepted the inescapable truth. I recognized the fine pink scar on his jawline, the slight bend to his nose, the tiny freckle on his right ear. This was not his evil twin. It was him. *He* was evil.

"You must have so many questions," he said. "I don't even know where to start. I just — I'm just so sorry about this. I wish I could explain — wish I could have explained two years ago, to you, if no one else. I wish I could explain what I'd give just to see you smile again."

How about your head on a stick?

"But in time, Max, it will all come out, and you'll understand what's happening. That's what I told Angel. I told her that everything is a test, even when you don't know it. That sometimes you just have to do what you have to do and know it will all be clearer later. All of this has been a test." He waved his hand vaguely, as if to encompass my entire experience.

I sat there, conscious that my sweatshirt was crusted with blood, that my face hurt, that I was hungry again — *quelle surprise* — and that I had never, ever wanted to kill anyone more, not even last summer when Iggy had shredded my only, favorite pair of non-Goodwill pants to make a fuse long enough to detonate something from fifty feet away.

I said nothing, had no expression on my face.

He glanced at me, then at the closed door. "Max," he said, with a new tone of urgency in his voice. "Max, soon some people will come in to talk to you. But I need to tell you something first."

That you are the devil incarnate?

"Something I couldn't tell you before, something I thought I'd have time to prepare you for later."

He looked around, as if to make sure no one else could hear. Guess he was forgetting all our surveillance lessons, about hidden mikes and heat sensors that can see through walls, and long-distance listening devices that could pick up a rat sneeze from a half mile away.

"The thing is, Max," he said, tons of heart-wringing emotion in his eyes, "you're even more special than I always told you. You see, you were created for a *reason.* Kept alive for a purpose, a special purpose."

You mean besides seeing how well insane scientists could graft avian DNA into a human egg?

He took a breath, looking deep into my eyes. I coldly shut down every good memory I had of him, every laugh we'd shared, every happy moment, every thought that he was like a dad to me.

"Max, that reason, that purpose is: You are supposed to *save the world.*"

62

Okay, I couldn't help it. My jaw dropped open. I shut it again quickly. Well. This would certainly give weight to my ongoing struggle to have the bathroom first in the morning.

"I can't tell you much more than that right now," Jeb said, looking over his shoulder again. "But I had to let you know the size of what we're dealing with, the enormity, the importance. You are more than special, Max. You're pre-ordained. You have a destiny that you can't imagine."

Maybe I can't imagine it because I'm not a complete nutcase.

"Max, everything you've done, everything you are, everything you can be, is tied into your destiny. Your life is worth the lives of thousands. The fact that you are alive is the most important thing anyone has ever accomplished."

If he was expecting a gushing response, he was gonna wait a long time.

He sighed heavily, not taking his eyes off me, disappointed at my lack of excitement over hearing that I was the messiah.

"It's okay," he said with sad understanding. "I can barely imagine what you must be feeling or thinking. It's okay. I just wanted to tell you myself. Later, others will come to talk to you. After you've had a chance to think about this, to realize what it could mean for you and the others. But for now, don't say anything to the rest of the flock. It's our secret, Maximum. Soon the whole world will know. But not just yet."

I was getting very good at saying nothing.

He stood up and helped me from my chair, a solicitous hand under my elbow that made my flesh crawl.

We walked in silence back to the row of crates, and he unlatched mine and waited patiently for me to crawl inside. *Such a gentleman.*

Latching it behind me, he leaned down to give me one last meaningful look. "Remember," he whispered. "Trust me. That's all I ask. Just trust me. Listen to your gut."

Well, how many times had I heard him say *that?* I wondered contemptuously as he walked away. Right now my gut was telling me I wanted to take his lungs out with a pair of pliers.

"You okay?" Angel asked anxiously, pressing her little face to the side of her cage.

I nodded, and met Fang's and Nudge's eyes across the way.

"I'm okay. Everyone hang tough, all right?"

Nudge and Angel nodded, concerned, and Fang kept

staring at me. I had no idea what he was thinking. Was he wondering if I was a traitor? Was he wondering if Jeb had managed to turn me — or if I had been in league with Jeb from the beginning?

He would find out soon enough.

63

Hours went by. In the dictionary, next to the word *stress,* there is a picture of a midsize mutant stuck inside a dog crate, wondering if her destiny is to be killed or to save the world.

Okay, not really. But there should be.

If you can think of anything more nerve-racking, more guaranteed to whip every fiber in your body up in a knot, you let me know.

I couldn't tell the others anything — not even in a whisper. If it amused Jeb to pretend that closed doors and lowered voices protected one against surveillance, that was fine. But I knew better. There could be cameras and mikes hidden anywhere, built into our crates. So I couldn't go over a plan, offer reassurance, or even freak out and say, "Oh, my God! Jeb is alive!"

When Angel whispered, "Where are Gazzy and Iggy?" I just shrugged. Her face fell, and I looked hard at her. *They got away. They're okay.*

She read my thoughts, gave a tiny nod, then gradually slumped against the side of her crate, worn out.

After that, all I could do was send meaningful glances.

For hours.

My headache was back, and when I shut my eyes all these images danced on the backs of my eyelids.

At one point a whitecoat came in and dumped another "experiment" into the crate next to mine. I glanced over, curious, then quickly turned away, my heart aching. It looked enough like a kid to make me feel sick, but more like a horrible fungus. Huge pebbly growths covered most of its body. It had few fingers and only one toe, stuck onto the end of a foot like a pod. Senseless blue eyes looked out at me, blinked.

Sometime in the next half hour, I realized the "experiment" was no longer breathing. It had died, right next to me.

Horror-struck, I looked across at Angel. She was crying. She knew.

Finally, much later, the door to the lab opened. A crowd came in, and I heard human voices and Eraserlike croons and laughs. They wheeled a big flatbed cart to our aisle.

"I count only four," a man said in a prissy, concerned voice.

"Two bought it," Ari said, sounding triumphant. "Back in Colorado. This is what's left." He kicked my cage, making the bars rattle. "Hi, Max. Miss me?"

"Is the Director quite sure about this?" a woman asked. "It seems a shame — there's so much more we can learn from them."

"Yes," said a third whitecoat. "It's just too risky. Given how uncooperative the little one has been."

I caught Angel's eye and gave her a thumbs-up, proud of her resistance. She sent a weak grin back at me.

Then her cage was grabbed roughly and swung onto the cart like luggage. She winced as her bruised cheek hit the side, and fury flamed in me again.

In the next second, Ari grabbed my crate and swung me up next to her on the cart, letting me drop with a crash that made me bite my lip hard. Like I needed another head wound. He grinned through the bars, letting me see his long yellow fangs. "Strong, like bull," he bragged.

"Your dad must be so proud," I said snidely, and he angered instantly, punching my cage so hard I almost toppled over.

"Easy," murmured a whitecoat, earning herself a murderous snarl from Ari.

Then two more Erasers loaded Nudge and Fang on next to us. With Ari trailing behind, looking angry, they pushed us through wide double doors. The hall outside was painfully bright and overlaid with the smells of floor cleaner and office machines.

Clutching the bars of my crate, I peered out, trying to recognize a doorway, an office — anything that would tell me what section of the School we were in. The Erasers poked their fingers through our bars, trying to scratch us, taunting, literally rattling our cages. I wondered how much strength it would take to grab an Eraser finger and snap it.

We took a sharp left turn and got pushed through more double swinging doors, and then we were outside. I inhaled eagerly, but even outdoors at the School the air was tainted and foul.

Squinting, I shifted from side to side in my cage, looking for landmarks. Behind us was the lab building. Ahead of us, maybe a hundred yards away, was a low redbrick building. We were in the yard in back of the School.

The yard I used to look out at, in the dead of night, from our lab window.

The yard where Erasers were trained to bring down prey and tear it limb from limb.

Which was probably why they were laughing.

64

The funny thing about facing imminent death is that it really snaps everything else into perspective.

Like right now. My choices were to either give in and let them kill all of us or fight back with everything I had.

I chose the second one, 'cause I'm just funny that way.

In the split second I had to ponder what form my "fighting to the death" would take, a shadow blotted out the sun.

"Got your running shoes on, piggy?" Ari asked, pushing his hairy fingers through the bars of my cage and wiggling them. "Feeling like a little exercise? Wanna race? Wanna play food fight? You're the food!"

I grinned evilly. Then I leaned over and chomped hard on Ari's fingers. He sucked in a deep breath, then yelled in awful pain. I gathered my strength and bit down harder, until I actually felt my teeth break his skin, tasted his horrible blood. But you know what? I didn't care. Seeing Ari hurt was worth it.

After the car wreck, biting anything hurt majorly, but I shut out the pain and put every ounce of my fury into my aching jaws. Ari was shaking my cage, slamming it with his other hand, and my head was getting snapped around like a paddleball.

But I hung on, thinking pit bull thoughts.

The whitecoats were yelling at me now. Still screaming, Ari began savagely kicking my cage. Suddenly, I unclenched my teeth and let go. His next kick smashed my crate sideways. It rolled over a couple of times.

I landed upside down, right next to Angel's crate door. Being smarter than the average bear, it took me only a few seconds to unlatch it.

"Go!" I ordered. "Go! Don't argue!"

She edged her door open and scrambled out just as Ari slammed down on top of my crate in a murderous rage. I braced myself as best I could, but he was tearing into the crate, roaring with pain. The crate tumbled sideways on the grass, and for just a split second, I caught a glimpse of the sky. It was streaked with dark, fast-moving storm clouds. Then I was batted upside down again, making me feel like laundry in a dryer.

Ari was screaming furiously, calling me awful names and shaking his bleeding fingers so that flecks of gore spattered me through the bars.

But I was smiling now. My first really good smile in days.

I knew what the storm clouds were.

They were hawks — led by Iggy and the Gasman, who else? And they were storming the School to save us.

65

Call me crazy, but there's just something cheering about seeing huge raptors tear into Eraser flesh.

Just as Ari, ignoring the latch in his murderous rage, finally succeeded in ripping it open, he was dive-bombed by a hawk with razor-sharp talons and a huge grudge against wolves. As I popped out, I saw him swatting at it, screaming like a big weenie as the bird sliced into the back of his neck.

"Angel! Get out of here!" I yelled, racing to her.

Two whitecoats were chasing her, but I got there first. I elbowed one out of the way, grabbed Angel's waist, and *threw* her up into the sky.

Then I managed to unlatch Fang's crate. The whitecoats fell on me, but a regular grown-up versus an angry Max doesn't stand a chance. I backhanded one across the jaw, feeling teeth knock loose. The other I kicked right under his double chin. His head jerked back, and he dropped like a brick.

Fang burst out of his cage, then grabbed a whitecoat and slammed him against the cart. He drew back a fist and punched, looking cold and determined. The whitecoat's eyes rolled back, and he crumpled.

Getting to Nudge took no time. She tumbled out of her crate just as Iggy and the Gasman led their hawk swarm in for round two.

Close by, one of the female whitecoats was struggling to her feet. I darted toward her, then jumped into the air, my right leg already swinging out in a huge roundhouse kick. I hit her in the chest, *wham!* She sank to her knees, unable to breathe, a stunned look on her face.

"Think of this as an occupational hazard, you witch!" I snarled, then spun to check on the rest of the flock.

Fang was venting his hostility on Ari, who crouched defensively on the ground, his arms wrapped around his head. Fang smashed him sideways with a kick, then punched the side of Ari's head. For good measure, Fang hoisted a crate and crashed it down on the wicked Eraser. Now it looked as though Ari had been caught in a cage.

I shot into the air, feeling exhilarated as fierce hawks rushed past me. I counted four whitecoats, Ari, and three other Erasers on the ground, two Erasers still standing. One of them pulled out a gun, but promptly had his wrist muscles slashed by an unforgiving beak. *Ooh. That had to hurt.*

"Fang!" I bellowed. "Iggy! Gazzy! Let's go! Go, go, go!"

Almost reluctantly, they pulled high into the air. Iggy moved through the hawks. By some unspoken message, he communicated that our battle was over. Those beautiful birds swerved gracefully and rocketed upward, making my ears ring with their wild calls.

"One, two, three, four, five," I counted, rounding up my

own flock and urging them higher. "Fang! Get Angel!" Angel had managed to stay airborne all this time, but she was sagging and losing altitude. Immediately, the Gasman flew to one side, Fang to the other, and they held her as they rose.

More whitecoats and Erasers streamed out of the building, but we were too high and moving too fast for them to hurt us. *So long, cretins,* I thought. *School is out — forever.*

"Max!"

That voice tugged my gaze downward.

Jeb stood there. He must have gotten caught in the hawk attack, because his white coat was torn, his shoulder red with blood. "Maximum!" he yelled again. The expression on his face wasn't anger — it was something that I didn't recognize.

"Max! *Please!* This was all a test! Don't you get it? You were *safe* here! This was only a *test!* You have to trust me — I'm the only one you *can* trust! Please! Come back — let me explain!"

I looked at him, the man who had saved my life four years ago, taught me practically everything I knew, comforted me when I cried, cheered me on when I fought, held my hair back when I was heaving my Wheaties, the closest thing I ever had to a dad.

"I don't think so," I said tiredly. Then I pushed down hard and let my wings carry me far away, up to where my family was waiting.

66

Two hours later, Lake Mead came into view, along with the cliff top covered with the huge hawks who had rescued us. The six of us, together again, landed gratefully on the scraped-out ledge.

Angel collapsed onto the cool, dust-covered floor of the cave. I sank down next to her, stroking her hair.

"I thought I would never see you again," she said, and a single tear rolled down her face. "They did all kinds of stuff to me, Max. Terrible. Terrible. Terrible."

"I would *never* quit trying to get you back," I told her, feeling like my heart was going to overflow. "There's no way I would ever let them keep you. They would have to kill me first."

"They almost did," she said, her voice breaking. I gathered her to me and held her for a long time.

"This is how it should be forever," Iggy said. "All of us together."

I looked up to where Fang was leaning against a wall, facing the canyon. He felt my gaze and turned. I held out my left fist. Almost smiling, he came and stacked his left fist on top of it. One by one, the others joined us, and I disentangled my right hand from Angel's hair and tapped the backs of theirs.

"I'm just . . . so thankful," I said. Nudge looked at me with faint surprise. Okay, so I'm not the most mushy person ever. I mean, I love my family and I try to be nice to them, but I don't go around telling them how much I love them all the time.

Maybe I should fix that.

"I mean," I said, feeling really self-conscious, "this made me realize how much we all need one another. I need *all* of you. I love you all. But five of us, or three of us, or two of us isn't *us*. Us is all six."

Fang was examining his sneakers with great interest. Iggy was nervously tapping long white fingers against his leg. But my little guys got what I was saying.

Nudge threw her arms around my neck. "I love you too, Max! I love all of us too."

"Yeah, me too," said the Gasman. "I don't care if we have our house, or a cliff ledge, or a cardboard box. Home is wherever we all are, together." I hugged him, and he nestled against me, looking happy.

Later on, we all slept, and awoke in the night to heavy rain, a miracle in the desert. We scrambled up to the ledge and let the rain pour down on us, washing off blood, dirt, and memories. Even raindrops hitting my nose hurt, but I held my arms open to the sky and felt clean and cold and shivery.

I shivered, and Fang briskly rubbed my shoulders. I looked at him, his eyes as dark as the desert sky. "Jeb knows our house," I said very softly.

Fang nodded. "Can't ever go back. Guess we need a new home."

"Yes," I said, thinking. I closed my eyes and opened my mouth slightly, inhaling the chill, rain-washed air. I opened my eyes. "East," I said, feeling the rightness of it. "We'll go east."

PART 4

*NEW YAWK,
NEW YAWK*

67

Blue, blue sky, above the clouds. The air is colder, but the sun is warmer up this high. The air is thin and light, like champagne. You ought to try it sometime.

I felt happy. The six of us were homeless, aimless, on the run — and might be for the rest of our lives, however long or short they might be. But . . .

Yesterday we'd escaped the hounds of hell at the School, after all. We'd had the pleasure of seeing our friends the hawks do some slice 'n' dice on the whitecoats and the Erasers.

We had Angel back.

I glanced over at her — she was still a mess. It would take her a while to heal after what they had done to her. Every time I thought about it, chains of anger tightened around me, till I felt like I couldn't breathe. Sensing me looking at her, she turned and smiled. One whole side of her face was green and yellow — a healing bruise.

"God!" Nudge said, speeding up a bit to catch my slipstream. "It's just so, so . . . you know?" She swooped down gracefully, then rose again and pulled alongside.

"Yeah, I know," I said, grinning at her.

"I mean, the air, and we're up so high, and no one's after us, and we're all together, and we hit IHOP for breakfast." She looked over at me, her brown eyes bright and untroubled. "I mean, God, we're just up here, and it's so cool, and down below kids are stuck in school or, like, cleaning their rooms. I used to hate cleaning my room."

Back when she had a room. I sighed. *Don't think about it.*

Then, in the next second, I choked. I think I made some kind of sound, then a blinding, stunning pain exploded behind my eyes.

"Max?" Nudge screamed.

I couldn't think, couldn't speak, couldn't do a thing. My wings folded like paper, and I started to drop like a hailstone.

Something was incredibly wrong.

Already.

68

Tears streamed from my eyes, and my hands clutched my head to keep the pain from splitting my skull wide open. The only semicoherent thought I had was *Please let me go splat soon, so this freaking pain will stopstopSTOP.*

Then Fang's arms, ropy and hard, scooped me up, and I felt myself rising again. My wings were mushed between us, but nothing mattered except that my brain had been replaced by a bursting nova of raw agony. I had just enough consciousness to be embarrassed at hearing myself moan pitifully.

Death would have been so great just then.

I don't know how long Fang carried me. Slowly, slowly, the pain leached away. I could almost open my eyes a slit. I could swallow. Cautiously, wincing, I let go of my head, half expecting huge shards of skull to come away in my hands.

I blinked up at Fang, his dark eyes looking down at me. He was still flying *and* carrying me.

"Man, you weigh a freaking *ton*," he told me. "What've you been eating, *rocks?*"

"Why, is your head missing some?" I croaked. His mouth almost quirked in a smile, and that's when I knew how upset he'd been.

"Max, are you okay?" Nudge's face was scared, making her look really young.

"Uh-huh," I managed. *I just had a stroke or something.*

"Find a place to land," I told Fang. "Please."

69

An hour or so later, I thought that I had recovered — *but from what?* We were making camp for the night.

"Yo, watch it!" I said. "Clear more of that brush away — we don't want the whole forest to burn down."

"Guess you're feeling like your old self," Fang murmured, kicking some dead branches away from where Iggy was lighting a fire.

I shot him a look, then helped Nudge and Angel surround the pile of kindling with big stones. Why was the blind guy playing with matches, you ask? Because he's good at it. Anything to do with fire, igniting things, exploding things, things with fuses, wicks, accelerants . . . Iggy's your man. It's one of those good/bad things.

Twenty minutes later, we were exploring the limits of what could be cooked on sticks over an open fire.

"This isn't half bad," the Gasman said, eating a curled piece of roasted bologna off his stick.

"Don't do bananas," Nudge warned glumly, shaking some warm mush off into the bushes.

"S'mores," I cooed, mashing a graham cracker on top of

the chocolate-and-marshmallow sandwich I had balanced on my knee. I took a bite, and pure pleasure overwhelmed my mouth.

"This is nice," the Gasman said happily. "It's like summer camp."

"Yeah, Camp Bummer," said Fang. "For wayward mutants."

I nudged his leg with my sneaker. "It's better than that. This is cool."

Fang gave me an "if you say so" look, and turned his bacon over the fire.

I stretched out with my head against my balled-up sweatshirt. Time to relax. I had no idea what that pain had been, but I was fine now, so I wasn't going to worry about it.

What a lie. My knees were practically knocking together. The thing is, the "scientists" back at the School had been playing with risky stuff, combining human and non-human DNA. Basically, the spliced genes started to unravel after a while, and the organisms tended to, well, self-destruct. The flock and I had seen it happen a million times: The rabbit-dog combo had been such bad news. Same with the sheep–macaque monkey splice. The mouse-cat experiment had produced a huge, hostile mouse with great balance and an inability to digest either grain or meat. So it starved to death.

Even the Erasers, as successful as they were, had a huge downside: life span. They went from embryo to infant in five weeks, and from infant to young adult in about four years. They fell apart and died at around six years, give or take. But they were being improved all the time.

How about us? How long would we last? Well, as far as I knew, we were the oldest recombinant beings the School had ever produced.

And we could devolve and expire at any time.

And maybe it had started happening to me today.

"Max, wake up," said Angel, tapping my knee.

"I'm awake." I pulled myself up, and Angel crawled over and climbed into my lap. I put my arms around her and stroked her tangled blond curls away from her face. "What's up, Angel?"

Her large blue eyes looked solemnly into mine. "I've got a secret. From when I was at the School. It's about us. Where we came from?"

70

"What do you mean, sweetie?" I asked softly. *What fresh hell is this?*

Angel twisted the hem of her shirt in her fingers, not looking at me. I clamped down on any thoughts I had, so Angel couldn't pick up on my alarm.

"I heard stuff," she said, almost whispering.

I gathered her closer. When the Erasers had taken her, it felt like someone had chopped my arm off. Getting her back had made me whole again.

"Stuff people said or stuff people *thought?*" I asked.

"Stuff people thought," she said. I noticed how tired she looked. Maybe this should wait till tomorrow.

"No, I want to tell you now," she said, obviously reading *my* thoughts. "I mean, it's just stuff I sort of heard. I didn't understand all of it — chunks were missing. And it was from a couple different people."

"From Jeb?" I asked, my throat tight.

Angel's eyes met mine. "No. I didn't get anything from him at all. Nothing. It was like he was dead."

Angel went on. "They kept doing tests, you know, and

they were all thinking about me, about the flock, like, wondering where you were and if you would try to come get me."

"Which we *did*," I said proudly.

"Yeah," she agreed. "Anyway, I found out that another place has information about us — like where we came from."

My brain snapped awake. "Whaat?" I said. "Like our life span? Or where they got our DNA?" Did I even want to know our life span? I wasn't sure.

Angel nodded.

"Well, spill it!" Iggy, who must have been awake and listening to us, demanded in that sensitive way of his. I shot him a look — which was useless, of course. And now everyone was awake.

"They have files on us," Angel said. "Like, the main files. They're in New York. At a place called the Institute."

"The Institute?" I asked. "In New York City or upstate New York?"

"I don't know," Angel said. "I *think* it was called the Institute. The Living Institute or something."

Fang was looking at me, still and intent. I knew he had already decided to go check it out, and I nodded briefly.

"There's more," Angel said. Her small voice wavered, and she pressed her face into my shoulder.

"You know how we always talk about our parents but didn't really know if we were made in test tubes?" Angel said. I nodded.

"I saw my name in Jeb's old files," Nudge insisted. "I really did."

"I know, Nudge," I said. "Listen to Angel for a minute."

"Nudge is right," Angel blurted. "We did have parents — real parents. We weren't made in test tubes. We were born, like real babies. We were born from human mothers."

71

I think if a twig had snapped right then, we all would have leaped ten feet into the air.

"You've sat on this since yesterday?" Iggy sounded outraged. "What's the matter with you? Just because you're the youngest doesn't mean you have to be the dumbest."

"Look," I said, taking a breath, "let's all calm down and let Angel talk." I brushed her curls out of her face. "Can you tell us everything you heard?"

"I only got bits and pieces," she said uncomfortably. "I'm sorry, everybody. I've just felt yucky . . . and it all makes me really, really sad too. I don't wanna cry again. Awhh, I'm crying again."

"It's okay, Angel," Fang said in his low, quiet voice. "We understand. You're safe now, here with us."

Nudge looked as if she was about to explode, and I sent her a glance that said, *Okay, just hang on.* The Gasman edged closer to me and took hold of my belt loop for comfort. I put one arm around him and held on to Angel with the other.

"It sounded like," Angel began slowly, "we came from different places, different hospitals. But they got us after we were born. We *weren't* test-tube babies."

"How did they get us?" Fang asked. "And how did they get the bird genes into us?"

"I didn't really understand," said Angel. "It sounded like — like they got the genes into us *before* we were born somehow." She rubbed her forehead. "With a test? An amino . . . ammo . . ."

"Amniocentesis?" I asked, cold outrage creeping down my spine.

"Yeah," said Angel. "That's it. And somehow they got the bird genes into us with it."

"It's okay, just keep going," I said. I could explain it to them later.

"So we got born, and the doctors gave us to the School," Angel went on. "I heard — I heard that they told Nudge's mom and dad that she had died. But she hadn't."

Nudge made a gulping sound, her large brown eyes full of tears. "I *did* have a mom and dad," she whispered. "I *did!*"

"And Iggy's mom —"

I saw Iggy tense, his acute hearing focused on Angel's small voice.

"Died," Angel said, and took in a shuddering breath. "She died when he was born."

The look of stunned grief on Iggy's expressive face was

awful to see. I didn't know what to do, what to say. I just wanted to take away everyone's pain.

"What about us?" the Gasman asked. "How could they get both of us, two years apart?"

Angel wiped her eyes. "Our parents gave us to the School *themselves,*" she said, and started crying again, her thin shoulders shaking.

The Gasman's mouth dropped open, his eyes as round as wheels. "What?"

"They *wanted* to help the School," Angel said, gasping out the words through her sobs. "They *let* them put bird genes in us. And gave us away for money."

My heart was breaking. The Gasman tried so hard to be brave, but he was just a little kid. He leaned against me, burying his face in my shirt, and burst into tears.

"Did you hear anything about me? Or Max?" Fang was stripping the bark off a stick. His tone was casual, but his shoulders were tight, his face stiff.

"Your mom thought you died, like Nudge," Angel said. "She was a teenager. They don't know who your dad was. But they told your mom you died."

The stick Fang was holding snapped in two, his knuckles white in the darkness. I saw pain in his dark eyes. Pain and sadness, and the reflection of our fire.

I cleared my throat. "What about me?" I'd always dreamed of having a mom. Even — and this is so awesomely embarrassing that I'll never admit I said it — hoping

227

that someday she would show up and be so wonderful and *marry Jeb*. And take care of all of us. I know. Pathetic, isn't it?

Angel blinked up at me. "I didn't hear anything about you, Max. Nothing. I'm real sorry."

72

"I can't believe it," the Gasman said for the *thirtieth* time. "They gave us away. They must be sick. Sick jerks. I'm *glad* I don't know them."

"I'm sorry, Gazzy," I said for the thirtieth time, digging down *deep* for my last shred of patience. I totally, totally felt for him, but I had reached my limit about thirteen times ago.

Anyway, I ruffled his fine, light hair and hugged his shoulders. His face was dirty and streaked with tears. I wished we could just go back to our mountain house. The Erasers knew where it was, had swarmed all over it. We could never go back. But right now, I so wished I could just stick Gazzy under a hot shower, then tuck him into bed.

Those days were gone, baby.

"Angel? It's late, sweetie. Why don't you try to get some sleep? Actually, we could all use an early night."

"I'm going to sleep too," said Nudge, her voice still thick from crying. "I just want this day to end."

I blinked. That was the shortest sentence I'd ever heard her utter.

The six of us gathered around. I held out my left fist, and Fang put his on top of it, and everyone else did too. When we had a stack, we tapped the backs of one another's fists with our right hands.

We always do it, wherever we are. Habit.

Angel curled up in her spot, and I covered her with my sweatshirt. The Gasman lay down next to her, and then Nudge settled down too. I knelt next to her and tucked her collar around her neck.

I almost always go to sleep last — like I have to make sure everyone else is down. I started to bank the fire, and Fang came and helped me.

"So maybe you were hatched after all," Fang said. The six of us had always teased one another, saying we'd hatched out of eggs.

I laughed drily. "Yeah. Maybe so. Maybe they found me in a cabbage patch."

"In a way, you're lucky," he said quietly. "Not knowing is better."

I hate the way he can read my mind, since he doesn't even have mind-reading abilities.

"It leaves all the possibilities open," he went on. "Your story could be worse, but it could also be a hell of a lot better."

He sat back on his heels, watching the fire, and then extended his wings a bit to warm them. "A teenager, jeez," he said in disgust. "She was probably a crack addict or something."

He never would have said that if the others were awake. Some things we trusted only each other to understand.

"Maybe not," I said, covering the fire with ashes. "Maybe she was a nice kid who just made a mistake. At least she wanted to actually wait the nine months and have you. Maybe she would have kept you or let a really nice family adopt you."

Fang snorted in disbelief. "On the one hand, we have a mythical nice family that wants to adopt me. On the other, we have a gang of insane scientists desperate to do genetic experiments on innocent children. Guess which hand I get dealt?"

Tiredly, he lay down next to Gazzy and closed his eyes, one arm over his forehead.

"I'm sorry, Fang," I mouthed silently.

I lay down myself, reaching out my foot to touch Nudge, putting an arm around Angel. I was too tired to worry about my brain attack earlier. Too tired to wonder how we would find the Institute in New York. Too tired to care about saving the world.

73

"Yo!" I said loudly. "Up and at 'em!"

You'll be relieved to hear that my brief descent into weary lack of caring was totally gone by the time the sun fried my eyelids the next morning.

I got up, started the fire going again — because that's the kind of selfless, wonderful leader I am — then started affectionately kicking the flock awake.

There was much grumbling and groaning, which I ignored, instead carefully balancing a pan of Jiffy Pop popcorn over a branch on the fire. Popcorn for breakfast! Why not? It's a *grain*. It's like, like, *grits,* but with high self-esteem.

Plus, no one can sleep through the machine-gun sound of popcorn popping. Soon the rest of the flock was gathering glumly around the fire, rubbing sleep out of their eyes.

"We're headed for the Big Apple, guys. The city that never sleeps. I think we're maybe six, seven hours away."

Twenty minutes later, we were taking off, one by one. I was last, after Angel, and I ran about twenty feet, then leaped into the air, beating my wings hard. I was maybe ten feet off the ground when it happened again: Some unseen force shoved an unseen railroad spike through my skull.

I cried out, falling, then smacked into the ground hard enough to knock my breath away.

I curled up in a fragile ball of pain, holding my head, feeling tears dripping down my cheeks, trying not to scream.

"Max?" Fang's gentle fingers touched my shoulder. "Is it like before?"

I couldn't even nod. It was all I could do to hold my head together so my brains wouldn't splatter all over my friends. A high, keening sound reached my ears. *It was me.*

Behind my eyes, bursts of red and orange flooded my brain, as if fireworks were exploding inside me. Then it was as though someone had jacked a movie screen directly into my retinas: Lightning-fast images shot through me so fast it made me feel sick. I could hardly make any of them out: *blurred buildings, fuzzy landscapes, unrecognizable people's faces, food, headlines from papers, old stuff in black-and-white, psychedelic stuff, swirly patterns . . .*

I don't know how long it went on — years? Gradually, gradually, I realized I could move, and as soon as I could, I crawled over to some bushes and barfed my guts up.

Then I lay gasping, feeling like death. It was a while before I could open my eyes and see blue sky, puffy white clouds — and five worried faces.

"Max, what is the *matter* with you?" Angel said, sounding as scared as she looked.

"Think you should see a doctor?" Fang asked mildly, but his eyes were piercing.

"Oh, yes, *that's* a good idea," I said weakly. "We need to let *more* people in authority know about us."

"Look," Fang began, but I cut him off.

"I'm okay now," I said, lying through my teeth. "Maybe it's a stomach bug or something." Yeah, the kind of stomach bug that causes *brain cancer*. The kind of bug you get when your whole genetic makeup is about to unravel. The bug you get before you die.

"Let's just go to New York," I said.

74

After giving me a long, level look, Fang shrugged and motioned to the Gasman to take off. Reluctantly, he did, and the others followed. "After you," Fang said, jerking his thumb toward the sky.

Gritting my teeth, I got to my feet and ran shakily, opening my wings and leaping into the air again, half braced for another explosion of pain. But it was okay. I still felt like I might hurl, and I thought about how awful that would be in midair.

"Are you okay?" Nudge asked once we were airborne. I nodded.

"I've been thinking about my mom and dad," she said. Her tawny wings beat in unison with mine, so we just barely missed each other on the downstrokes. "I bet — if they've been thinking I died eleven years ago, then I bet they would be pretty happy to see me again, right? I mean, if all this time they wished I had gone home with them and grown up — then they would be pretty happy to see me, wouldn't they?"

I didn't say anything.

"Unless . . ." She frowned. "I mean — I guess I'm not what they would be expecting, huh? It's not my fault or anything, but I mean, I've got *wings.*"

Yep, I thought.

"They might not want me if I have wings and am so weird and all," Nudge said, her voice dropping. "Maybe they just want a normal daughter, and if I'm weird, they wouldn't want me back anyway. What do you think, Max?"

"I don't know, Nudge," I said. "It seems like if they're your parents, then they should love you no matter what, even if you're different."

I thought about how Ella had accepted me just the way I was, wings, weirdness, and all. And Dr. Martinez was always going to be my perfect image of a mom. She'd accepted me too.

Now I was gulping, trying not to cry. Because I hadn't experienced *enough* emotion already this morning. I muttered a swear word to myself. After I'd heard Angel cussing like a sailor when she stubbed her toe, my new resolution was to watch my language. All I needed was a six-year-old mutant with a potty mouth.

I thought about how Ella and her mom and I had made chocolate-chip cookies. From scratch. From, like, a bag of flour and real eggs. Not store-bought, not even slice 'n' bake. The way they'd smelled when they were baking was in-cred-i-ble. It had smelled like — home. Like what a real home should smell like.

They'd been the best dang cookies I'd ever had.

75

"Oh, my God," I muttered, staring at the lights below us. Most of New York City is at the bottom part of a long, thin island — Manhattan Island, actually. You could tell exactly where it began and ended, because suddenly the dark landscape was ablaze with lights. Streaming pearls of headlights moved slowly through the arteries of the city. It looked like every window in every building had a light burning.

"That's a *lot* of people," Fang said, coming up beside me.

I knew what he was thinking: We all tend to get a little claustrophobic, a little paranoid when we're around lots of people. Not only had Jeb constantly warned us about interacting with anyone for any reason, but there was always the possibility that one of those strangers could suddenly morph into an Eraser.

"Oh, my gosh, oh, my gosh," Nudge was saying excitedly. "I want to go down there! I want to walk on Fifth Avenue! I want to go to museums!" She turned to me, her face alight with anticipation. "Do we have any money left? Can we get something to eat? Can we, like, go shopping?"

"We have some money," I told her. "We can get something to eat. But remember, we're here to find the Institute."

Nudge nodded, but I could tell half of my words had gone right out her other ear.

"What's that sound?" Iggy asked, concentrating. *"It's music.* Is there music below us? How could we hear it, way up here?"

Central Park was a big, relatively dark rectangle below us. At one end, in a clearing, I could see an enormous crowd of people. Huge floodlights were shining over them.

"I think it must be a concert," I told Iggy. "In the park. An outdoor concert."

"Oh, so cool!" Nudge said. "Can we go? Please, Max, please? A real concert!" If it's possible for someone to bounce up and down with excitement while flying, Nudge was doing it.

The park was pretty dark. There were hundreds of thousands of people down there. Even Erasers would have a hard time finding us in that crowd.

I made an executive decision. "Yes. Try to come down right behind a floodlight's beam, so we won't be seen."

We landed silently among a group of thick-trunked oaks. We took a moment to shake out our legs, and fold in our wings and cover them with windbreakers. After a quick head count, I led the way toward the crowd, trying to look casual, like, *Fly? Me? Nah.*

The music was unbelievably loud: Speakers taller than

Iggy were stacked on top of one another, three high. To me it felt as if the actual ground was vibrating.

"What concert is this?" Iggy asked, yelling in my ear.

I peered over tens of thousands of heads to see the raised stage. Thanks to my raptorlike vision, I had no trouble making out the musicians. And a banner that said Natalie and Trent Taylor. "It's the Taylor Twins," I reported, and most of the flock whooped and whistled. They loved the Taylor Twins.

Angel kept close to me, her small hand in mine, as we stood among the crowd. We were enough on the edge that we avoided the sardine effect of the people closer to the stage. I think we all would have freaked out if we'd been that hemmed in, that unable to move. Iggy put the Gasman on his shoulders and gave him his lighter to burn, like thousands of other people. The Gasman swayed in time to the music, holding the lighter high.

Once he looked down at me, and his face was so full of happiness I almost started crying. How often had I seen him look like that? Like, twice? In eight years?

We listened to Natalie and Trent until the concert ended. As soon as the rivers of people began to flow past us, we melted into the shadows of the trees. The branches above us were thick and welcoming. We flew up into them, settling comfortably.

"That was awesome," Nudge said happily. "I can't believe how many people there are, all crowded into one place. I mean, listen. . . . *There's no silence, ever.* I can hear people and traffic and sirens and dogs barking. I mean, it was always so quiet back at home."

"Too quiet," said the Gasman.

"Well, I hate it," Iggy said flatly. "When it's quiet, I can tell where the heck things are, people are, where echoes are bouncing off. Here I'm just surrounded with a thick, smothering wall of sound. I want to get out of here."

"Oh, Iggy, no!" Nudge cried. "This place is so cool. You'll get used to it."

"We're here to find out what we can about the Institute," I reminded both of them. "I'm sorry, Iggy, but maybe you'll get a little more used to it soon. And Nudge, this isn't a pleasure trip. Our goal is to find the Institute."

"How are we gonna do that?" Angel asked.

"I have a plan," I said firmly. God, I was really going to have to get all this lying under control.

76

Basically, if you put a fence around New York City, you'd have the world's biggest nontraveling circus.

When we woke up at dawn the next morning, there were already joggers, bicyclers, even horseback riders weaving their way along the miles and miles of trails in Central Park. We slipped down out of the trees and casually wandered the paths.

Within an hour, speed skaters were rushing by, street performers were setting up their props, and the paths were almost crowded with dog walkers and moms pushing jogging strollers.

"That lady has six white poodles!" Nudge hissed behind her hand. "Who needs six white poodles?"

"Maybe she sells them," I suggested, "to kids with big wide eyes."

"Something smells awesome," Iggy said, swiveling his head to detect the source. "What is that? It's over there." He pointed off to my left.

"There's a guy selling food," I said. "It says honey-roasted peanuts."

"I am so there," said Iggy. "Can I have some money?"

Iggy, Angel, and I went to buy six small bags of honey-roasted peanuts (they really did smell like heaven), and Fang, Nudge, and the Gasman went to look at a clown selling balloons.

We were walking over to join them when something about the clown caught my eye. She was watching a sleek, dark-haired guy strolling down a path. Their gazes met.

A chill went down my back. Just like that, my enjoyment of the day burst. I was swept into fear, anger, and an intense self-preservation reflex.

"Iggy, heads up," I whispered. "Get the others."

Beside me, Angel was wound tight, her hand clenching mine hard. We walked fast toward the others. Fang, doing an automatic sweep of the area, saw my urgent expression. In the next moment he had clamped a hand on Nudge's and the Gasman's shoulders and spun them around to walk quickly away.

We met on the path and sped up our pace. One glance behind me showed the dark-haired guy following us. He was joined by a woman who looked just as intent and powerful as he did.

A flow of heroically suppressed swear words ran through my brain. I scanned the scenery for escape routes, a place where we could take off, a place to duck and cover.

They were gaining on us.

"Run!" I said. The six of us can run faster than most

grown men, but the Erasers had also been genetically enhanced. If we couldn't find an out, we were done for.

Now there were three of them — they'd been joined by another male-model type. They had broken into an easy trot and were closing the space between us.

Paths merged into other paths, sometimes narrowing, sometimes widening. Again and again, we almost crashed into bikers or skaters going too fast to swerve.

"Four of them," Fang said. "Pour it on, guys!"

We sped up. They were maybe twenty yards behind us. Hungry grins marred their good-looking faces.

"*Six* of them!" I said.

"They're too fast," Fang informed me unnecessarily. "Maybe we should fly."

I bit my lip, keeping a tight grip on Angel's hand. *What to do, what to do. They were closer, and even closer* —

"Eight of them!" said Fang.

77

"Left!" Iggy said, and without question we all hung a sudden left. How he knew it was there, I have no idea.

Our path suddenly opened into a wider plaza surrounded by vendors selling all kinds of stuff. Some brick buildings were on the left, and a big crowd of kids was passing through a metal gate.

I caught a glimpse of a sign: Central Park Zoo.

"Merge!" I whispered, and just like that, we melted smoothly into the horde of schoolkids. Fang, Iggy, Nudge, and I ducked down to be shorter, and we all wormed our way into the middle of the group, so we were surrounded by other kids. None of them seemed to think it was weird we were there — there must have been more than two hundred of them being herded through the gate.

I repressed an urge to moo and peeped over a girl's shoulder. The Erasers had spread out and were searching for us, looking frustrated.

One of the big creeps tried to push past the policeman at the zoo gate, but the cop blocked his way. "School day only," I heard him say. "No unauthorized adults. Oh, you're a chaperone? Yeah? Show me your pass."

With a low snarl, the Eraser backed away and rejoined his companions. I grinned: stopped in his tracks by a New York cop. Go, boys in blue!

We reached the entry gate: *the moment of truth.*

We got waved in!

"Pass, pass, pass," the gate person muttered, motioning us through without looking at us.

Inside the zoo, we scrambled off to one side, then paused for a moment and slapped high fives.

"Yes!" the Gasman said. "School day only! Yes! I love this place!"

"The zoo!" Nudge said, practically quivering with excitement. "I've always wanted to see a zoo! I've read about 'em — I've seen them on TV. This is so great! Thanks, Max."

I hadn't had anything to do with it, but I smiled and nodded: magnanimous Max.

"Come on, let's get farther in," said Iggy, sounding nervous. "Put some distance between us and them. Jeez, was that a lion? Please tell me it's behind bars."

"It's a *zoo,* Iggy," Nudge said, taking his arm and leading him. "*Everything* is behind bars."

Like we used to be.

78

"Oh, man, look at the polar bear!" The Gasman pressed his face against the glass of the enclosure, watching as the huge white bear swam gracefully in its big pool. The bear had an empty steel beer keg to play with, which it was batting through the water.

I'll just tell you flat out: We'd never seen any of these animals before, not in real life. We didn't grow up going on field trips, having Sunday outings with the 'rents. This was a completely different, foreign world, where kids swarmed freely through a zoo, animals were in habitats and weren't undergoing genetic grafting, and we were strolling along, not hooked up to EEG monitors and blood pressure cuffs.

It was wild.

Like this bear. Two bears, actually. A big main bear and a smaller backup bear. They had a pretty large habitat, with huge rocks, an enormous swimming pool, toys to play with.

"Man," said Gazzy wistfully. "I'd love to have a pool."

Or, hey! How about a house? Safety? Plenty of food? Those were about as impossible as a swimming pool. I reached out and rubbed Gazzy's shoulder. "That would be really cool," I agreed.

All these animals, even though they were stuck in enclosures, probably bored out of their minds, possibly lonely, still had it so much better than we'd had it at the School. I felt edgy and angry, nervous, still coming off my adrenaline high after being chased by the Erasers. Seeing all these animals made me remember too much about when I was little, when I lived in a cage so small I couldn't stand up.

Which reminded me: We were here to find the Institute, whatever that was. In just a short while, we might know who we were, where we came from, how our whole lives had happened.

I rubbed my hand across my mouth, really starting to feel twitchy and kind of headachy. But Nudge, the Gasman, Angel, and Iggy were having a great time. Nudge was describing everything to Iggy, and they were laughing and running around. Just like normal kids. I mean, except for the retractable wings and all.

"This place gives me the creeps," Fang said.

"You too? I'm going nuts," I admitted. "It's flashback city. And I have —" I started to say "a headache," but then didn't want to complain or have Fang tell me to see a doctor again "an overwhelming desire to set all these animals free."

"Free to do what?" Fang asked drily.

"Just to be *out*, to escape," I said.

"Out in the middle of Manhattan?" Fang pointed out. "Free to live without protection, without someone bringing them food, with no idea of how to take care of themselves? They're better off here. Unless you want to fly to Greenland with a polar bear on your back."

Logic is just so incredibly annoying sometimes. I shot Fang a look and went to round up everyone.

"Can we leave?" I asked them, trying not to whine. Very unbecoming in a leader. "I just — want to get out of here."

"You look kind of green," the Gasman said with interest.

I *was* starting to feel nauseated. "Yeah. Can we split before I upchuck in front of all these impressionable kids?"

"Over here," Fang said, motioning us to a big crevice between two huge manufactured rocks. It led back to a path that must have been for the zookeepers — it was empty and roped off.

I managed to get out of there without crashing, screaming, or throwing up. What a nice change.

79

"You know what I like about New York?" the Gasman said, noisily chewing his kosher hot dog. "It's full of New Yorkers who are freakier than we are."

"So we blend?" Iggy asked.

I glanced over at him. He was licking an ice-cream cone that was like a mini him: tall, thin, and vanilla. He was already just over six feet tall — not bad for a fourteen-year-old. With his height, his pale skin, and his light reddish-blond hair, I'd always felt he was the most visible of all of us. But here on this broad avenue, we were surrounded by gorgeous supermodels, punk rockers, Goths, and leatherites, suits, students, people from every other country — and, well, yeah, six kids with bulky windbreakers, ratty clothes, and questionable hygiene didn't really stick out.

"More or less," I said. "Of course, that won't help with the Erasers." Automatically, I did a perimeter sweep, a 360 around us to pick up signs of trouble.

"Speaking of which," Fang said, "we seem to be dealing with version 6.0."

"I was thinking the same thing," I said. "This year's crop

looks more human. And there are females. Which is a bummer." Even as I said the words, I was examining every face we passed, looking for a hint of feral sleekness, a cruel light in the eyes, a hard slash of a mouth.

"Yeah. We all know how bloodthirsty females are. Dirty fighting and so on," Fang said.

I rolled my eyes. What a comedian.

"Can I have a burrito?" Nudge asked as we approached yet another street vendor. She faced me, bouncing backward down the sidewalk. "What's a nish? I can have a burrito, right?"

"Ka-nish," I corrected her. "It's like a square of mashed potatoes, fried." I was scanning every building — for what, I didn't know. A big sign that said The Institute?

"What's sauerkraut?" Angel asked.

"You don't want it," I said. "Trust me."

We each got a burrito, hot and wrapped in foil.

"I like being able to just buy food as we walk along," Nudge said happily. "If you walk a couple blocks, there's someone selling food. And delis. I love delis! They're everywhere! Everywhere you go, there's everything you need: food, delis, banks, subway stops, buses, cool stores, fruit stands right on the street. This is the best place, I'm telling you. Maybe we should always live here."

"It would certainly be convenient for the Erasers," I said. "They wouldn't have to track us down in the middle of nowhere."

Nudge frowned, and Angel took my hand.

"But you're right, Nudge," I said, sorry for raining on her parade. "I know what you mean." But it was costing money, and we were running out. *And we had a mission.*

Suddenly, I stopped dead, as if I'd been poleaxed.

Fang examined my face. "That pain?" he asked quietly, glancing around as if planning where to take me if I suddenly crumpled.

I shook my head and inhaled deeply. *"Cookies!"*

He looked at me blankly.

I spun in a circle to see where the aroma was coming from. Duh. Right in front of us was a small red storefront. Mrs. Fields. The scent of cookies right out of the oven wafted out onto the street. It smelled like Ella's house, like safety, like home.

"I must have cookies," I announced, and went into the store, Angel trotting at my side.

They were fabulous.

But not as good as homemade.

80

"So what's your big plan for finding the Institute?" Iggy asked.

"I'm tired of walking," Nudge said. "Can we just sit for a minute?" Without waiting for an answer, she sank onto some broad stone steps in front of a building. She rested her head in her hands and closed her eyes.

"Uh . . ." *Just walk around until we see it* didn't seem like a good response. But Iggy had hit the nail on the head: I didn't know how to find the Institute. I didn't know what it looked like or even, really, if it was in New York City.

The Gasman and Angel sat down next to Nudge. I was struck once again by what incredibly cute kids they are — for mutants.

"How about a phone book?" Fang suggested. "Every once in a while I see one."

"Yeah, that's a possibility," I said, frustrated by not coming up with something better. We needed an information system of some kind — like a computer we could hack into. A large marble lion caught my eye; this building had two of them. Very fancy-schmancy.

I blinked and saw four lions, like images superimposed on one another. They flickered in front of my eyes, and I shook my head a bit. I blinked again, and everything was normal. A heavy weight settled on my chest — my brain was malfunctioning again.

"So what are we going to do?" Iggy asked.

Yeah, leader, lead.

Stalling for time, worried that my head might explode at any moment, I looked up at the building in front of us. It had a name. It was called the New York Public Library of Humanities and Social Sciences. Hello. A *library*.

I jerked my head at the building. "We're going to start in here," I said briskly, and clapped twice to get the younger set on its feet. "I figure they've got computers, databases . . ." I let my voice trail off and started purposefully up the steps. Nudge, Gazzy, and Angel followed me.

"How does she do that?" I heard Fang ask Iggy.

81

Inside, the library was awesome. None of us had ever been inside one, and we were staring like the out-of-town yokels we were.

"May I help you?" A young guy was standing behind a polished wooden counter. He looked faintly disapproving, but not like he wanted to rip our lungs out, so I figured he wasn't an Eraser.

"Yes." I stepped forward, looking as serious and professional as a fourteen-year-old mutant who had never been in a library can look. "I was hoping to find information about a certain institute that I *think* is in New York." I smiled at him, putting real warmth into it, and he blinked. "Unfortunately, I don't know the whole name or where in New York it is. Is there a computer I could use to search? Or some sort of database?"

He glanced over all of us. Angel stepped up next to me and put her hand in mine. She smiled sweetly at the guy, looking, well, angelic.

"Fourth floor," the guy said after a pause. "There are computers in a room off the main reading room. They're free, but you have to sign in."

"Thank you so much," I said, smiling again. Then we hustled to the elevators.

The Gasman punched number four.

"Well, aren't you the charmer?" Fang muttered, not looking at me.

"What?" I asked, startled, but he didn't say anything. We rode upward, hating being in a small enclosed space. Sweat was breaking out on my brow by the time the doors slid open on the fourth floor, and we leaped out as if the elevator had been pressurized.

We immediately found a bank of computers with instructions on how to surf the Net. All we had to do was sign in at the desk. I signed "Ella Martinez" with a flourish, and the clerk smiled at me.

That was the last cheerful thing that happened for the next hour and a half. Fang and I searched in every way we could think of and found a million institutes of one kind or another, in Manhattan and throughout New York state, but none of them seemed promising. My favorite? The Institute for Realizing Your Pet's Inner Potential. Anyone who can explain that to me, drop a line.

Angel was lying under the desk at our feet, murmuring quietly to herself. Nudge and the Gasman were playing hangman on a piece of scrap paper. Violence occasionally broke out, since neither of them could spell their way out of a paper bag.

Iggy was sitting motionless in a chair, and I knew he was listening to every whisper, every scraped chair, every rustle of fabric in the room, creating an invisible map of what was happening all around him.

I typed in another search command, then watched in dismay as the computer screen blurred and crashed. A string of orange words, *fail, fail, fail,* scrolled across the screen before it finally went black and winked out.

"It's almost closing time, anyway," Fang said.

"Can we sleep here?" Iggy said softly. "It's so quiet. I like it in here."

"Uh, I don't think so," I said, looking around. I hadn't realized that most people had left — we were the only ones in the room. Except for a guard, in uniform, who had just spotted us. She started walking toward us, and something about her, her tightly controlled pace, made my inner alarms go off.

"Let's split," I muttered, pulling Iggy out of his chair.

We skittered out of there, found the stairs, and raced down as fast as we could. I was expecting Erasers at any moment. But we burst out into the dim late-afternoon light and ran down the stone steps without anyone following us.

82

"Can we take the subway back to the park?" Nudge asked tiredly.

It was late. We'd decided to sleep in Central Park again. It was huge, dark, and full of trees.

"It's only about eighteen blocks to walk," I said. But Angel was starting to fade too — she wasn't back to a hundred percent by a long shot. "Let's see how much it would cost."

Five steps down the subway entrance, I was already tense. Nudge, Angel, and the Gasman were too tired to hate being in an enclosed space, but Fang, Iggy, and I were twitching.

The fare was two dollars a person, except kids under forty-four inches, who were free. I looked at Angel. Even though she was only six, she was already over four feet tall. So that was twelve dollars.

Except the fare booth was empty. So we'd have to use the automatic fare machine. That is, if we were going to be troubled about a small thing like hopping over the turnstile when no one was looking.

Once we were inside, ten minutes went by with no train. Ten loooong minutes with me feeling like I was about to start screaming and climbing the walls. If we'd been followed, if Erasers came . . .

I saw Iggy turn his head, listening to something from inside the dark tunnel.

"What?" I asked.

"People," he answered. "In there."

"Workers?"

"I don't think so."

I peered into the blackness. Now that I concentrated, I could hear voices too. And way down the line, I saw what looked like the flickering of a fire — its reflected glow from around a bend in the tunnel.

I made a snap decision, which always makes the flock feel so safe and comfortable.

"Let's go," I said, and I jumped off the platform and onto the tracks leading into the darkness.

83

"What does that mean?" the Gasman asked, pointing at a small metal plaque that said Stay off the third rail!

"It means the third rail has seven hundred volts of direct current running through it," Fang said. "Touch it and you're human popcorn."

"Okay," I said. "Good tip. Everyone stay off the third rail."

Then I shot Fang a look that said, Thank you for that lovely image. He almost grinned at me.

Iggy felt the train first. "Everyone off the rails," he said, standing still until I took his arm. We all stepped over to a yucky, disgusting wall and pressed ourselves as flat against it as possible.

Thirty seconds later, a train rushed past so fast that its slipstream made us sway toward it. I kept my knee shoved against Angel so she wouldn't be pulled off her feet.

"Well, that was fairly nerve-racking," I said as we gingerly peeled ourselves off the wall.

"Who's there?" The voice was querulous, aggressive,

and rough, as if its owner had spent the last fifty years smoking cigarettes. Maybe he had.

We walked forward, on the alert, wings starting to unfold a tiny bit in case we suddenly needed to go airborne.

"Nobody," I called convincingly as we turned the bend of the tunnel.

"Whoa," the Gasman breathed.

Before us was a city. A small, ragged city in Manhattan's basement. Groups of people clotted a large concrete cavern. The ceiling was three stories above us and dripped with paint stalactites and humid condensation.

Several unwashed faces looked toward us, and someone said, "Not cops. *Kids.*"

They turned away, uninterested, except for one woman who seemed to be wearing about five layers of clothing. "You got food?" she barked.

Silently, Nudge pulled a napkin-wrapped knish out of her pocket and handed it over. The woman sniffed it, looked at it, then turned her back to us and started eating.

Here and there the cavern was dotted with fifty-gallon oil drums in which people had made fires. It was a warm spring night, but the fires provided the only light and helped get rid of the dank chill that was creeping up my legs.

It was a whole new world, made up of homeless people, people who didn't fit in anywhere, runaways . . . We saw a handful of kids who looked around our age.

I realized that my head was aching. It had been growing worse all evening, and now I just wanted to go to sleep.

"Over there," said the knish woman, pointing. We looked and saw a narrow concrete ledge built into a wall. It was hundreds of feet long, and people were sleeping on it, sitting on it, marking off their territory with old blankets or cardboard boxes. The woman had pointed out a thirty-foot-long section that seemed unoccupied.

I looked at Fang, and he shrugged. It wasn't as nice as the park, but it was warm, dry, and seemed somewhat safe. We scrambled up the ledge, with me boosting Angel. Keeping our backs to everyone, we stacked our fists and tapped twice. Almost instantly, Nudge lay down, pillowing her head on her hands.

Fang and I sat with our backs against the wall. I dropped my head into my hands and started rubbing my temples.

"You okay?" Fang asked.

"Yeah," I muttered. "I'll be better tomorrow."

"Go to sleep," said Fang. "I'll take the first watch."

I gave him a grateful smile, and soon I was out, out, out — with no idea how we would ever know it was morning.

84

The brain explosion came again while I was sleeping.

One moment I was lost in a dream in which I was strolling lazily through a field of yellow flowers, like a dopey shampoo commercial, and the next I had jackknifed into a sitting position, holding my head and feeling like this was it: Death had finally come for me, and it wasn't taking no for an answer.

My breaths were tight hisses. Jagged shards of pain ripped through my skull, and I heard myself whimper. *Please let it be fast,* I begged God. Please just end it, end it, end it now. Please, please, please.

"Max?" Fang's low voice, right by my ear, seeped through the waves of agony. I couldn't respond. My face was awash with tears. If I had been standing on a cliff, nothing could have kept me from throwing myself off. With my wings tucked *in*.

Inside my brain, images flashed incomprehensibly, making me sick, assaulting my senses with pictures, words, sounds. A voice speaking gibberish. *Maybe it was mine.*

As if from a great distance, I felt Fang's hand on my

shoulder, but it was like watching a movie — it seemed totally unrelated to what I was going through. My teeth were clenched so hard my jaw ached, and then I tasted blood — I had bitten into my lip.

When was I going to see the proverbial tunnel of white light I'd heard about? With people waiting for me at the other end, smiling and holding out their hands? Don't kids with wings go to heaven?

Then an angry voice filtered through the pain: *"Who's screwing with my Mac?"*

85

Just as before, the pain slowly ebbed, and I almost cried with frustration: If it was ending, I wasn't dead. If I wasn't dead, I could go through this again.

Images flashed across the backs of my eyes, but they were unfocused and undecipherable. If I had been alone, I would have started bawling. Instead I had to desperately try to keep it together, try not to wake the younger ones (if I hadn't already), try not to give our position away.

"Who are you?" The angry voice came again. "What are you doing? You've crashed my whole system, worthless dipstick!"

Ordinarily, I would have been on my feet by now, pushing Angel and the others in back of me, an angry snarl on my face.

However, tonight I was crumpled in a humiliated, whimpering ball, holding my head, eyes squeezed shut, trying not to sob like a complete weenie.

"What are you talking about?" Fang asked, an edge of steel in his voice.

"My system crashed. I've tracked the interference, and

it's comin' from *you*. So I'm tellin' you to knock it off — or else!"

I drew in a deep, shuddering breath, totally mortified that a stranger was seeing me like this.

"And what's wrong with *her*? She trippin'?"

"She's fine," Fang snapped. "We don't know anything about your computer. If you're not brain-dead, you'll get out of here." No one sounds colder or meaner than Fang when he wants to.

The other guy said flatly, "I'm not going nowhere till you quit messing with my Mac. Why don't you get your girlfriend to a hospital?"

Girlfriend? Oh, God, was I going to catch it later about that. It was enough to make me lever up on one arm, then pull myself to a sitting position.

"Who the hell are *you?*" I snarled, the effect totally ruined by the weak, weepy sound of my voice. Blinking rapidly, finding even the dim tunnel light painful, I struggled to focus on the intruder.

I got a hazy impression of someone about my age; a ragged-looking kid wearing old army fatigues. He had a dingy PowerBook attached to straps around his shoulders like a xylophone or something.

"None of your beeswax!" he shot back. "Just quit screwing up my motherboard."

I was still clammy and nauseated, still had a shocking headache and felt trembly, but I thought I could string a complete sentence together. "What are you talking about?"

"This!" The kid turned his Mac toward us, and when I saw the screen I actually gasped.

It was a mishmash of flashing images, drawings, maps, streams of code, silent film clips of people talking. It was exactly the stuff that had flooded my brain during my attack.

PART 5

THE VOICE — MAKE THAT MY VOICE

86

My eyes flicked to the kid's grimy face. "Who *are* you?" I demanded again, still sounding shaky.

"I'm the guy who's gonna kick your butt if you don't quit messing with my system," the kid said angrily.

In the next moment, his computer screen cleared totally, turning the same dull green as his fatigues. Then large red words scrolled down: *Hello, Max.*

Fang's head whipped around to stare at me, and I focused helplessly on his wide, dark eyes. Then, as if connected, our heads turned to stare again at the computer. Onscreen, it said, *Welcome to New York.*

Inside my head, a voice said, *I knew you'd come. I've got big plans for you.*

"Can you hear that?" I whispered. "*Did* you hear it?"

"Hear what?" Fang asked.

"That voice?" I said. My head ached, but the pain was better, and it looked as if I might avoid barfing. I rubbed my temples again, my gaze fixed on the kid's Mac.

"What's the deal?" the kid asked, sounding a lot less

belligerent and much more weirded out. "Who's Max? How are you doing this?"

"We're not doing anything," Fang said.

A new pain crashed into my brain, and once again the computer screen started flashing disconnected images, gibberish, plans, drawings, all chaotic and garbled.

Peering at the screen, wincing and still rubbing my temples, I spotted four words: *Institute for Higher Living.*

I looked at Fang, and he gave the slightest nod: He'd seen them too.

Then the screen went blank once more.

87

The kid quickly started typing in commands, muttering, "I'm gonna track this down. . . ."

Fang and I watched, but a couple minutes later the geek stopped, flicking his computer in frustration. He looked at us with narrowed eyes, taking in everything: the drying blood on my chin, the other kids sleeping near us.

"I don't know how you're doing it," he said, sounding resigned and irritated. "Where's your gear?"

"We don't have any gear," Fang said. "Spooky, isn't it?"

"You guys on the run? You in trouble?"

Jeb had drilled it into us that we shouldn't ever trust anyone. (We now knew that included *him*.) The geek was starting to make me extremely nervous.

"Why would you think that?" Fang asked calmly.

The kid rolled his eyes. "Let me see. Maybe because you're a bunch of *kids* sleepin' in a *subway tunnel*. Kind of clues me in, you know?"

Okay, he had a point.

"What about you?" I asked. "You're a kid sleeping in a subway tunnel. Don't you have school?"

The kid coughed out a laugh. "MIT kicked me out."

MIT was a university for brainiacs — I'd heard of it. This kid wasn't old enough.

"Uh-huh." I made myself sound incredibly bored.

"No, really," he said, sounding almost sheepish. "I got early admission. Was gonna major in computer technology. But I spun out, and they told me to take a hike."

"What do you mean, spun out?" asked Fang.

He shrugged. "Wouldn't take my Thorazine. They said, no Thorazine, no school."

Okay, I'd been around wack-job scientists enough to pick up on some stuff. Like the fact that Thorazine is what they give schizophrenics.

"So you didn't like Thorazine," I said.

"No." His face turned hard. "Or Haldol, or Melleril, or Zyprexa. They all suck. People just want me to be quiet, do what I'm told, don't make trouble."

It was weird — he reminded me a little bit of us: He'd chosen to live a hard, dirty life, being free, instead of a taken-care-of life where he was like a prisoner.

Course, we weren't schizo. On second thought, I had a voice talking inside my head. Better not make any snap judgments.

"So what's up with your computer, man?" Fang asked.

The kid shrugged again. "It's my bread and butter. I can hack into anything. Sometimes people pay me. I do jobs when I need money." All of a sudden his mouth snapped shut. "Why? *Who wants to know?*"

"Chill out, dude," Fang said, frowning. "We're just having a chat."

But the kid had started to back away, looking angry. "Who sent you?" he asked, his voice rising. "Who are you? You just leave me alone! You just stay away!"

Fang raised his hands in a "calm down" gesture, but the kid had turned and run. In about fifteen seconds we could no longer hear his sneakers on the ground.

"It's always refreshing to meet someone crazier than us," I said. "We seem so normal afterward."

"*We?*" Fang said.

"Wha's up?" Iggy asked sleepily, pulling himself upright.

I sighed but forced myself to tell Iggy about the kid's computer, the Voice in my head, the images that flashed through me during one of my attacks. I tried to sound nonchalant, so he wouldn't know I was quaking in my boots.

"Maybe I'm going crazy," I said lightly. "But it will lead me to greatness. Like Joan of Arc."

"But controlling other people's computers?" Iggy said skeptically.

"I don't see how," I said. "But since I have no clue about who or what could possibly be causing it, I guess I can't rule anything out."

"Hmm. Do we think it's connected to the School or the Institute?" Fang asked.

"Well, either that or I was born this way," I said sarcastically. "On the off chance I *wasn't,* let's really, really try to

273

find the Institute tomorrow. At least now we know what name to look for."

The Institute for Higher Living.

Catchy, huh?

88

Have you ever woken up about a hundred times more exhausted than you were when you went to sleep?

The next morning — at least, I assumed it was morning, since we were all waking up — I felt like one of the twelve dancing princesses, who danced all night, wore holes in their shoes, and had to sleep it off the next day. Except, oh, yeah: a) I'm not a princess; b) sleeping in a subway tunnel and having another brain attack aren't that much like dancing all night; and c) my combat boots were still in good shape. Other than that, it was *exactly* the same.

"Is it morning?" Angel asked, yawning.

"I'm hungry" were, predictably, Nudge's first words.

"Okay, we'll get you some chow," I said tiredly. "Then it's off to find the Institute."

Fang, Iggy, and I had agreed to not tell the younger kids about the hacker or about my latest brain attack. Why make 'em worry?

It took a couple minutes for us to wend our way through the subway tunnels, back up into light and air.

You know you've been breathing something less than primo when the New York street smells really fresh and clean.

"It's so bright," the Gasman said, shielding his eyes. Then, "Is that honey-roasted peanuts?"

Their incredible scent was impossible to resist. You could have an Eraser selling those peanuts, and we'd probably still go. I focused my eyes on the vendor. No. Not an Eraser.

We got some peanuts, and then we walked down Fourteenth Street, chomping, as I tried to figure out a sensible way to comb the city. First, a phone book. We saw a phone kiosk up ahead, but it had only a chain where the phone book had been. Would a store let us use theirs? *Hey! Information!* I dug some change out of my pocket and picked up the phone. I dialed 411.

"In New York City, the Institute for Higher Living," I said when the automated operator came on.

"We're sorry. There is no listing under that name. Please check and try again."

Frustration was my constant companion. I wanted to scream. "What the he-eck are we supposed to do *now*?" I asked Fang.

He looked at me, and I could tell he was mulling over the problem. He held out a small waxed-paper bag. "Peanut?"

We kept walking and eating, gazing in constant amazement at the store windows. Everything you could buy in the world was for sale on Fourteenth Street in New York.

Of course, we couldn't afford any of it. Still, it was awesome.

"Smile, you're on *Candid Camera,*" said Fang, pointing at a window.

In an electronics store, a short-circuit camera was displaying passersby on a handful of TV screens. Automatically, we ducked our heads and turned away, instinctively paranoid about anyone having our images.

Suddenly, I winced as a single sharp pain hit my temple. At the same time, words scrolling across the TV screens caught my eye. I stared in disbelief as *Good morning, Max,* filled every screen.

"Jeez," Fang breathed, stopping dead in his tracks.

Iggy bumped into him, saying, "What? What is it?"

"Is that you?" the Gasman asked me. "How do they know you?"

Playing is learning, Max, said the Voice inside my head. It was the same one as last night, and I realized I couldn't tell if it was adult or child, male or female, friend or foe. Great.

Games test your abilities. Fun is crucial to human development. Go have fun, Max.

I halted, oblivious to the gobs of people streaming around us on the street. "I don't want to have fun! I want some answers!" I blurted without meaning to — the crazy girl talking back to her little Voice.

Get on the Madison Avenue bus, said the Voice. *Get off when it looks fun.*

89

I don't know about the *rest* of you who have little voices, but something about *mine* made me feel completely compelled to listen to it.

I blinked and discovered the flock gazing at me solemnly, watching me sink further into total insanity right before their eyes.

"Max, are you okay?" Nudge asked.

I nodded. "I think we should get on the Madison Avenue bus," I said, looking for a street sign.

Fang looked at me thoughtfully. "Why?"

I turned slightly so the others couldn't see me and mouthed, "The Voice."

He nodded. "But Max," he whispered, barely audible, "what if this is all a trap?"

"I don't know!" I said. "But maybe we should do what it says for a while — to see."

"Do what *what* says?" the Gasman demanded.

I had started walking toward the corner. I heard Fang say, "Max has been hearing a voice, inside her. We don't know what it is." So much for not worrying the others.

"Like her conscience?" Nudge asked. "Do the TVs have anything to do with it?"

"We don't know," said Fang. "Right now it wants us to get on the Madison Avenue bus, apparently."

The bus stop was fourteen blocks away. We got on, and I pushed our fares into the machine. The driver waved us through, saying, "Pass, pass, pass" in a bored voice.

I hoped the Voice didn't want me to keep spending money — we were dangerously low.

For people who get nervous in small, confined spaces or surrounded by other people, riding a bus is pretty much a living nightmare. It was so crowded we had to stand in the aisle with people pressed up against us. I figured we could always kick a window out and jump, but the whole thing frayed my few remaining nerves. My head was swiveling constantly, scanning for Erasers suddenly morphing out of our fellow passengers.

Well, Voice? I thought. *What now?*

I'm sure this will surprise you, but the Voice did not answer.

Next to me, Angel trustingly held my hand, watching the city go past the bus windows. It was up to me. I had to keep everyone safe. I had to find the Institute. If my brain attacks killed me, Fang would take over. But until then, I was numero uno. I couldn't let the flock down. *Do you hear that, Voice? If you're going to make me let everyone down, you're going to be sorry you ever ... entered my brain.*

Oh, my God, I was so freaking nuts.

"Okay, people," the bus driver said over the PA system. "Fifty-eighth Street! This is where the fun is!"

Startled, I looked at Fang, then started hustling everyone out the back door of the bus. We stepped into the sunlight. The bus pulled noisily away, leaving us choking on its exhaust. We were at the bottom of Central Park.

"What —" I began, then my eyes widened as I saw a large glass-fronted building across the street. Behind its glass were an enormous teddy bear, a huge wooden soldier, and a fifteen-foot-tall ballerina up on one pointed toe.

The sign said AFO Schmidt.

The world's most amazing toy store.

Well, okay.

90

We poor, underprivileged, pathetic bird kids had never been in a toy store.

And AFO Schmidt is where kids think they've died and gone to heaven. Right inside the front door was a huge two-story clock covered with moving figures. The song "It's a Small World" was playing loudly, but I figured that was to keep out the riffraff.

I had no idea why we were here. It seemed too much to hope for that somehow this little romp was getting us closer to finding the Institute, but I made the executive decision to see where it took us.

A life-size stuffed giraffe surrounded by other life-size stuffed animals led the way to the whole stuffed-animal area, which was practically as big as our old house.

I looked down at Gazzy and Angel to see them staring, wide-eyed and slack-jawed, at too many fabulous toys to even comprehend.

"Iggy," the Gasman said, "there's a *whole room* of Lego and Bionicle."

"Go with them," I told Fang. "And let's keep an eye out for each other, okay?"

He nodded and followed the boys into the Lego room, while I trailed after Angel and Nudge, who were picking up one stuffed animal after another.

"Oh, my gosh," Nudge was saying, holding a small stuffed tiger. "Oh, Max, isn't he the cutest thing? Oh, his name is Samson."

I dutifully agreed that he was in fact the cutest thing and kept glancing around for either an Eraser or some kind of clue my Voice might point me to.

"Max?" Angel tugged on my sleeve. I turned to her, and she held up a small stuffed bear. It was dressed as an angel, with a white gown and little wings on its back. A tiny gold wire halo floated above its head.

Angel's eyes were pleading with me. I checked its price tag. The pleasure of owning this small stuffed bear could be hers for only forty-nine dollars.

"I'm so sorry, Angel," I said, bending down to her eye level. "But this bear is forty-nine dollars. We're almost out of money — I don't have anywhere near that. I'm really sorry. I wish I could get it for you. I know it's an angel, just like you." I stroked her hair and handed her the bear back.

"But I want it," Angel snapped at me, which was completely out of character for her.

"I said no. That's it, kiddo."

I wandered a few feet away, still within eyeshot of the

girls, to look at a "mystical" display. There were Magic 8 Balls, and when you shook them, an answer would float to the surface of a little window. I shook one. "Very likely" was its prediction. Unfortunately, I had forgotten to ask it a question.

There was a game called Ca-balah!, a Gypsy Fortune-teller game, and the old favorite: a Ouija board. I breathed out, my hands in my pockets, and looked around the store. Maybe we should sleep here tonight.

Out of the corner of my eye, I detected a slight movement, and my raptor gaze locked on it. It was the little Ouija doohickey, the thing that "spirits" are supposed to guide across the board, pointing to certain letters, but everyone knows it's really the kids doing it.

This one was moving with nothing touching it.

I looked around: No one was near. Angel was almost twenty feet away, not looking at it, still holding the angel bear. I waved my hand over it — there were no wires. It had touched the *S* and then the *A.* I lifted the game board and held it up, in case it was being moved by a magnet underneath. The pointer reached the *V* and headed toward the *E.*

Save.

I put the board back down as if it were red-hot.

The small black triangle paused on the *T,* then moved to the *H.* Then the *E.*

The.

It slid very slowly toward the *W,* and I frowned. It

moved up and over to the *O*, and my jaw clenched. By the time it reached the *R*, I was ready to throw the board across the store. Grimly, I watched as it finished. The *L*. The *D*. The *M*, the *A*, the *X*.

Save the world, Max.

91

"Fang!"

He whirled, saw my face, and instantly tapped Iggy's and the Gasman's hands. They joined me and Nudge under the huge clock.

"Let's get out of here," I muttered. "A Ouija board just told me to save the world."

"Gosh, you're, like, famous," said the Gasman, clearly not feeling the ominous dread that I was.

"Where's Angel?" Fang asked.

I reached out for her and grabbed air. My head whipped around, and I rushed back to the stuffed-animal section. Already, panic was flooding my senses — it had been barely more than a week since she'd been kidnapped. . . .

I skidded to a stop by a life-size chimpanzee hanging from a display. In front of me, Angel was talking to an older woman. I'd never seen an Eraser that old, so my heartbeat ticked down a couple notches.

Angel looked sad, and she held up the angel bear to show the woman.

"What's she up . . ." Fang began.

The woman hesitated, then said something I couldn't hear. Angel's face lit up, and she nodded eagerly.

"Someone's buying something for Angel," Iggy said quietly.

Angel *knew* we were watching her, but she was refusing to meet our eyes. The five of us followed them to the checkout counter, and I watched in disbelief as the woman, seeming a bit bemused, took out her wallet and paid for Angel's bear. Angel was practically jumping up and down with happiness. She bounced on her heels, clutching the bear to her chest, and I heard her say "Thank you" about a thousand times.

Then, still looking slightly confused, the woman smiled, nodded, and left the store.

We swarmed around our youngest family member.

"What was that about?" I asked. "Why did that woman buy you that bear? That thing cost *forty-nine dollars!*"

"What did you say to her?" Iggy demanded. "No one's buying *us* stuff."

"Nothing," Angel said, holding her bear tightly. "I just asked that lady if she would buy me this bear, 'cause I really, really wanted it and I didn't have enough money."

I started shepherding everyone out the front door before Angel asked someone to buy her the life-size giraffe.

Outside, the sun was bright overhead, and it was time for lunch. Time to get us back on track.

"So you just asked a stranger to buy you an expensive toy, and she did?" I asked Angel.

Angel nodded, smoothing her bear's fur down around its ears. "Yeah. I just asked her to buy it for me. You know, *with my mind.*"

92

Fang and I exchanged a look. This was a little scary. Actually, a lot scary.

"Um, what do you mean, exactly?" I asked Angel. Okay, so she can pick up on most people's thoughts and feelings. But this was the first I'd heard of her *sending* a thought.

"I just asked her, in my mind," Angel said absently, straightening the bears' small white wings. "And she said okay. And she bought it for me. I'm going to call it Celeste."

"Angel, are you saying that you influenced that woman so she would buy you the bear?" I asked carefully.

"Celeste," Angel said. "What's *influenced?*"

"To have an effect on something or someone," I said. "It sounds like you sort of *made* that woman buy you the bear —"

"Celeste."

"*Celeste*, whether she wanted to or not. Do you see what I'm saying?"

Angel frowned and shrugged, looking uncomfortable. Then her brow cleared. "Well, I *really* wanted Celeste. More than anything in the whole wide world."

Like that made it okay.

I opened my mouth to explain the life lesson that was screaming to be learned here, but Fang caught my eye. His expression said, Save it, and I shut up and nodded, waiting to hear his thoughts later.

And now, back to our mission. If only I had one freaking clue as to how to find the Institute.

We stopped and bought falafel for lunch, keeping an eye out for danger as we walked along eating. Angel tucked her bear — Celeste — into the waistband of her pants so she'd have both hands free.

Angel is only six, and God knows her upbringing hasn't exactly been normal. Still, I thought she was old enough to know the difference between right and wrong. I thought she knew that *influencing* that woman to buy her Celeste was wrong. But she had done it anyway.

Which I found disturbing.

I winced and grabbed my temple just as the silky Voice said, *It's just a toy, Max. Kids deserve toys. Don't you think you deserve a toy too?*

"I'm too old for toys," I muttered angrily, and Fang glanced at me in surprise.

"Did you want a toy?" the Gasman asked, confused.

I shook my head. Don't mind me, folks. Just talking to my little Voice again. But at least my head didn't hurt nearly as bad this time.

I'm sorry it hurts sometimes, Max. I don't want to hurt you. I want to help you.

I clamped my lips together so I wouldn't answer it. When I wanted information, it was silent; when I didn't want to hear from it, it got chatty.

It was almost as irritating as Fang.

93

I was starting to seriously freak out. Everywhere we went, something from the Other Side got to me. If it wasn't a voice in my head, it was a TV screen in a window. It was a hacker kid in a subway tunnel, the contents of my brain displayed on his computer. Bus drivers telling us where the fun was. The Erasers. What's that saying — you're not paranoid if somebody really is chasing you?

"We're surrounded," I muttered, staring at the toes of my boots as we walked along.

I felt Fang do a 360 next to me.

"We're wasting time," I finally said in frustration. "We need to find the Institute. Discover our histories and destinies. We don't need to go to toy stores. We've got to get serious about this."

All in good time, Max.

Fang started to answer me, but I held up a finger — one sec.

You need to learn how to relax. Relaxation facilitates learning and communication. Studies have shown it. But you're not relaxing.

JAMES PATTERSON

"Of course I'm not relaxing!" I hissed under my breath. "We need to find the Institute! We're running out of money! We're constantly in danger!"

The others had stopped and were watching me with alarm. Fang was probably ready to drag me to the funny farm.

I was totally losing my mind, right? Something had damaged my brain — I'd had a stroke or something, and now I was hearing voices. It made me different from the rest of the flock. Too different. I felt alone.

Just one voice, Max. Not voices. Calm down.

"What's wrong, Max?" asked the Gasman.

I took a deep breath and tried to get a grip. "I feel like I'm about to explode," I said honestly. "Three days ago, Angel said she'd heard there was more info about us in a place called the Institute, in New York. *More info.* This could be what we've always wanted to know."

"'Cause we might find out about our parents?" Iggy said.

"Yes," I answered. "But now we're here, and really weird things are happening, and I'm not sure —" With no warning, the hairs on the back of my neck stood up.

"Hello, kids!"

Directly in front of us, two Erasers leaped out of the doorway of a building.

Angel screamed, and I instinctively grabbed her arm, jerking her back hard. In a split second, I had swung around and we were racing down the sidewalk at top speed. Fang and Iggy were behind us, Nudge and the Gasman on either side. The sidewalks were full of people, and it was like an obstacle course.

"*Cross!*" I yelled, and darted into the street. The six of us whisked between two passing taxis, whose drivers honked angrily. Behind us, I heard a loud *thunk!* and a startled, half-choked cry.

"Bicycle messenger took an Eraser out!" Fang shouted.

Can you giggle while racing for your life and protecting a six-year-old? I can.

But two seconds later, a heavy clawed hand grabbed my hair, yanking me backward, right off my feet. Angel's hand was ripped out of mine, and she screamed bloody murder. You think you understand those words — *bloody murder?* Trust me; you don't.

94

Without pausing, the powerful Eraser swung me up over his shoulder. Talk about being dead meat.

I smelled his harsh animal smell, saw his bloodshot eyes. He was laughing, happy to have caught me, and his long yellow fangs actually looked too big for his mouth. Angel was still screaming.

Bloody murder!

I kicked and yelled and hit and punched and scratched, but the Eraser just laughed and started tearing down the sidewalk while people stared. "Is this a movie?" I heard someone ask.

Nah — this is too original for Hollywood. They do sequels.

Lifting my head, I saw Fang, dark and determined, streaking toward us. He was keeping pace, but he wasn't catching up. If a car was waiting, I was a goner. I struggled as hard as I could, chopping at the Eraser, punching and scratching, and it was infuriating how little effect I had on the beast. Had they been bred to have no pain receptors?

"Fang!" I bellowed, seeing him even farther away than

he had been. We were outpacing him. Dimly, I could still hear Angel's high-pitched shrieking. Every nasty swear word I knew came pouring out of my mouth, punctuated with punches and chops and kicks. The Eraser didn't even slow down.

The next thing I knew, we were going down, suddenly and with no warning, as if someone had cut the Eraser's legs out from under him. He hit the ground with a sickening thud, and I cracked my head against the sidewalk so hard I saw fireworks. My legs were pinned, and I frantically started kicking, scrambling out from under him.

He didn't move. *Had he knocked himself out? How?*

I scrabbled back into a trash can, snapped onto all fours, and stared at the Eraser. He was completely still, his eyes open and glassy. Blood trickled out of his mouth, which had morphed halfway to a wolf's snout. A few curious people had paused to watch us, but most kept on walking, talking into their cell phones. Life as usual in New York City.

Fang roared up and pulled me hard to my feet, starting to drag me away.

"Wait!" I said. "Fang — I think he's dead."

Fang looked from me to the Eraser, then nudged his boot against the still form. It didn't move, didn't blink. Still holding my hand, Fang knelt and put his fingers against the Eraser's wrist, wary and alert for movement.

"You're right," he said, standing. "He's dead. What'd you *do* to him?"

"Nothing. I was whaling on him, but it didn't do squat. Then he went down like a ton of bricks."

The crowd thickened and moved a bit closer as the rest of the flock raced up. Angel leaped into my arms and burst into tears. I held her tight and shushed her, telling her it was all right, I was safe.

Fang flipped the Eraser's collar back, just for a second. We both saw the tattoo on the back of his neck: 11-00-07.

Just then, a cop car pulled up, lights flashing, siren wailing.

We started to fade into the background, edging away through the crowd.

"Crazy drug addict!" Fang said loudly.

Then we strode quickly, turning the first corner we came to. I put Angel down and she trotted next to me, keeping up, sniffling. I held her hand tight and gave her a reassuring smile, but actually I was shaking inside. That had been so freaking close.

We *had* to find the Institute and get the heck out of here — back to the desert. Somewhere they couldn't ever find us. It was late, though. We were almost to the park, where we planned to sleep. In the street beside us, cars and taxis passed, unaware of the high drama that had just taken place.

"So he was five years old," Fang said quietly.

I nodded. "Made in November, year 2000, number seven of a batch. They're not lasting too long, are they?" How much longer would *we* last? All of us? Any of us?

I took a deep breath and looked around. My eye was

caught by a taxi with one of those flashing-red-dot signs on top that advertise Joe's Famous Pizza, or a cleaning service, or a restaurant. This one had the words racing across its face: "Every journey begins with one step."

It was like a taxi–fortune cookie. Every journey, one step. One step. I blinked.

I stopped where I was and looked down, where my feet were taking one step at a time on this long, bizarre journey.

Then I noticed a stunted, depressed tree set into a hole in the sidewalk. A metal grate protected its roots from being trampled. Barely visible between the bars of the grate was a plastic card. I picked it up, hoping I wouldn't see a burning fuse attached to it.

It was a bank card, the kind you can use at an ATM. *It had my name on it: Maximum Ride.* I tugged on Fang's sleeve, wordlessly showed him the card. His eyes widened a tiny bit, so I knew he was astonished.

And voilà, my ol' pal the Voice popped up just then: *You can use it if you can figure out the password.*

I looked up, but the mystic taxi was long gone.

"I can use it if I can figure out the password," I told Fang.

He nodded. "Okay."

Swallowing, I tucked the card into my pocket.

"Let's just get into the park," I said. "Nice, safe Central Park."

95

"How can the Voice know where I am and what I can see?" I whispered to Fang. All six of us had settled onto the wide, welcoming branches of an enormous oak tree in Central Park. Almost forty feet in the air, we could talk softly with no one hearing us.

Unless the tree was wired.

Believe me, I had lost my ability to be surprised by stuff like that.

"It's inside you," Fang answered, settling back against the tree's trunk. "It's wherever you are. If it's tapped into any of your senses, it knows where you are and what you're doing."

Oh, no, I thought, my spirits sinking. I hadn't considered that. Did that mean nothing I did was ever private anymore?

"Even in the bathroom?" The Gasman's eyes widened with surprise and amusement. Nudge suppressed a grin as I gave Gazzy a narrow-eyed glare. Angel was smoothing Celeste's gown and neatening the bear's fur.

I took out the bank card and examined it. I still had the

one we'd stolen from the jerk in California, and I compared them. The new one seemed just as legit as the old one. I stuck the old one into a deep fissure in the tree's bark — couldn't use it again anyway.

"So we need to figure out the password," I muttered, turning the new card over and over in my hands. Great. That should only take about a thousand years or so.

I was beyond tired. I also had an impressive knot on my head from whacking the sidewalk. Because, you know, I didn't have enough head problems lately.

Wordlessly, I held out my left fist. Fang put his on top, then Iggy, then Nudge. Gazzy leaned way over from his branch and managed to barely touch us. Angel leaned down and put her fist on Gazzy's, and then Celeste's paw on top of her fist. I heard Gazzy sigh. Or *something*. We all tapped hands, then got comfy on the wide branches. Angel was directly above me, her small foot hanging down to touch my knee. I saw her tuck Celeste firmly against the tree. Kinda sweet.

The evening air washed over me. My last thought was that I was thankful we were together and safe for at least one more night.

96

"It is unlawful to climb trees in Central Park," boomed a tinny but very loud voice.

My eyes popped open and instantly met Fang's dark ones. We looked down.

A black-and-white was parked below, its lights flashing. Like in New York they didn't have any more important crimes to work on than a bunch of kids sleeping in a tree.

"How did they even know we were up here?" the Gasman muttered. "Who looks up into a tree?"

A uniformed cop was talking to us through a PA system. "It is unlawful to climb trees in Central Park," she repeated. "Please come down at once."

I groaned. Now we had to shimmy clumsily down instead of just jumping and landing like the amazing super-duper mutants we were.

"Okay, guys," I said. "Get down; try to look *normal.* When we're on the ground, we'll make a run for it. If we get separated, connect up at, like, Fifty-fourth Street and Fifth Avenue. *Comprende?*"

They nodded. Fang went down first, and Iggy followed

him, carefully feeling his way. Man, for big adolescent kids, they were some awesome, squirrelly climbers.

Angel went next, then Nudge, then Gazzy, and I went last.

"There are signs posted everywhere clearly stating that climbing trees is forbidden," one cop began pompously. We started to back away slowly, trying to look as if we weren't really moving.

"Are you runaways?" asked the female cop. "We'll take you somewhere. You can make phone calls, call your folks."

Uh, officer, there's a little problem with that . . .

Another cruiser pulled up, and two more police people got out. Then a walkie-talkie buzzed, and the first cop pulled it out to answer it.

"Now!" I whispered, and the six of us scattered, tearing away from them as fast as we could.

"Celeste!" I heard Angel cry, and I whirled to see her turning back to pick up her little bear. Two cops were racing toward it.

"No!" I yelled, grabbing her hand and pulling her with me. She almost fought me, planting her feet and trying to unbend my fingers from around her wrist. I swung her up into my arms and took off, tossing her to Fang when I reached him.

With a fast glance back, I saw that the female cop had picked up the bear and was staring after us. Behind her, the others were jumping into their cruisers. Just as I sped around a corner, I saw a tall cop sliding into his car. I blinked hard, twice, and my heart seemed to freeze. *It was Jeb. Or was it?* I shook my head and ran on, catching up to the others.

"Celeste!" Angel cried, reaching back over Fang's shoulder. "Celeste!" She sounded heartbroken, and it killed me to make her leave her toy behind. But if I had to choose between Angel and Celeste, it was going to be Angel every time. Even if she hated me for it.

"I'll get you another one!" I promised rashly, my legs pumping as I kept up with Fang.

"I don't want another one!" she wailed, putting her arms around Fang's neck and starting to cry.

"Have we lost 'em?" the Gasman called back over his shoulder.

I looked back. Two police cars with lights and sirens were weaving through the heavy traffic toward us.

"No!" I put my head down and ran faster.

Sometimes it felt as if we would never be free, be safe. Never, ever, as long as we lived. Which might not be that much longer, anyway.

97

We headed south and east, out of the park, hoping to get lost among the ever-present crowds of people jamming the streets.

Fang put Angel down and she dutifully ran, her small face white and streaked with tears. I felt really, really bad about Celeste. Iggy ran next to me, his hand out to barely brush against me. He was so good at keeping up, following us, that it was easy to forget sometimes that he was blind. We passed Fifty-fourth Street — the police were still behind us.

"Inside a store?" Fang asked, pulling up beside me. "Then out through a back exit?"

I thought. If only we could take off, get airborne — leave the ground and the noise and the crowds and the cops behind, be up in the blue, blue sky, free. . . . My wings itched with the urge to snap open, unfurl to their full size, catch the sun and wind in them.

"Yeah, maybe so," I shot back. "Let's turn east on Fifty-first."

We did. Then we pounded down the pavement. Really

fast. I almost laughed when I realized it was a one-way street going the wrong way: The cruisers would have to take a detour.

If only we could find a safe haven before they caught up to us. . . .

"What's *that?*" Nudge called, pointing.

I skidded to a halt, the way they do in cartoons. In front of us was an enormous gray stone building. It soared up into the sky, all pointy and lacy on top, not like a sky-scraper. More as if gray stone crystals had grown toward the sky, stretching up and thinning out as they went. There were three arched doors, with the middle one being the biggest.

"Is it a museum?" Gazzy asked.

I scanned for a sign. "No," I said. "It's Saint Patrick's Cathedral. It's a church."

"A church!" Nudge looked excited. "I've never been in one. Can we go?"

I was about to remind her that we were running for our lives, not playing tourist, but then Fang said quietly, "Sanc-tuary."

And I remembered that in the past, churches used to be safe havens for people — cops weren't allowed in them. Like hundreds of years ago. That probably wasn't the case anymore. But it was huge and full of tourists, and it was as good a place to try to get lost as any.

98

A steady stream of people was filing through the huge middle double doors. We merged with them and tried to blend in. As we passed through the door, the air was instantly cooler and scented with something that smelled ancient and churchy and just . . . *religious,* somehow.

Inside, people split up. One group was gathering for a guided tour, and others were simply milling around, reading plaques, picking up pamphlets.

It was incredibly quiet, considering it was a building the size of a football field, full of hundreds of people.

Toward the front, people were sitting or kneeling in pews, their heads bowed.

"Let's go," I said softly. "Up there."

The six of us walked silently down the cool marble-tile floor toward the huge white altar at the front of the church. Nudge's mouth was wide open, her head craned back as she stared at the sunlight filtering through all the stained-glass windows. Above us the ceiling was three stories high and all arched and carved like a palace.

"This place is awesome," breathed the Gasman, and I

nodded. I felt good in here, safe, even though Erasers or cops could just stroll through the doors like anybody else. But it was enormous inside, and crowded, and yet there was good visibility. Not a bad place at all. *A good place.*

"What are those people doing?" Angel whispered.

"I think they're praying," I whispered back.

"Let's pray too," Angel said.

"Uh —" But she had already headed toward an empty pew. She eased her way to the middle, then reached down and pulled out the little kneeler thing. I saw her examine the other people for the proper form, then she knelt and bowed her head onto her clasped hands.

I bet she was praying for Celeste.

We filed into the pew after her, kneeling awkwardly and self-consciously. Iggy brushed his hand along Gazzy, light as a feather, then mimicked his position.

"What are we praying for?" he asked softly.

"Um — anything you want?" I guessed.

"We're praying to God, right?" Nudge checked to make sure.

"I think that's the general idea," I said, not really having much of a clue. And yet, an odd sensation came over me, like, if you were ever going to ask for anything, this would be the place to do it. With the high, sweeping ceiling, all the marble and glory and religion and passion surrounding us, it felt like this was a place where six homeless kids just might be heard.

"Dear God," said Nudge under her breath, "I want real

parents. But I want them to want me too. I want them to love me. I already love *them*. Please see what you can do. Thanks very much. Love, Nudge."

Okay, so I'm not saying we were pros at this or anything.

"Please get Celeste back to me," Angel whispered, her eyes squeezed tightly shut. "And help me grow up to be like Max. And keep everyone safe. And do something bad to the bad guys. They should not be able to hurt us anymore."

Amen, I thought.

With surprise, I saw that Fang's eyes were shut. But his lips weren't moving, and I couldn't hear anything. Maybe he was just resting.

"I want to be able to see stuff," Iggy said. "Like I used to, when I was little. And I want to be able to totally kick Jeb's butt. Thank you."

"God, I want to be big and strong," the Gasman whispered, and I felt my throat close up, looking at his flyaway pale hair, his eyes shut in concentration. He was only eight, but who knew when his expiration date was? "So I can help Max, and other people too."

I swallowed hard, blinking fast to keep any tears at bay. I breathed in heavily and breathed out, then did a surreptitious 360. The whole cathedral was calm, peaceful, Eraser-free.

Had that been Jeb I saw, back with the cops? Were the cops really cops or were they goons from the School — or from the Institute? What a bummer that Angel had dropped Celeste. Jeez, the kid finally gets to have one thing she cares about, and then fate rips it from her hands.

"Please help Angel about Celeste," I found myself muttering, and realized I had closed my eyes. I had no idea who I was talking to — I'd never really thought about if I believed in God. Would God have let the whitecoats at the School do what they had done to us? How did it work, exactly?

But I was on a roll now, so I went with it. "And help me be a better leader, a better person," I said, moving my lips with no sound. "Make me braver, stronger, smarter. Help me take care of the flock. Help me find some answers. Uh, thanks." I cleared my throat.

I don't know how long we were there — till my kneecaps started to go numb.

It was like a beautiful peace stole over us, the way a soft breeze would smooth our feathers.

We liked this house. We didn't want to leave.

99

I gave serious thought to staying in that cathedral, hiding, sleeping there. There were choir lofts way up high, and the place was huge. Maybe we could do it. I turned to Fang.

"Should we —" I winced as a sharp pain burst in my head. The pain wasn't as bad as before, but I shut my eyes and couldn't speak for a minute.

The images came, sliding across my brain like a movie. There were architectural drawings, blueprints, what looked like subway lines. Double helixes of DNA twisted and spiraled across my screen, then were overlaid with faded, unreadable newspaper clippings, staccato chunks of sound, colored postcards of New York. One image of a building stayed for a few seconds, a tall, greenish building. I saw its address: Thirty-first Street. Then a stream of numbers floated past me. Man, oh, man, oh, man — what did it mean?

I took a couple deep breaths, feeling the pain ease away. My eyes opened in the dim light of the cathedral. Five very concerned faces were watching me.

"Can you walk?" Fang asked tersely. I nodded.

We went out through the tall doors behind a group of Japanese tourists. It was too bright outside, and I shaded my eyes, feeling headachy and kind of sick.

As soon as we were away from the crowd, I stopped. "I saw Thirty-first Street, in my head," I said. "And a bunch of numbers."

"Which means . . ." Iggy prompted.

"I don't know," I admitted. "Maybe the Institute is on Thirty-first Street?"

"That would be nice," said Fang. "East or west?"

"I don't know."

"Did you see anything else?" he asked patiently.

"Well, a bunch of numbers," I said again. "And a tall, kind of greenish building."

"We should just walk all the way down Thirty-first Street," said Nudge. "The whole way, looking for that building. Right? I mean, if that's the building you saw, maybe it was for a good reason. Or did you see a whole lot of buildings, or a whole city, or what?"

"Just that building," I said.

Nudge's brown eyes widened. Angel looked solemn. We all felt the same: twitchy with nervous anticipation and also overwhelmed with dread. On the one hand, the Institute might very well hold the key to everything — the answer to every question we'd ever had about ourselves, our past, our parents. We might even find out about the mysterious director the whitecoats had mentioned. On the other hand, it felt like we were voluntarily going up to the School and ringing the doorbell. Like we were delivering ourselves to evil. And those two feelings were pulling us all in half.

You never know until you know, my Voice chimed in.

100

"So do we have money? I hope?" the Gasman asked as we passed a street vendor selling Polish sausage.

"Maybe," I said, pulling out the bank card. What do you think?" I asked Fang. "Should we try this?"

"Well, we need money, for sure," he said. "But it might be a trap, a way for them to track where we are and what we're doing."

"Yeah." I frowned.

It's okay, Max. You can use it, said my Voice. *Once you get the password.*

Thank you, Voice, I thought sourly. Any hopes of you just *telling* me the freaking password? Of course not. God forbid anything should come easily to us.

We had to have money. We could try begging, but we'd probably get the cops called on us ASAP. Runaways and all that. Getting jobs was out of the question also. Stealing? It was a last resort. We weren't to that point yet.

This bank card would work at any number of different banks. Taking a deep breath, I swerved over to an ATM. I swiped the card and punched in "maxride."

No dice.

Next I tried our ages: 14, 11, 8, 6.

Wrong.

I tried typing in "password."

Wrong. The machine shut down and told me to call customer service.

We kept walking. In a way, it was like we were deliberately slowing ourselves down, to give us time to buck up for the Institute. Or at least, that's what my inner Dr. Laura thought.

"What about, like, the first initial of all of our names?" the Gasman suggested.

"Maybe it's something like 'givememoney,'" Nudge said.

I smiled at her. "It has to be shorter than that."

Beside me, Angel was walking with her head down, her little feet dragging.

If I had money, I could get her another Celeste.

In the next block, at a different ATM, I tried the first initials of all our names: "MFINGA." Nope.

I tried "School" and "Maximum."

It told me to call customer service.

Farther on, I keyed in "Fang," "Iggy," and "Gasman."

In the next block, I tried "Nudge" and "Angel," then on a lark I tried today's date.

They really wanted me to call customer service.

I know what you're thinking: Did I try our birthdays or our Social Security numbers?

No. None of us knew our actual birth dates, though we had each picked a day we liked and called it our birthday. And the nut jobs at the School had mysteriously neglected to register any of us with the Social Security Administration. So none of us could retire any time soon.

I stopped in front of the next ATM but shook my head in frustration. "I don't know what to do," I admitted, and it was maybe the second time those words had ever left my lips.

Angel looked up tiredly, her blue eyes sad. "Why don't you try 'mother'?" she asked, and started tracing a crack on the sidewalk with the toe of her sneaker.

"Why do you think that?" I asked, surprised.

She shrugged, her arm moving to hold Celeste tighter and then falling emptily to her side.

Fang and I exchanged glances, then I slowly swiped the bank card and punched in the numbers that would spell out "mother."

WHAT KIND OF TRANSACTION DO YOU WANT TO MAKE? the screen asked.

Speechless, I withdrew two hundred dollars and zipped it into my inside pocket.

"How did you know that?" Fang asked Angel. His tone was neutral, but tension showed in his walk.

Angel shrugged again, her small shoulders drooping. Even her curls looked limp and sad. "It just came to me," she said.

"In a voice?" I asked, wondering if *my* Voice was hopping around.

She shook her head no. "The word was just in my head. I don't know why."

Once again, Fang and I looked at each other but didn't say anything. I didn't know what was on his mind, but I was thinking again about how Angel had been at the School for a few days before we rescued her. Who knows what happened there? What kind of foul, disgusting experiments? Maybe they'd planted a chip in her too.

Or worse.

101

A few more blocks, and we turned left, walking toward the East River. Inside me, the tension mounted. My breath was coming in short huffs. Every step was bringing us closer to what could be the Institute: the place where the secrets of our lives might be revealed, all our questions answered.

And here's the thing: I wasn't even sure I wanted my questions answered. What if my mom had given me away on purpose, like Gasman and Angel's? What if my parents were horrible people? Or what if they were wonderful, fabulous people who didn't want a freak mutant daughter with thirteen-foot *wings?* I mean, not knowing almost seemed easier.

But we walked along, examining each building. Again and again the others looked at me, only to see me shake my head no. We walked down several *looong* blocks, and with each step, I was getting more and more uptight, and so was everyone else.

"I wonder what the Institute is like," Nudge said nervously. "I guess it's like the School. Will we have to break in? How do they hide the Erasers from all the normal people? What kind of files on us do you think they have? Like actual parent names, you think?"

"For God's sake, Nudge, my ears are bleeding!" Iggy said with his usual tact.

Her sweet face shut down, and I put my arm around her shoulders briefly. "I know you're worried," I said softly. "I am too."

She smiled at me, and then I saw it: 433 East Thirty-first Street.

It was the building from the drawing in my brain.

And if you don't think *that's* a weird sentence, maybe you should reread it.

The building rose tall, maybe forty-five stories, and had a greenish facade, kind of old-fashioned looking.

"Is this it?" Iggy asked.

"Yep," I said. "Are we ready?"

"Aye, Captain!" Iggy said firmly, and saluted.

I so wished he could see me roll my eyes at him.

We marched up the steps and pushed through revolving doors. Inside, the lobby was all polished wood, brass, and big tropical plants. The floor was smooth granite tiles.

"Here," said Fang softly, pointing to a large display board behind glass. It listed all the offices and companies in the building, and their floors and room numbers.

There was no Institute for Higher Living. There was no institute of any kind.

Because that would have been too easy, right?

I rubbed my forehead, holding back bitter words of

disappointment. Inside, I felt like crying and yelling and stomping around, and then getting into a hot shower and crying some more.

Instead, I took a deep breath and tried to think. I looked around. No other office lists anywhere.

At the reception desk, a woman sat behind a laptop computer. A security guard had another desk across the lobby.

"Excuse me," I said politely. "Are there any other companies in this building that aren't on the board?"

"No." The receptionist looked us over, then went back to typing something incredibly urgent — like her résumé for another job. We turned away just as the receptionist made a sound of surprise. Glancing back, I saw that her computer screen had cleared. The pit of my stomach started to hurt.

There's a pot of gold beneath every rainbow, filled her laptop screen in big red letters. The message broke up into smaller letters that then scrolled across the screen over and over, filling it.

Pot of gold beneath every rainbow . . . Okay, did leprechauns work here? Was Judy Garland going to burst into song? Why couldn't I just get some straight information? Because it was a puzzle, a test. I literally gnashed my teeth. Beneath every . . . Hmm.

"Does this building have a basement?" I asked.

The receptionist frowned at me and looked us over again with a harder gaze.

"Who are you?" she asked. "What do you want?" She lifted her chin and caught the eye of the security guard. *Were they Erasers?* They definitely *could* be Erasers. This whole building might be full of despicable wolf men.

"Never mind," I muttered, pushing the others toward the revolving doors. The security guard was already on our tails, and just as we all got through, I jammed a ballpoint pen into the door channel. The guard was trapped inside one section and started throwing his weight against the glass.

On the street, we hit the ground running.

102

My lungs were burning. Know the feeling? About six blocks later, we slowed to a walk. No one seemed to be following us, no cop cars had emerged from the traffic, no sign of Erasers. My head was pounding and it hurt like crazy. I felt like I needed a time-out from life.

With no warning, the Gasman turned and punched a mailbox. "This sucks!" he yelled. "Nothing ever goes right! We get hassled everywhere! Max's head is busted, Angel lost Celeste, we're all hungry — I hate this! I hate everything!"

Stunned, I shut my gaping jaw and went over to him. When I put my hand on his shoulder, he pushed it away. The others crowded around — it was so unusual for Gazzy to break down like this. He was always my little trouper.

Crap.

The flock was watching me, waiting for me to tell the Gasman to snap out of it, get it together.

Stepping forward, I wrapped my arms around Gazzy, surrounding him. I rested my head against his and just held him tight. I smoothed his light hair with my fingers and felt his narrow back shaking.

"I'm sorry, Gazzy," I murmured. "You're right. This has really sucked. I know it's hard sometimes. Listen, what would make you feel better right now?" I swear, if he'd said, *Check into the Ritz,* I would have done it.

He sniffled and straightened a bit, wiping his face on his grubby sleeve. I resolved to get us new clothes soon. 'Cause I was Ms. Bank Card.

"Really?" he said, sounding very small and young.

"Really."

"Well, I just want — I just want to, like, sit down somewhere and eat a lot of food. Not just get food while we're walking. I want to *sit down* and *rest* and *eat.*"

I looked solemnly into his eyes. "I think that can be arranged."

103

We ended up back near Central Park, searching for a place to eat. A diner on Fifty-seventh Street looked good, but there was a half-hour wait. Then, off the street inside the park, we saw a restaurant. Millions of tiny blue lights covered the oak trees that surrounded it. The sign said, Parking for Garden Tavern, This Way. Plunked among the trees was a huge building with tons of plate glass windows overlooking the park.

Gazzy said excitedly. "This looks *great!*"

It was also the last place on earth I wanted us to go. Too big, too flashy, too expensive, and no doubt full of trendy grown-ups. We were not going to blend. We would not be inconspicuous.

And yet, the Gasman wanted to eat here. And I had promised him pretty much anything he wanted.

"Uh, okay," I said, already feeling dread and anxiety seeping from my pores. Fang pulled open the heavy glass door, and we stepped inside.

"Whoa," Nudge said, her eyes wide.

From the reception area, we could see three different

dining rooms. There was the Prism Room, which was dripping with crystals, basically: chandeliers, candelabras, faceted windows. Door number two led to the Garden Room, which was like a lush, overgrown rainforest, but with tables, chairs, and waiters. The third one was the Castle Room, for those of us who needed to feel regal while we chowed. They all had soaring ceilings with rafters. The Castle Room had an open fireplace big enough to roast a steer.

I was glad to see we weren't the only kids — though we *were* the only ones without a grown-up.

"May I help you?" A tall, blond, modelly woman glanced at us, then looked to see who we were with. "Are you waiting for your parents?"

"No," I said. "There's just us." I smiled. "Can we have a table for six, please? I'm treating everybody with my birthday money." Another lie, another smile.

"Um, okay," said the hostess. She led us to a table in the Castle Room, way back by the kitchen. Since the kitchen would be a useful escape route, if necessary, I didn't quibble.

She passed out large, very fancy menus as we scrambled into our seats. "Jason will be your server today." With one last, uncertain glance, she left us.

"Max, this is so, so great," Nudge said excitedly, clutching her enormous menu. "This is the nicest place we've ever eaten!"

Since we've Dumpster-dived for lunch on many occasions, this was an understatement.

Fang, Iggy, and I were miserable. Nudge, Gazzy, and Angel were ecstatic.

Actually, the Castle Room would have been neat, if I didn't hate crowds, sticking out, grown-ups, feeling paranoid, and spending money.

On to the menu. I was relieved to see that they had a kids' section.

"Are you waiting for your parents?" A short, stocky waiter with slicked-back red hair — Jason — was standing next to Iggy.

"No, there's just us," I said.

He frowned slightly and gave us a once-over. "Ah. Are you ready to order?"

"Anyone know what they want?" I asked.

The Gasman looked up. "How many chicken tenders are on a plate?"

Jason looked almost pained. "I believe there are four."

"I better have two orders, then," said the Gasman. "And this fruit cocktail. And two glasses of milk."

"Two orders for yourself?" Jason clarified.

The Gasman nodded. "With fries. To start."

"I want a hot-fudge sundae," said Angel.

"Real food first," I said. "You need fuel."

"Okay," Angel said agreeably, then blinked and looked up at Jason. "We're not spoiled rich brats," she said. "We're just hungry."

Jason started, then his face flushed and he shifted his feet.

"I want this prime rib thing," Angel said, looking at the adult side of the menu. "And all this stuff that goes with it. And a soda. And lemonade."

"The prime rib is sixteen ounces," our waiter said. "It's a *pound* of meat."

"Uh-huh," Angel said, wondering what he was getting at.

"She can handle it," I said. "She's a big eater. Nudge? What do you want?"

"This lasagna primavera," Nudge decided. "I might need two. It comes with salad, right? And bread? Some milk. Okay?" She looked at me, and I nodded.

Jason just stood there — he thought we were pulling his leg. "Two lasagnas?"

"You might want to start writing this stuff down," I suggested. I waited till he had noted their orders, then said, "I'll start with the shrimp cocktail. Then the maple-glazed roast pork loin, with the cabbage and potatoes and everything. The house salad with bleu cheese dressing. And a lemonade and an iced tea."

Jason wrote it all down, as if he were enduring an hour-long eye-poke.

"The lobster bisque," Fang said. "Then the prime rib. A big bottle of water."

"The spaghetti and meatballs," Iggy said.

"That's on the children's menu," our waiter said, sounding tense. "For our patrons twelve and under."

Iggy looked ticked off.

"How about the rack of lamb?" I said quickly. "It comes with potatoes and spinach, and a merlot-rosemary sauce."

"Fine, okay," Iggy said, irritated. "Plus a couple glasses of milk and some bread."

Jason lowered his pad and looked at us. "This is a great deal of food for just the six of you," he said. "Maybe you've overordered."

"I understand your concern," I said, my tension starting to get the better of me. "But it's okay. Just bring it, please."

"You'll have to pay for all of it, whether you eat it or not."

"Yeah, that's *usually* how a restaurant works," I said slowly, with exaggerated patience.

"This is going to really add up," he persisted unwisely.

"I *get* it," I said, trying unsuccessfully to keep my cool. "I *get* the concept. Food costs *money*. *Lots* of food costs *lots* of money. Just bring us what we ordered. Please."

Jason looked at me stiffly and stalked away toward the kitchen.

"I love this place," Fang said with a straight face.

"Did we order too much?" Angel asked.

"No," I said. "It's fine. I guess they're not used to hearty eaters."

An underling brought us two baskets of bread and set out small dishes of olive oil. Even she seemed skeptical.

My fingers curled into claws on the white tablecloth. And it all kind of went downhill from there.

104

"Good afternoon." A man in a suit and tie had materialized at my elbow. Jason was with him.

"Hello," I said warily.

"I am the manager. Is there something I can help you with?" he asked.

Was this a trick question? "Well, I don't think so," I said. "Unless the kitchen is out of something we ordered."

"Yes, well," said the manager. "You seem to have ordered an unusual quantity of food. We wouldn't want to be wasteful with it, or present you with a shocking bill because your eyes were bigger than your stomachs." He gave a small artificial laugh.

"Well, that is just so sweet of you," I said, close to my breaking point. "But we're pretty hungry. It seems like we should just order and get what we ordered, you know?"

This didn't go over as well as you would think.

The manager took on a look of forced patience. "Perhaps you would be happier in some other restaurant," he said. "Broadway is nearby."

I couldn't believe this. "No freaking *duh*," I snapped,

finally losing it. "But we're *in* this one and we're *hungry*. Now, I have the money, we brought our appetites with us; are you going to give us what we ordered or not?"

The manager looked like he had just sucked on a lemon. "*Not,* I believe," he said, signaling to a burly guy loitering by the doors.

Great, just great. I rubbed my forehead.

"This is stupid," Iggy said angrily. "Let's just split. Gasser, we'll go someplace that isn't run by Nazis, okay?"

"Okay," said the Gasman uncertainly.

Angel looked up at the manager. "Jason thinks you're full of hot air and that you smell like a sissy," she said. "And what's a *himbo?*"

Jason stifled a choking sound and turned red. The manager turned to glare at him.

"Fine," I said, standing up and throwing my napkin down. "We're going. The food's probably lousy here, anyway."

That was when the cops showed up.

Who called the cops?

Were they real cops?

I wasn't planning to stay around and ask them.

105

Remember how the kitchen was going to provide a useful escape route? That would have worked great if the cops hadn't split up, two coming in the front, two more coming in through the — you guessed it — kitchen.

All around us, tables of people were staring open-mouthed. This was probably the most exciting thing that had happened to them all week.

"Up and away," Fang said, and I nodded reluctantly.

Nudge and Iggy looked surprised, Gazzy grinned, and Angel got that determined look on her face.

"Right, kids," said a female cop, weaving her way through the tables. "You have to come with us. We'll call your folks down at the station."

Jason shot me a superior smile, and suddenly I was furious. How hard would it be for someone to cut us just one break? Without stopping to think, I snatched up the bowl of olive oil and upturned it on his head. His mouth opened in an *O* as pale green oil streaked down his face.

If that surprised him, what happened next would rock his world.

Moving fast, as only a mutant bird kid could, I jumped up on a chair, stepped onto our table, then threw myself into the air, snapping my wings open and pushing down hard. I dropped alarmingly toward the ground — hadn't had a running takeoff, which is always best — but surged upward again with the next stroke and rose toward the high raftered ceiling.

Angel joined me, then Iggy, the Gasman, Nudge, and Fang.

Looking down, I couldn't help laughing at everyone's faces. "Astonished" doesn't cover it. They were stunned, dumbstruck, completely freaked out.

"Jerk!" the Gasman yelled, and pelted the manager with pieces of bread.

Fang was circling the ceiling, looking for a way out. I saw that the cops had started to recover and were fanning out.

I won't lie to you — it was hilarious. Yes, we were in trouble, yes, this was a disaster, and so on and so forth, but I have to say, seeing all those upturned faces, the looks, was about the best thing that had happened to us since we'd come to New York.

"Up here!" Fang shouted, and pointed to one of the stained-glass skylights.

"Come on, guys!" I yelled, just as I realized that flashes from cameras were going off — seriously bad news. *"Let's go!"*

Fang ducked his head, covered it with his arms, and flew straight up through the window. It burst with a rainbow-colored crash, and bits of glass sprinkled down.

Iggy was right behind Nudge, his fingers brushing her ankle, and they flew through next, tucking their wings in at the last second to fit.

"Angel, go!" I ordered, and she shot through, her small white wings looking just like Celeste's. "Gasser! Move it!" I saw him swoop down one last time to grab someone's abandoned dessert. Shoving an entire éclair into his mouth, he nodded and aimed himself through the window. I went last, and then I was in the open air, stretching my wings, filling my lungs. I knew we had just made a crucial, devastating mistake and that we'd have to pay for it.

But you know what? It was almost worth it.

The *looks* on all those faces . . .

106

"To the trees," I told Fang, and he nodded, making a big circle to head north. It was a hazy day, but we weren't high enough to be out of sight. I hoped no one was looking up. Yeah, right.

We dropped down into a tall maple, breathing hard.

"That went well," said Fang, brushing glass dust off his shoulders.

"It was my fault," said the Gasman. He had chocolate on his face. "I'm the one who wanted to go there."

"It was their fault, Gazzy," I said. "I bet those weren't even real cops. They had an eau de School air about them."

"You didn't think before you dumped the olive oil on the waiter, did you?" Fang asked.

I scowled at him.

"I'm still . . ." Nudge began, then let her voice trail off. I'm guessing she was about to say "hungry," but then realized it wasn't a good time.

But we *were* still hungry. We *did* have to have food. As soon as my adrenaline calmed down, I would go find a grocery store or something.

"People were taking pictures," Iggy said.

"Yeah," I said miserably. "As an unqualified disaster, this ranks right up there."

"And it's getting worse," said a smooth voice.

I jumped about a foot in the air, then clutched my branch and looked down.

Our tree was surrounded by Erasers.

Without meaning to, I shot a stricken glance at Iggy: He was usually our early-warning system. If he hadn't heard these guys coming, then they'd materialized out of nowhere.

One Eraser stepped forward, and I caught my breath. *It was Ari.*

"You keep showing up like a bad penny," I said.

"I was about to say the same thing to you," he replied with a feral smile.

"I remember back when you were three years old," I went on conversationally. "You were so cute — before you got huge and wolfy."

"Like you ever paid attention to me," he said, and I was surprised to hear sincere bitterness in his voice. "I was trapped in that place too, but you shut me out."

My mouth dropped open. "But you were normal," I blurted. "And Jeb's son."

"Yeah, Jeb's son," he snarled. "Like he even knows I'm alive. What did you think happened to me while you were off playing house with *my* father? Did you think I just disappeared?"

"Okay, there's *one* knot unraveled," Fang muttered under his breath.

"Ari, I was ten years old," I said slowly. "Is all this back history why you're tracking us now? Why you're trying to *kill* us?"

"Of course not." Ari spit on the ground. "I'm tracking you 'cause that's my job. The back history is helping me enjoy it." He smirked.

I shot him the bird. (Get it? *I* shot him the — never mind.)

He was morphing, and when he smiled, his muzzle seemed to split in half, like a dog's. From behind his back he pulled something small, with brown fur and two white —

"Celeste!" Angel cried, and started to scramble down.

"Angel, no!" I shouted, and Fang yelled, *"Stay put!"*

But my baby jumped, landing lightly on the ground a few feet from Ari.

The other Erasers surged forward, but Ari snapped up his hand to hold them back. They stopped, coiled tightly, their cold, wolfish eyes locked on Angel.

Ari shook Celeste playfully, and Angel stepped forward.

I dropped down to the ground, adrenaline pouring into my veins. Again the Eraser team lunged, and again Ari held them back.

"Touch her and I'll kill you," I promised, my hands curled into fists.

Ari smirked, his dark curly hair catching the last bit of

afternoon sun. He shook Celeste again, and Angel quivered by my side.

"Give me the bear," Angel said, low and intense.

Ari laughed.

Angel took a half step forward, but I grabbed her collar.

"Give. Me. The. Bear." Angel sounded odd, not like herself, and she was staring intently into Ari's eyes. His smile faded, and a look of confusion crossed his face. I remembered how Angel had influenced the woman to buy Celeste for her.

"You're —" Ari began, then seemed to choke slightly, coughing, putting his hand to his throat. "You're —"

"Drop the bear *now,*" Angel said, hard as concrete.

Seemingly against his will, Ari's clawed, powerful hand unclenched, and Celeste fell to the ground.

Almost faster than my eyes could follow, Angel snatched Celeste and leaped back up into the tree.

I blinked and wondered if I looked as surprised as Ari did.

The other Erasers sprang into motion, as if it had taken them a few seconds to realize Angel was gone. Ari's arm shot out, and an Eraser crashed into it.

"You have your orders!" he barked at the team. "Don't ever question them!" He turned back to look at me thoughtfully. "You can't question them," he said in a normal tone, speaking directly to me. "Even if they seem stupid. Even if you'd rather just rip the flock apart."

An Eraser made an eager, hungry sound, and it was all I could do not to shudder.

Ari leaned closer to me, as if catching my scent, like prey. "Your day is coming, bird girl," he whispered. "And I'm going to finish you off myself."

"Don't sharpen your fangs just yet, dog boy."

He opened his mouth to say something but then cocked his head and pressed a finger against his ear, as if hearing something.

"The Director wants to see us," he barked at his team. "Now!"

After one last lingering look at me, he turned and followed the other Erasers. They melted into the twilight shadows like smoke.

107

Up in the tree, Angel was clutching Celeste tightly, murmuring softly to her.

"I heard them mention the Director at the School," Nudge said. "Who is it?"

I shrugged. "Some big, very bad person." One of many who were after us. I wondered if it was Jeb, our fake father. Our savior and then our betrayer.

"You okay?" Iggy asked. I saw his white-knuckled hold on his branch and gave him a gentle tap with my boot.

"Hunky-dory," I said. "But I want to get out of here right now."

In the end, we settled in the top floor of a ninety-story apartment building that was being built on the Upper East Side. The first seventy or so floors had been windowed in, but up here it was just an empty shell with piles of drywall and insulation. Huge gaping holes gave us a great view of the East River and Central Park.

Nudge and I went to a local grocery store, then schlepped three heavy bags of groceries back to the others. It was breezy up in our aerie, but private and safe. We watched the last of the sun go down and ate. My head was aching, but not too badly.

"I'm tired," Angel said. "I want to go to bed."

"Yeah, let's try to get some sleep," I said. "It's been a long, relatively yucky day." I held out my left fist, and we all stacked up. Tapping our hands seemed so familiar, so comforting, connecting us.

The Gasman and I cleared construction debris away, and Iggy and Fang moved stacks of drywall to make wind-breaks. In the end we had a cozy space, and the flock was asleep within ten minutes.

Except me.

How were the Erasers tracking us so easily? I looked hard at my left wrist, as if staring at it would make my chip float to the surface of my skin. I myself could be a beacon without knowing it, without being able to do a thing about it — except leave the flock and strike out on my own. The Erasers were tracking us but not killing us. Why had Ari stopped them today?

And what in the world was happening with Angel? Her telepathic powers seemed to be growing. I groaned to myself, picturing a strong-willed Angel demanding birthday presents; junk food before dinner; stupid, trendy clothes.

Don't borrow trouble, Max, said my Voice.

Long time no hear, I thought.

Worry is unproductive. You can't control what happens

to Angel. You can save the world, but the only thing you can control is you. Go to sleep, Max. It's time to learn.

Learn what? I started to ask, but then, as if someone had flicked a switch, I sank into unconsciousness.

108

When I blinked awake the next morning, I was greeted by newspapers and breakfast in bed.

"Wha'?" I mumbled.

"We got breakfast," Fang said, taking a bite of muffin. "You were out for the count."

As I took my first bite of muffin, I became aware of the quivering tension around me. "What else?"

Fang nodded toward the newspapers.

"I figured you got 'em for the comics," I said, pulling the pile closer.

Up to now, our main survival strategy had been to stay inconspicuous, to hide as much as possible. I guess having our pictures plastered on the front page of the *New York Post* under the huge, screaming headline "Miracle or Illusion? Superhumans or Genetic Freaks?" blew that strategy out of the water.

Fang had gotten four different papers, and fuzzy pictures of us swooping gaily around the Garden Tavern were on every front page.

"Saw them when we were out," Fang explained, draining his juice. "Guess we better lie low for a while."

"Yes, thank you, Tonto," I said irritably. I mean, would it kill him to speak in full sentences? I checked out the *New York Times.* Under a blurry photo, it said, "No one has taken credit for what may be this year's most unusual stunt . . ."

Finally, I sighed and picked up my muffin again. "The upshot is, we might as well glow in the dark in terms of staying inconspicuous. So it looks like it's ix-nay on the Institute, at least for a while." I felt so frustrated I could have screamed.

"Maybe we could wear disguises," the Gasman suggested.

"Yeah, like glasses and funny noses," Angel agreed.

I smiled at them. "You think?"

109

That afternoon, we had to venture out to get food again. Six pairs of glasses with funny noses hadn't materialized, so we went as is.

At the nearest deli, we stocked up on sandwiches, drinks, chips, cookies, anything we could carry and eat at the same time.

"So I'm thinking we should leave the city as soon as it gets dark," I said to Fang.

He nodded. "Where to?"

"Not too far," I said. "I'm still bent on getting to the bottom of the Institute, so to speak. Maybe upstate a bit? Or somewhere by the ocean?"

"*You!*"

I recoiled and dropped my soda as a young guy with a mohawk haircut jumped in front of us. Nudge bumped into my back, and Fang went very still.

"You guys are perfect!" he said excitedly.

How nice that *someone* thought so. But who was this wing nut?

"Perfect for what?" Fang asked with deadly calm.

The guy waved a skinny tattooed arm at a storefront. Its sign said, U 'Do: Tomorrow's styles today.

"We're having a makeover fest!" the guy explained, sounding like we had just won a million dollars. "You guys can have total makeovers for *free* — as long as your stylist gets to do whatever he or she wants."

"Like what?" Nudge asked with interest.

"Makeup, hairstyle, everything!" the guy promised ecstatically. "Except tattoos. We'd need a note from your parents."

"So that's out," I said under my breath.

"I want to do it!" Nudge said. "It sounds so fun! Can we do it, Max? I want a makeover!"

"Uh . . ." I saw a couple teenage girls emerging from U 'Do. They looked wild. I bet their own friends wouldn't have recognized them.

Hello.

"I'm up for it," I said briskly, as Fang's eyes widened a fraction of an inch. I gave him a meaningful look. "We'd love to be *made over*. Make us look completely different."

PART 6

WHO'S YOUR DADDY, WHO'S YOUR MOMMA?

110

"That is so cool," Nudge said approvingly as I turned to let her see the back of my new jean jacket. Of course, I would have to cut huge slits in it to let my wings out, but other than that, it was great.

I looked at her and grinned. She looked so *not* Nudge, I was still startled every time I saw her. Her dark brown supercurly hair had been blow-dried perfectly straight and cut in layers. Then they'd streaked it with blond highlights. The difference was incredible — she'd gone from scruffy adolescent to slightly short fashion model in under an hour. I'd never noticed that she had the potential to be gorgeous when she grew up. If she grew up.

"Check this out!" The Gasman had outfitted himself in camouflage, down to his sneakers.

"Okay by me," I said, giving him a thumbs-up.

In this barnlike secondhand shop, we were in the process of completing our total physical transformation. Some of Gazzy's pale blond hair had been bleached white. They'd spiked it with gel and colored just the spiky tips bright blue. The sides were supershort.

"I still wish you'd let me get 'Bite Me' shaved into the back of my head," he complained.

"No," I said, straightening his collar.

"Iggy got *his* ear pierced."

"Nein," I said.

"But everyone does it!" he said in a perfect imitation of his stylist.

"O-nay."

He made an exasperated sound and went over by Fang, whose hair had been cut short also, except for one long chunk that flopped over in front of his eyes. It had been highlighted with several mottled tan shades and now it looked exactly like a hawk's plumage. Quelle coinkydink. In this store, he'd exchanged his basic black ensemble for a slightly different basic black ensemble.

"I like this," said Angel, holding up something froufrou. I'd already outfitted her in new cargo pants and a T-shirt, and she'd picked out a fluffy blue fleece jacket.

"Um," I said, looking at it.

"It's so pretty, Max," she coaxed. "Please?"

I wondered if I would be able to tell if she was putting thoughts into my head. Her eyes were wide and innocent looking.

"And Celeste really likes it too," Angel added.

"The thing is, Angel," I said, "I'm not sure how *practical* tutus are — given how much we're on the run and all."

She looked at the tutu and frowned. "I guess."

"We ready?" Iggy asked with a touch of impatience. "Not that I don't adore shopping."

"You look like you stuck your finger in a light socket," the Gasman said.

Iggy's strawberry-blond hair was spiked like Gazzy's and tipped with black on the ends.

"Really?" Iggy asked. "Cool!" He'd gotten his ear pierced before I'd noticed: His thin gold wire loop was the only thing I'd had to pay for.

We walked out into the late afternoon. I felt free and happy, even though the Institute was on hold at the moment. I bet not even Jeb would recognize me.

My stylist had picked up my long braid and simply whacked it off. Now my hair floated in feathery layers. No more hair getting in my eyes when I flew. No spitting wisps out of my mouth in the middle of an escape.

Not only that, but they'd streaked it with chunky strands of hot pink and, despite my protest, gone to town with makeup. So now I looked both totally different and about twenty years old. Being five-eight helped.

"There's a little park up here," Fang said, pointing.

I nodded. It would be darker than the street, and we'd have enough room to take off. Five minutes later, we were rising above the city, leaving the lights and noise and energy behind. It felt fabulous to stretch my wings out, stroking hard, feeling so much faster and smoother and cooler than I did on the ground.

Just for fun I flew in huge, banking arcs, taking deep breaths, enjoying the feel of my newly weightless hair. The stylist had called it "wind-tossed."

If only she knew.

111

Up this high, I could clearly see the outline of Manhattan. Right across the East River was Long Island, which was much, much bigger than New York City. We flew above its coast as the sun went down, barely able to see the curly ridges of white-capped waves breaking along the shore.

After an hour and a half, we saw a long stretch of black beach with few lights, which meant few people. Fang nodded at me, and we aimed downward, enjoying the heady rush of losing altitude. Roller coasters had nothing on us.

"Looks good," Fang said, scoping out the beach after we landed on the soft sand. It was undeveloped, with no attached parking lots. Huge boulders sealed off both ends, so it seemed even safer. Plus, other large boulders formed a natural outcropping that created a bit of shelter maybe thirty yards inland.

"Home, sweet home," I said drily, taking off my new backpack.

I rummaged in it for food, passed out what we had, and sank down on a large chunk of driftwood. Twenty minutes later, we stacked fists, tapped, and then curled up in the sand beneath the outcropping.

I winced slightly as the Voice drifted into my head. *Time to learn,* it said.

Then I was pulled into unconsciousness as if getting dragged beneath a wave. Dimly, I heard bits of foreign languages that I didn't understand, and the Voice said, *This is on a need-to-know basis, Max. You need to know.*

112

The ocean. Another new and incredible experience. We'd grown up in lab cages until four years ago, when Jeb had stolen us. Then we'd been in hiding, avoiding new experiences at all costs.

Now we were doing something different every day. It was a trip.

"A crab!" the Gasman yelled, pointing at the surf by his feet. Angel ran over to see, holding Celeste so her back paws barely touched the water.

"Cookie?" Iggy asked, holding out a bag.

"Don't mind if I do," I said. This morning I had toned down my appearance a tad, then Nudge and I had hit the closest town. We'd stocked up on supplies at a mom-and-pop store that sold their own fresh homemade cookies.

My mission, and I chose to accept it, was to find chocolate-chip cookies as good as the ones I'd made with Ella and her mom. So I'd brought back a couple dozen.

I took a bite of cookie and chewed. "Hmm," I said, trying not to spit crumbs. "Clear vanilla notes, too-sweet chocolate chips, distinct flavor of brown sugar. A decent cookie, not spectacular. Still, a good-hearted cookie, not pretentious." I turned to Fang. "What say you?"

"It's fine."

Some people just don't have what it takes to appreciate a cookie.

"I give them a seven out of ten," I pressed on dutifully. "Though warm from the oven, they lack a certain je ne sais quoi. My mission will continue."

Iggy laughed and rummaged in a bag for an apple.

Nudge ran up, her clothes wet past her knees. "This place is so cool," she said. "I love the ocean! I want to be a scientist who studies the ocean when I grow up. I would go out to sea, and scuba dive, and find new things, and *National Geographic* will hire me."

Sure, Nudge. Probably around the same time I become president.

Nudge ran back to the water, and Iggy got up and ambled after her.

"They're happy here," Fang said, looking at them.

I nodded. "What's not to like? Fresh air, peace and quiet, the ocean. Too bad we can't stay here."

Fang was quiet for a moment. "What if we were safe here?" he asked. "Like, we just knew no one would come hassle us. Would you want to stay?"

I was surprised. "We have to find the Institute," I said. "And if we find out anything, the others will want to track down their parents. And then, do we find Jeb and confront him? And who's the Director? Why did they do this to us?

Why do they keep telling me I'm supposed to save the world?"

Fang held up his hand, and I realized my voice had been rising.

"What if," Fang said slowly, not looking at me, "what if we just forgot about all that?"

My jaw dropped open. You live with someone your whole life, you think you know them, and then they go and drop a bomb like this. "What are you —" I started to say, but then the Gasman ran up with a live hermit crab, which he plopped in my lap, and then Angel wanted lunch. I didn't have a chance to grab Fang's shoulders and yell, "Who are you and what have you done with the real Fang?"

Maybe later.

113

The next morning, Fang came back from town and placed the *New York Post* at my feet with a little bow. I flipped through the paper. On page six, I saw "Mysterious Bird-Children Nowhere to Be Found."

"Well, good for us," I said. "We've gone two days without causing a huge commotion in a public place and getting our pictures splashed all over the news."

"We're going swimming!" Nudge said, tapping Iggy's hand twice. He got up and followed her, Angel, and Gazzy down to the water.

The sun was shining, and though the ocean was still pretty cold, it didn't bother them. I was glad they were having this little vacation, where they could just have fun and eat and swim without stressing out about everything.

I was still stressing, of course.

Next to me, Fang read the paper, absently working his way through a can of peanuts. I watched the younger kids playing in the water. Iggy started a sand castle, built by touch, just out of reach of the waves.

How come the Erasers hadn't found us yet? Sometimes

they tracked us so easily, and other times, like now, we seemed to be truly hidden. Did I have a homing signal in my implanted chip or not? If I did, why weren't the Erasers here by now? It was like they were just toying with us, keeping us on our toes, like a game. . . .

Like a game. Like a freaking *game*.

Just like Jeb had said back at the School. Just like the Voice kept telling me, that everything was a *game*, that you learn through playing, that everything, every single thing, was a test.

I felt like a neon sign had just lit up right in front of my face. For the first time, I finally, *finally* understood that this all might *be* a huge, twisted, sick, important game.

And I had been cast as a major player.

I sifted coarse sand through my fingers, thinking hard. Okay. If this was a game, were there only two sides? Were there any double agents?

I opened my mouth to blurt my thoughts out to Fang but stopped. He glanced at me, his dark eyes curious, and suddenly I felt a cold dread. I dropped my gaze, feeling my cheeks heat.

What if we *weren't* all on the same team?

Part of me felt ashamed for even having that thought, and part of me remembered how many times my adorable paranoia had saved our butts.

I glanced out at the water, where Angel was splashing the Gasman and laughing. She dove beneath the surface, and Gazzy started chasing her.

Had Angel been different since we'd gotten her back from the School? I groaned and dropped my head into my hands. It was all too much. If I couldn't trust these five people, then my life wasn't worth living.

"Your head hurt?" Fang asked with quiet alertness.

Sighing, I shook my head no, then looked back at the ocean. I depended on Fang. I needed him. I *had* to be able to trust him.

Did I?

Gazzy was staring at the surface of the water, turning this way and that, seeming confused. Then he looked up at me, panic on his face.

Angel hadn't come back up. She was still under water.

I started running.

114

"Angel!" I yelled, plunging into the water. I reached Gazzy and grabbed his shoulder. "Where did she go down?"

"Right here!" he said. "She dove that way! I saw her go under."

Fang splashed in behind me, and Nudge and Iggy made their way over. The five of us peered into the cold gray blue water, able to see only a few inches down. A wave broke over us.

"This would be an excellent time for one of us to develop X-ray vision," I muttered, a cold hand closing around my heart. I felt the strong tug of an underwater current pulling at my legs, saw how the wind was rippling the water out to sea.

"Angel!" Nudge yelled, cupping her hands around her mouth.

"Angel!" I shouted, wading through the water, taking big strides, praying I would brush against her.

Fang was sweeping his arms through the water, his face close to the surface. We fanned out, squinting from the sun's glare, taking turns diving into the surf.

My throat closed, and I felt like I would choke. My voice was a strangled rasp; my eyes stung from the glare and the salt.

We had covered a big circle, maybe thirty yards out, and still there was no sign of her. *My Angel.* I glanced back at the shore, as if I would see her walking out onto the sand toward Celeste, who waited for her by a piece of driftwood.

Endless minutes ticked by.

I could feel the undertow pulling at my whole body. I couldn't stop picturing Angel's body being pulled out to sea, her eyes wide with terror. Had we come so far only to lose her now?

"Do you see *anything?*" I cried to Fang.

He shook his head, keeping his eyes on the water, sweeping his arms back and forth.

Once again, we swept the whole area, taking in every detail of the water, the beach, the open sea.

And did it again.

And again.

I saw *something* and blinked, then looked harder.

What was — was it — oh, God! Hundreds of yards away, a small, wet cornrowed head popped out of the water. I stared. Angel stood up in waist-high water and waved at us.

My knees almost buckled. I had to catch myself before I did a face-plant in the water.

Angel and I surged toward each other, the others catching up.

"Angel," I could barely whisper, unbelieving, when I was finally close enough. "Angel, where were you?"

"Guess what?" she said happily. "I can breathe under water!"

115

I grabbed Angel into my arms, hugging her wet, chilly body against me. "Angel," I murmured, trying not to cry, "I thought you had drowned! What were you doing?"

She wriggled closer, and I steered her to shore. We collapsed on the wet sand, and I saw the Gasman fighting back tears too.

"I was just swimming," Angel said, "and I accidentally swallowed some water and started to choke. But I didn't want Gazzy to find me. We were playing hide-and-seek," she explained. "Under water. So I just stayed under, and then I realized that I could sort of swallow water and stay under and not choke."

"What do you mean, swallow water?" I asked.

"I just swallow it and then go like this." Angel blew air out of her nose, and I almost laughed at the face she made.

"It comes out your nose?" Fang asked.

"No," Angel said. "I don't know where the water goes. But air comes out my nose."

I looked at Fang. "She's extracting oxygen from the water."

"Can you show us?" Fang asked.

Angel got up and trotted to the shore. She plunged in when the water was waist high. I was inches away from her, determined she wasn't going to get lost again, even for a second.

She knelt down, took a big mouthful of water, and stood up. She seemed to swallow it, then blew air out of her nose. My eyes bulged until I thought they'd just fall out: Rivulets of seawater were seeping out of invisible pores on each side of Angel's neck.

"Holy moly," the Gasman breathed.

Nudge explained to Iggy what was happening, and he whistled, impressed.

"And I can do it and stay under and just keep swimming," Angel said. She wiggled her shoulders, unfolding her wings so they could dry in the bright sunlight.

"I bet I can do it too!" the Gasman said. " 'Cause we're siblings."

He dropped down into the water and scooped up a big mouthful. Then he swallowed it, trying to blow out air.

He gagged, then choked and started coughing violently. Seawater streamed out his nose, and he gagged again and almost barfed.

"You okay?" I asked when he had finally shuddered to a halt.

He nodded, looking wet, miserable, nauseated.

"Iggy," I said, "touch Angel's neck and see if you can feel anything, those pores that water comes through."

Like a feather, Iggy skimmed his fingertips over her fair skin, all around her neck. "I can't feel a thing," he said, which surprised me.

So we all had to try it, just in case. No one except Angel could do it. I'll spare you the revolting details, but let me just say that's one stretch of ocean you won't catch me swimming in for a while.

So Angel could breathe under water. Our abilities kept unfolding, as if certain things had been programmed to come out at different times, like when we reached certain ages. In a way it felt like being kinged in checkers — all of a sudden you had more strength, more power than you had before.

How weird.

Not weird, Max, my Voice suddenly chimed in. *Divine. And brilliant. You six are works of art. Enjoy it.*

Well, I would, *I thought bitterly, if I wasn't so busy* running for my life *all the time.* Jeez. Works of art or freaks? Glass half empty, glass half full. Like I wouldn't give up my wings in a second to have a regular life with regular parents and regular friends.

A tinkling laugh sounded in my head. *Come on, Max,* said the Voice. *You and I both know that isn't true. A regular family and a regular life would bore you to tears.*

"Who asked you?" I said angrily.

"Asked me what?" said Nudge, looking up in surprise.

"Nothing," I muttered. And there you have it. Some people get cool abilities like reading minds and breathing under water, and some people get annoying voices locked inside their head.

Lucky me.

What do you wish you could do, Max? asked the Voice. *If you could do anything?*

Hmm. I hadn't thought about it. I mean, I could already fly. Maybe I would want to be able to read minds, like Angel. But then I would know what everyone thought, like if someone really didn't like me but acted like they did. But if I could do anything?

Maybe you would want to be able to save the world, the Voice said. *Did you ever think of that?*

No. I frowned. *Leave that to the grown-ups.*

But grown-ups are the ones destroying the world, the Voice said. *Think about it.*

116

"Look who's come to the seashore."

The low voice, smooth and full of menace, woke me from sleep that night. My body tightened like a longbow and I tried to jump up, only to be held down by a big booted foot on my throat.

Ari. Always Ari.

In the next second, Fang and Iggy woke, and I snapped out my free hand to wake Nudge.

Adrenaline dumped into my veins, knotting my muscles. Angel woke and seemed to take off straight into the air with no running start. She clutched Celeste tightly, hovering about twenty feet above us. I saw her look around, saw her face take on an expression that had disaster written all over it.

I looked around too.

And gasped despite myself.

We were surrounded by Erasers, more Erasers than I'd ever seen before. Literally hundreds and hundreds of them. They'd been growing these things in quantities I could hardly imagine.

Ari leaned down and whispered, "You're so pretty when you're sleeping — and your mouth is shut. But what a shame to cut your hair."

"When I want your opinion, I'll ask for it," I spat, struggling against his boot.

He laughed, then reached down and stroked my face with one claw. "I like 'em feisty."

"Get off her!" Fang launched himself at Ari, taking him by surprise. Ari outweighed Fang by a hundred pounds, easy, but Fang was coldly furious and out for blood. He was scary when he was like that.

Iggy and I leaped up to help and were instantly grabbed by Erasers.

"Nudge and Gazzy — U and A," I yelled. "Now!"

Obeying without question, the two of them leaped into the air and flapped hard, rising to hover next to Angel. Erasers snapped at their legs, but they'd been quick and were out of reach. I was so proud, especially when Nudge snarled down meanly.

I struggled, but three Erasers held me in a tight, foul embrace. "Fang!" I screamed, but he was beyond hearing, locked in battle with Ari, who raked his claws across Fang's face, leaving parallel lines of red.

The six of us are superhumanly strong, but even we don't have the sheer muscle mass of a full-grown Eraser. Fang was badly outmatched but managed to chop Ari's collarbone.

Ari yelped and bared his teeth, then pulled back and

swung hard, catching Fang upside of his head. I saw his head snap sideways and his eyes close, then he dropped like a dead weight onto the sand.

Ari seized Fang's head and brought it down hard on a rock. And then he did it again.

"Leave him *alone!* Stop it! Please stop it!" I screamed, a mist of fury swimming before my eyes. I struggled against the Erasers holding me and managed to stomp on one's instep. He yelped a curse and corkscrewed my arm until tears rolled down my cheeks.

Fang's eyes opened weakly. Seeing Ari over him, he grabbed sand and threw it into Ari's face. Fang scrambled to his feet and launched a roundhouse kick at Ari that caught him square in the chest. Ari staggered back, wheezing, then recoiled fast and cracked Fang with an elbow. Blood sprayed from Fang's mouth, and again he went down.

I was crying by now but couldn't speak: An Eraser's rough, hairy paw was clapped over my mouth.

Then Ari bent over Fang's body, his muzzle open, canines sharp and ready to tear Fang's throat. "Had enough," he growled viciously, "of life?"

Oh, God, oh, God, not Fang, not Fang, not Fang —

"Ari!"

My eyes went wide. I knew that voice too well.

Jeb. My adopted father. Now my worst enemy.

117

I stared with the fiercest, most righteous anger and hatred as Jeb Batchelder easily moved through the crowd of Erasers, parting them as if he were Moses and they were the Red Sea. It was still bizarre to see him — I'd been so used to mourning, not despising, him.

Ari paused, his rank and deadly mouth open over Fang's neck. Fang was] unconscious but still breathing.

"Ari!" Jeb said again. "You have your orders."

Jeb walked toward me, keeping one eye on Ari. After endless seconds, Ari slowly, slowly drew back from Fang, leaving his body crumpled unnaturally on the sand.

Jeb stopped in front of me.

He'd saved my life more than once. He'd saved all our lives. Taught me to read, how to make scrambled eggs, how to hot-wire cars. Once I'd depended on him as if he were the very breath in my lungs: He was my one constant, my one certainty.

"Do you get it now, Max?" he asked softly. "Do you see the incredible beauty of the game? No child, no adult, no one has ever experienced anything like what you're feeling. Do you see why all this is necessary?"

The Eraser holding me peeled his fingers away from my mouth so I could speak. Instantly, I spit hard, clearing my mouth and throat of tears. I hit Jeb's shoe.

"No," I said, keeping my voice steady, though everything in me was shrieking, desperate to run to Fang. "I don't get it. I'll never get it. I want to get *out* of it."

His heartbreakingly familiar face looked strained, as if he was losing patience with me. Tough. "I told you, you're going to save the world," he said. "That's the purpose of your existence. Do you think an ordinary, untrained fourteen-year-old could do that? No. You've got to be the best, the strongest, the smartest. You've got to be the ultimate. *Maximum.*"

I yawned and rolled my eyes, knowing he'd hate that, and Jeb's jaw tightened in anger. "Do not fail," he said, a hard note in his voice. "You did okay in New York, but you made serious, rather stupid mistakes. Mistakes cost you. Make better decisions."

"You're not my dad anymore, Jeb," I said, putting as much annoying snideness into my tone as possible. "You're not responsible for me. I do what I like. I named myself — Maximum Ride."

"I'll *always* be responsible for you," he snapped. "If you think you're actually running your own life, then maybe you're not as bright as I thought you were."

"Make up your mind," I snapped back. "Either I'm the greatest or I'm not. Which is it?"

He motioned with his hand, and the Erasers let me and Iggy go. Ari turned and smirked at me, then blew me a kiss.

I spit at him. "Daddy always loved me best!" I hissed, and his face darkened.

He took a fast step toward me, paws coiled into fists, but was pushed along by a rough, hairy wave of the other Erasers. They swept him up and shuffled off around the large boulder at the end of our beach. Jeb was with them. No, he was *one* of them.

118

Stumbling badly, my shoulder feeling like it was on fire, I made my way down the beach. Before I moved Fang, I felt his neck to see if it was broken. Then I carefully turned him over. Blood trickled from his mouth.

"Fang, you have to wake up," I whispered.

The others ran over. "He looks really bad," Gazzy said. "He should see a doctor."

Nothing seemed broken — maybe his nose — but he was still out cold. I lifted his head into my lap and used my sweatshirt to dab at the bloody stripes on his face.

"We could carry him, you and me," said Iggy, his long, pale hands floating over Fang, cataloging bruises, lumps, blood.

"Where to?" I asked, hearing my bitterness. "It's not like we can check him into a hospital."

"No hospi'l," Fang mumbled, his eyes still shut.

Relief flooded through me.

"Fang!" I said. "How bad?"

"Pre'y bad," he said fuzzily, then, groaning, he tried to shift to one side.

"Don't move!" I told him, but he turned his head and spit blood out onto the sand. He raised his hand and spit something into it, then opened his eyes blearily.

"Tooth," he said in disgust. "Feel like crap," Fang added, touching the knots on the back of his head.

I tried to smile. "You look like a kitty cat." I made whisker motions on my face, indicating where Ari had raked his. He looked at me sourly.

"Fang," I said, my voice breaking. "Just live, okay? Live and be okay."

With no warning, I leaned down and kissed his mouth, just like that.

"Ow," he said, touching his split lip, then he and I stared at each other in shock.

Mortification heated my face. I glanced up to see Nudge and the Gasman gaping at me. Luckily, Iggy was blind, and Angel was getting Fang water.

Gazzy looked from me to Fang to Iggy, clearly thinking that he was sunk now that I had obviously severed all ties with reality.

Slowly, Fang levered himself into a sitting position, his jaw tight, sweat breaking out on his face. "Man," he said, and coughed. "This feels pretty bad."

It was about the most he'd ever admitted to, painwise. He stood clumsily and took the water from Angel. Taking a swig, he rinsed his mouth and spit it out onto the sand.

"I'm going to kill Ari," Fang said.

119

Fang and the rest of us made it back to Manhattan without dropping out of the sky due to injury, exhaustion, or both.

"You macho thing, you," I said when we finally landed in the darkness of Central Park. He looked worn out, clammy, and pale, but he had flown all the way with no complaint.

"That's me," he said, but he gave me a long look, like, I haven't forgotten what you did, meaning *the Kiss*.

I blushed furiously, embarrassed beyond belief. I would never live that down.

"Are you really okay, Fang?" Nudge asked, the most touching concern in her voice. Nudge doted on Fang.

He looked like he'd fallen off a cliff, with huge purple bruises distorting his face, the awful scratches Ari had left on his cheeks, the stiff, pained way he moved.

"I'm cool," he said. "Flying helped loosen me up some."

"Look, let's find a place to hunker down, catch some Zs, and then take another shot at the Institute," I said. "We've got to figure it out — we can't stop now. Right, guys?"

"Yeah, right," Nudge said. "Let's do it, get it over with. I want to know about my mom. And other stuff. I want to know the whole story, good or bad."

"Me too," said Gazzy. "I want to find my parents so I can tell'm what total scuzzes they are. Like, '*Hi, Mom and Dad, you're such scum!*'"

I decided we'd better stay underground for safety's sake. In the subway station, we jumped off the platform and walked quickly along the tracks. It looked familiar, and sure enough, a few minutes' walking brought us to a huge firelit cavern populated by homeless people and misfits. Home, sweet home, especially if you happen to be a sewer rat.

"Boy, does this look inviting," Fang said, rubbing his hands together.

I made a face at him as we climbed up onto the concrete ledge. Inside, I was glad that he had enough energy to be sarcastic.

Suddenly exhausted and emotionally wiped, I held out my left fist to make our bedtime stack. We did our thing, then Angel snuggled next to me. I checked to make sure the others, especially Fang, were okay, then I lay down, letting despair cover me like a blanket.

I was in the middle of another sleep-driven brain explosion when I felt myself surface to consciousness without opening my eyes. Not analyzing the impulse, I shot out my hand and grabbed *someone's wrist.*

Moving fast, still on instinct, I sat up and twisted the intruder's arm behind his back, my senses roaring to life.

"Cool it, sucker!" the arm's owner whispered furiously. I yanked upward, threatening to pop his arm out of its socket. I definitely could've done it.

Fang creaked upright next to me, his eyes alert, but his body moving stiffly.

"You're screwing with my Mac again," said the hacker, and I loosened my hold on him. "Jeez, what happened to *you?*" Directed at Fang.

"Cut myself shaving," Fang said.

The hacker frowned and rubbed his shoulder where I'd strained it. "Why'd you come back here?" he asked angrily. "You're totally wrecking my hard drive."

"Let me see," I said, and he grumpily opened his laptop.

The screen was covered with the *inside* of my head: images, words, photos, maps, mathematical equations.

The hacker scowled, seeming more perplexed than mad, though. "It's weird," he said. "You guys don't have a computer with you?"

"No," Fang said. "Not even a cell phone."

"What about a Palm Pilot?" the hacker asked.

"Nope," I said. "We're kinda more low-tech than that." Like, having Kleenex would be a huge step up for us.

"A memory chip?" he persisted.

I froze. Almost against my will, I slid my gaze over to Fang.

"What kind of memory chip?" I asked, striving for casual.

"Anything," the hacker said. "Anything that would have data on it that would interfere with my hard drive."

"If we did have a chip," I said carefully, "could you access it?"

"If I knew what it was," he said. "Maybe. What do you have?"

"It's small and square," I said, not looking at him.

"Like this?" The hacker held his fingers about three inches apart.

"Smaller."

His fingers were a half-inch apart. "You have a memory chip this small?"

I nodded.

"Let me see. Where is it?"

I took a deep breath. "In me. It's implanted in me. I saw it on an X-ray."

He stared at me with horror in his eyes. He turned off his laptop and closed the lid. "You have a memory chip that small *implanted* in you," he verified.

I nodded, guessing this was somewhat worse than having cooties.

He took several steps back. "A chip like that is bad news," he said slowly, as if I were stupid. "It might be NSA. I won't mess with it. Look, you stay away from me! Next thing, they'll be after *me*." He backed away into the darkness, his hands up as if to ward off evil. "I hate them! Hate them!" Then he was gone, back into the bowels of the tunnels.

"See ya," I whispered. "Wouldn't want to be ya."

Fang looked at me irritably. "I can't take you *any*-where."

I so wished he weren't all banged up — so I could whack him.

120

We tried to get some sleep — God knows we needed it. I kind of dozed off. Then I *wasn't* asleep, I knew that much. But I wasn't awake, exactly.

I'd been, like, sucked into another dimension, where I could feel my body, sort of, knew where I was, and yet was powerless to move or speak. I was in a movie, starring me, watching it all happen around me. I was going down a dark tunnel, or the tunnel was slipping by me, and I was staying still. Trains were rushing past me on both sides, so it was a subway tunnel.

I was thinking, *Okay, subway tunnel.* Yeah, so?

Then I saw a train station: Thirty-third Street. The Institute's building was on Thirty-first Street. In the darkness of the waking-dream subway tunnel, I saw a filthy rusted-over grate. I saw myself pulling the grate up. Fetid brown water gurgled below. *Bleah* — it was the sewer system, beneath the city.

Hello.

Beneath a rainbow . . .

Bingo, Max, said my Voice.

My eyes popped wide open. Fang was watching me with concern. "Now what?"

"I know what we have to do," I said. "Wake everyone up."

121

"This way," I said, walking in the darkness of the tunnels. It was as if a detailed map was imprinted on my retinas, so I could see it laid over reality, tracing the path we needed to follow. If this map effect was part of my life forever, I would go nuts, but right now it was dang useful.

One other thing I guess I should mention — I was really, really afraid now, more afraid than I'd ever been before, and I didn't even know why. Maybe I didn't want to know the truth. Also, my head was throbbing, and that had me a little crazy too. Was I approaching my expiration date? Was I going to die? Was I just going to fall over and be gone from the world and my friends?

"Did the Voice tell you about this, Max?" Nudge poked at me and asked.

"Kind of," I answered.

"Great," I heard Iggy mutter, but I ignored him. Every step was bringing us closer to the Institute — I could feel it. We were finally about to have our questions answered, and also possibly fight the worst fight of our lives. But our curiosity was *so* compelling: Who were we? How had they taken us from our parents? Who had grafted avian DNA into us and why? My mind shied away from the parent question. I really didn't know if I could stand to find out. But everything in me burned to know the other whys and wherefores. I wanted names. I wanted to know who was accountable. I wanted to know where they lived.

"Okay, now the tunnel splits," I said, "and we take the one with no tracks."

Angel's hand was in mine, small and trusting. The Gasman was still dopey with sleep, occasionally stumbling. Iggy had one finger in Fang's belt loop.

We were looking for a rusted grate set in the floor. In my dream, I had seen it at the crossroads of two tunnels, so it had to be here. But I didn't see it. I stopped, and the others stopped behind me.

"It has to be here," I said under my breath, peering into the darkness.

Don't think about what has to be, Max. Think about what is.

I set my jaw. *Can't you just tell me stuff straight out?* I thought. Why did everything have to be like, "What is the sound of one hand clapping" and all?

But okay. What *was* here, then? I closed my eyes and just *sensed* where I was, consciously letting any impression at all come to me. I felt like such a total dweeb.

Then I just walked forward, eyes shut, trying to sense where we should go. Instinctively, I felt I should stop. So I stopped. I looked down.

There, at my feet, was the dim outline of a large rusted grate.

Well, aren't *you* special, I told myself. "It's over here," I called.

The grate pulled up easily, its screws disintegrating into rusty powder as Fang, Iggy, and I pulled. It came loose, and we set it aside.

Below it was a manhole with rusted U-shaped hand-holds set into one side. I lowered myself over the edge and started climbing down into the sewer system of New York City.

What a destiny.

Finally, I had to ask the Voice a question. HAD TO ASK. *Am I going to die? Is that what this is all about?*

There was a pause, a long one, really agonizing, the worst.

Then the Voice decided to answer. *Yes, Max, you are going to die. Just like everybody else.*

Thank you, Confucious.

122

This may surprise you, but the sewer system of a burg with eight million people is even less delightful than you might imagine. We climbed down the manhole one by one and ended up standing on a grimy tiled ledge maybe two feet wide. Above us, the tunnel curved around, some fourteen feet across, and below our ledge was a swiftly moving current of filthy wastewater.

"Bleah," said Nudge. "This is so gross. When we get out of here, I want someone to spray me with, like, disinfectant."

Angel stuffed Celeste up under her shirt.

"Max?" said the Gasman. "Are those, um, rats?"

Lovely. "Yes, those do appear to be either rats or mice on steroids," I said briskly, trying not to shriek and climb the walls like a girly-girl.

"Jeez," said Iggy with disgust. "You'd think they'd want to live in a park or something."

Ahead of us was a four-way intersection of tunnels, like a big cross. I hesitated, then turned left. Several minutes later, I stopped, completely and utterly without a clue.

Hello, Voice? I thought. *A little help here, please.*

I had no hope that the Voice would respond, but if it did, it would probably say something like, If a tree falls in a forest, does it still —

I looked down, then sucked in my breath so fast I almost choked. *I was standing on a translucent platform suspended high over the sewer system.* I wanted to scream, feeling off-balance and scared. Below me I could see another Max, looking like a deer caught in headlights, and the rest of the flock staring at me. Fang reached out and took the other Max's arm, and I felt it, but no one was with me.

When are you going to trust me, Max? said the Voice. *When are you going to trust yourself?*

"Maybe when I don't feel completely *bonkers*," I snarled.

I swallowed hard and tried to get a grip. Tentatively, I glanced down again at the translucent surface. As I watched, faint lines of light tracked the path behind us, where we'd already been. Then the lines continued through the tunnels, like a neon This Way sign.

Quickly, I glanced up but saw only the yucky yellow-tiled arch covered with mold — no glass ceiling. Fang was still holding my arm, looking at me intently.

I gave him an embarrassed smile. "You must be so sick of looking at me with concern."

"It *is* getting stale," he said. "What happened? This time, I mean."

"I don't even want to explain," I said, wiping clammy sweat off my forehead. "You'd have me committed to a madhouse."

I stepped carefully around him and led the others forward. Some sections of the tunnel were lit dimly from open grates high above us, other parts were dark and dismal. But I was never lost, never uncertain, and after what felt like miles, I stopped again because it felt like it was time to. 'Cause, like, the feng shui was right, you know? Ugh.

As we stood staring around ourselves in the darkness, avoiding our chittering little rat friends, I saw why we were there.

Set into one cruddy, disgusting sewer wall was an almost completely hidden gray metal door.

"We're here, gang. We made it."

123

Don't get too excited. The door was locked, of course.

"Okay, guys," I said softly. "Can any of us open locks with our minds? Speak up now."

No one could.

"Iggy, then." I moved out of the way and pulled him gently to the door. His sensitive fingers reached out and skimmed the door, feeling its almost indistinguishable edges, hovering around the keyhole. Like someone was going to come down here with a *key*.

"Okay," Iggy muttered. He pulled his little lock-picking kit out of his pocket, as I knew he would. Even though I had confiscated it for *forever* only two months ago, after he picked the lock on my closet at home.

Home. Don't even think about it. *You no longer have a home. You're home-less.*

Carefully, Iggy selected a tool, changed his mind, took out another one. Angel shifted from foot to foot, looking nervously at the rats, who were growing creepily curious about us.

"They're going to bite us," she whispered, clutching my

hand, patting Celeste through her grimy shirt. "I can read their minds too."

"No, sweetie," I said softly. "They're just afraid of us. They've never seen such huge, ugly . . . creatures before, and they want to check us out."

I was rewarded with a tiny smile. "We're ugly to them. Right."

It took Iggy three minutes, which was a personal record for him, breaking the old four-and-a-half-minute record required by the three locks on my closet.

Iggy, Fang, and I gripped the edge of the door with our fingernails and pulled — there was no doorknob. Slowly, slowly, the immensely heavy door creaked open.

Revealing a long, dark, endless staircase ahead of us. Going down. Of course.

"Yeah, *this* is what we needed," Fang muttered. "A staircase going down to the Dark Place."

Iggy blew out his breath, less than thrilled. "You first, Max."

I put my foot on the first step.

You're on your own now, Max, said my Voice. *See you later.*

124

My headache was back, worse than before. "Let's keep it moving," I called over my shoulder.

Unlike the sewer, there wasn't even far-off light on the stairs, so it was pitch black. Fortunately, we could all see pretty well in the dark. Especially Iggy.

The steps seemed endless, and there was no handrail. I guess whoever built this wasn't too concerned with *safety*.

"Do you know what you're doing?" Fang asked softly.

"We're approaching our destination," I said, descending into the darkness. "We're homing in on the answers we've dreamed about getting our whole lives."

"We're doing what your Voice has told us to do," he said.

I was wary. "Yeah? The Voice has been okay so far, right?"

There was a bottom at last. "Here we are," I said, my heart pounding.

"There's a wall in front of you," said Iggy.

I reached out in the blackness, and a few feet away, my outstretched fingers touched a wall, then a door, then a doorknob. "Door," I said. "Might need you, Iggy."

I turned the knob, just to see, and lo and behold — the door began to open.

We were all silent. The door swung all the way open without a sound, and a gentle wash of fresh, cool air wafted over us. After the fetid, dank stench of the sewers, it was amazing.

Feeling like Alice in Wonderland falling down the rabbit hole, I stepped forward, my filthy shoes sinking into thick carpet. Yes, carpet.

Dim lights showed me another door, and, almost shrieking with tension, I opened it.

This all suddenly seemed horribly easy, suspiciously easy, scarily easy.

We went through this second door, then stopped and stared.

We were in a lab, a lab just like the one back at the School, thousands of miles away in California.

"We're in the Institute," I said.

"Uhm, is that a *good* thing?" asked Gazzy.

125

"Holy [insert a swear word of your choice here]," Fang said, stunned.

"No kidding," I said. There were banks of computers taller than me. And tables with first-class lab equipment. Dry-erase boards covered with diagrams — many of which I'd seen during my brain attacks. Things were in "sleep" mode, quietly humming but not working — it wasn't yet dawn.

We wove our way among the tables, trying to take it all in while quaking in our boots. I knew there were Erasers in this building — I could feel them.

Then I saw one computer still on, its screen bright, data being processed as we watched. This could be it — our chance to find out about our past, our parents, the whole amazing enchilada.

"Okay, guys," I said quietly. "Fan out, stay on guard, watch my back. I mean it! I'm going to try to hack in." I climbed on the lab stool in front of the counter and grabbed the computer mouse.

Password?

I cracked my knuckles, making Fang wince. Well, it could only be about a hundred million different things, I thought. How hard could it be?

I started typing.

I won't bore you with the whole list of what was rejected. I was thankful that the system didn't lock me out after three bad tries. But "School," "Batchelder," "Mother," "Eraser," "Flock," and a whole lot of others didn't cut it.

"This is pointless," I said, my nerves frayed.

"What's wrong, Max?" Nudge asked softly, coming to stand close to me.

"Who am I kidding?" I said. "There's no way for me to crack the password. We've come all this way for *nothing*. I'm such a loser! I can't stand it!"

Nudge leaned closer and touched the monitor with a finger, angling it so she could see better. She read the screen, her lips moving silently. I wanted to push her away, but I didn't want to be pointlessly mean.

Nudge closed her eyes.

"Nudge?" I asked.

Her hand fanned out on the monitor, as if pressing closer for warmth.

"Hello?" I said. "What are you doing?"

"Um, try big x, little j, little n, big p, the number seven, big o, big h, little j, and the number four," she said in a whisper.

I stared at her. Across the room, Fang was watching us, and my eyes met his.

Quickly, before I forgot, I typed in what she'd said, seeing the letters show up as small dots in the password box.

I hit *Enter*, and the computer whirred to life, a list of icons popping up on the left-hand side of the screen.

We were in.

126

I stared at Nudge, and she opened her eyes slowly. A bright smile crossed her face. "Did it work?"

"Yeah, it worked," I said, stunned. "Where'd you get it?"

"The computer," she said, looking pleased. "Like, when I touched it." She reached out and touched it again. "I can see the person who works here. It's a woman, with frizzy red hair. She drinks way too much coffee. She typed in the password, and I can feel it."

"Wow," I said. "Touch something else."

Nudge went to the next chair and put her hand on it. She closed her eyes and, a few moments later, smiled. "A guy sits here. A baldie. He bites his nails. He went home early yesterday." Opening her eyes, she looked at me happily. "I have a new skill!" she said. "I can do something new! This is so cool!"

"Good for you, Nudge," I said. "You saved our butts here."

Trying to focus despite this latest mind-blowing development, I skimmed icons and right-clicked my way into Explore. I searched for "avian," "School," "genetics" . . .

Then, oh, my God . . . *document files filled the screen.*

My fingers flew across the keyboard, searching out names, dates, anything I could think of to make a connection.

Origins. That looked promising, and I clicked on it. My eyes raced down the lines of text — and my throat closed. I almost went into shock on the spot.

I saw *our* names, names of hospitals, names of towns — even what looked like names of parents. Then I saw pictures of adults that seemed to go with the names. Were these our parents? They had to be. Oh, God, oh, God. This was it! This was exactly what we needed!

I hit *Print,* and pages started spewing out of the printer.

"What are you doing?" Fang asked, coming over.

"I think maybe I found something," I said breathlessly. I knew we shouldn't stop to look over the amazing pages here. "I'm going to print it, and then we should get the heck out of here. Start getting the others together."

I grabbed pages as they came out, folding them up and cramming them into all my pockets. I didn't even know how many there were, but finally the printer stopped. I was bursting to tell the others everything, but I didn't. I bit the inside of my cheek until it hurt. See why I'm the leader?

"Come on!" I said urgently. "Let's split! Let's go!"

"Uh, just a second, Max," said the Gasman, sounding really, really weird.

127

The Gasman was standing by a fabric-covered wall, and with typical curiosity, he had pulled the fabric aside. Slowly, we walked over to him, six sets of eyes opened wide as saucers.

When I was two feet away, my heart slammed to a halt inside my chest. I put my hand over my mouth to keep from screaming. Angel *did* scream, until Fang cupped a hand over her mouth.

Behind the curtain was a glass wall. Okay, no biggie.

But behind the glass was another lab room, with lab stations, computers, and . . . *cages.*

Cages with sleeping forms in them. Child-size forms. Dozens of them.

Mutants.

Just like us.

128

I couldn't speak. My gaze raked the glass wall, and I saw a small pad at eye level. I went over and pressed it in that cute don't-think-it-through way I have.

The glass wall opened, and we tiptoed through, our nerves as taut as rubber bands.

Sure enough, there were mutant kids sleeping in cages and in large dog crates. It brought my awful, gut-twisting childhood whooshing back to me, and I felt on the verge of having a panic attack. I'd forgotten about my headache for maybe a minute, but now it was back, throbbing as if my brain was getting ready to blow.

Angel was looking sadly into one cage, and I went to her. Out of hundreds of genetic experiments, only we and the Erasers had been at all viable — as far as I knew. The two little creatures asleep on their cage floor were clearly horrible failures and probably couldn't last much longer. What with some of their vital organs on the *outside* of their bodies and all. Kidneys, bowels, a heart. *Oh, the poor babies.*

"This is pathetic," Fang whispered, and I turned to see him looking at a large cat, like a serval or a margay. I'd never seen a real animal in one of the labs before. Just as I was wondering what its deal was, it woke up, blinked sleepily, then turned over and dozed off again.

I swallowed really, really hard. *It had human eyes.* And when I examined its paws more closely, I saw humanlike fingers beneath the retractable claws. Jiminy Christmas.

Glancing over, I saw Angel reading the card tacked to another small cage. Its doglike occupant was running in its sleep. "Hi, doggie," Angel whispered. "Hi, little doggie. You look like Toto. From *The Wizard of Oz*?"

I went over to Nudge, who was standing stiffly beside a cage. I looked in.

This one had wings.

I caught Fang's gaze, and he came over. When he saw the bird kid, he sighed and shook his head. I actually saw sadness and tenderness in his eyes. It made me want to hug Fang. But I didn't, of course.

"You know, we can't save them *all*," he told me softly.

"I'm supposed to save the whole world, remember?" I whispered back. "Well, I'm gonna start with these guys."

There you go, Max, said the Voice. *That's the difference between you and Fang.*

Don't you dare say anything bad about Fang, I thought. *He's usually right. He's probably right about this now.*

Is it important to be right or is it important to do what's right? That's one of the hardest lessons to learn.

Okay, whatever. I'm really busy right now.

"Start popping latches," I whispered to Iggy, who whispered to the Gasman, and so on.

I opened a cage and gently shook the creature inside awake. "Get ready to run," I whispered. "We're getting you out of here." The poor baby looked back at me uncomprehendingly.

Several creatures were awake and pressing against their cage bars, making weird noises I'd never heard before. We moved as fast as we could, opening doors. Finally, most of the prisoners were free, standing around, looking at the entrance to the lab with confusion or fear.

One cage held a large child who was gripping the bars. Fine features said this was probably a female. She had wings — I could see them tucked tight against her sides. She was older than the other winged child we'd seen.

I quickly unlatched the door to her cage. I jumped back when I heard a voice.

"Who are you? Why are you doing this?" she whispered.

"Kids don't belong in cages," I said to her. Then I called out in a loud voice, "Okay, everybody. Let's blow this joint."

129

"This way!" Nudge said, attempting to herd the mutants out of the lab. "Don't be afraid."

"I hear voices," Iggy said. "Be *very* afraid."

"Let's move it!" I ordered. My heart was pounding — *what was I doing?* Was I going to take care of all these kids? I could barely manage the ones I had.

I would think about that tomorrow.

"Nudge! Fang! Angel!" I called. "Out, out, out!"

They zipped past me, urging the others, and then we ran through the first door and across the deep carpeting to the second door. "Up the stairs!"

I didn't have Iggy's hearing, but I felt, sensed, that our little liberation party was about to be discovered. And that would be bad.

Plan ahead, Max. Think it out. Think on your feet.

Yes, Voice. Okay, we had steps, then sewer — I practically pushed the others up the dark stairs, one, two, three . . . One of the mutant kids freaked out and curled up in a ball, whimpering. I snatched it in one arm and kept climbing, two steps at a time. In my mind, I pictured the route we had to take.

Up ahead, Fang shoved open the last door, the one into the tunnel, and we all poured out after him, moving from cool, fresh air to a hot, fetid dampness that made my nose wrinkle.

"Where are we?" asked the bird girl we'd freed. She looked about ten years old and was one of the few who would speak.

"Sewer system, under a big city," I said shortly. "On our way out to fresh air and sunlight."

"But not just *yet*," Ari hissed from behind. "First we need to chat, Maximum. You and I. For old times' sake."

130

I went still and saw the bird girl's eyes widen in fear too. *Did she know Ari?* Slowly, I handed her the small whimpering mutant in my arms, then turned.

"Back again? What are *you* doing here?" I asked. "I thought Dad was keeping you on a short leash."

His hands curled into clawed fists.

I needed time. Behind me, I made "run!" motions with one hand. "So what happened, Ari?" I said, keeping his attention on me. "Who took care of you when Jeb left with us?"

His eyes narrowed, and I saw his canines growing visibly longer. "The whitecoats. Don't worry about it; I was in good hands. The best. Somebody was looking out for *me.*"

I frowned, wondering — "Ari, did Jeb give them permission to Eraserfy you or did someone just do it while he was gone?"

Ari's heavily muscled body quivered with rage. "What do you care? You're so perfect, the one successful recombinant. And I'm nobody, remember? I'm the boy who was left behind."

Despite everything, despite the fact that I could cheerfully have kicked his teeth in for what he had done to Fang, I did feel a pang of pity for Ari. It was true — once we were out of the School, I'd never given him a second thought. I didn't think about why Jeb had left him or what had happened to him.

"Someone did terrible things to you because Jeb wasn't there to protect you," I said quietly.

"Shut up!" he growled. "You don't know *anything!* You're dumb as a brick!"

"Maybe not. Someone wanted to see if Erasers would last longer if they didn't start from infancy," I went on. Ari was trembling now, his hands clenching and unclenching convulsively. "You were three years old, and they grafted DNA into you and they got a superEraser. Right?"

Suddenly, Ari lunged and swung out with one clubbed paw. Even with my speed-record reflexes, he managed to cuff my cheek hard enough to spin me against the gross tunnel wall. Something like pus stuck to my face.

I sucked in a breath, accepting that I was about to get the stuffing beat out of me. Ol' Jeb, though clearly an agent of the devil, had taught us the useful art of street fighting. Never fight fair — that's not how you win. Use every dirty trick you can. *Expect* pain. Expect to get hurt. If you're surprised by the pain, you just lost.

I turned slowly back toward Ari. "Out in the real world, you should be in second grade," I said, tasting salty blood inside my mouth. "If Jeb had protected you."

"Out in the real world, you would have been killed for the disgusting mutant freak you are."

Now the gloves were off. "And you're a . . . *what?*" I asked in mock polite confusion. "Face it, Ari. You're not just a big, hairy seven-year-old. You're much more of an obvious mutant freak than I am. And your *own father* let it happen."

"Shut up!" Ari yelled furiously.

I couldn't help it — I felt bad for him for a second.

But only for a second.

"You see, Ari," I said conversationally, then launched myself at him with a roundhouse kick that would have caved in the chest of an ordinary man. Ari merely staggered.

Staggered back a half-step. Not even a full one.

He cuffed me again, and I saw circles and stars. He punched me in the stomach. My God, he was as strong as a team of oxen. That would be strong, right?

"You're dead meat," Ari growled. "I mean that literally."

Then he surged toward me, claws out — *and he slipped.*

His boot slid on the slimy tunnel ledge and he fell heavily to his back. So hard I could hear the wind knocked out of him, a mighty gush of air.

"Get them out of here!" I shouted at Fang, barely turning my head, then instantly dropped my full weight onto Ari's chest.

I could hear my heart and feel adrenaline snaking through me, turning me into Supergirl. I remembered that Ari had hurt Fang bad out at the beach — and he'd enjoyed it.

Ari struggled to get up, wheezing like a large animal with pneumonia, trying to push me off. I grabbed his head with both hands, my face twisted with fury.

But he got away from me. He was so fast, faster than I was.

Ari punched me again, and I thought I heard a rib crack. He was taking me apart bit by bit. Why did he hate me so? Why did all of the Erasers hate us?

"Yes, Maximum, I *am* enjoying this. I want it to last a long, long time."

I was his pummeling bag now, and there was nothing I could do about it. You can't imagine the hurt and pain, or his strength, or the fury aimed at me.

The only thing saving me from destruction was the slippery footing in the tunnel, the grime under his feet.

Just then Ari lost his balance again, and I saw the smallest opening. A chance, at least.

I kicked him once more, this time in the throat. Solid, a good one.

Ari gagged and started to go down. I threw myself at him, grabbing his head, and we fell as one in slow motion. He was huge, heavy, and we dropped like lead. Wham! Butt, back, head . . . I held on tight — as Ari's neck slammed against the hard side of the tunnel. I heard a horrible, stomach-turning *crack* that vibrated up my arms. Ari and I stared at each other in shock.

"You really hurt me," he gasped rawly, terrible surprise in his voice. "I wouldn't hurt you. *Not like this.*" Then his head flopped down, and Ari went totally limp. His eyes rolled up and the whites showed.

"Max?" Iggy was trying to sound calm. "What was that?"

"I — I . . ." I gulped, sitting on Ari's barrel chest, still holding his head, "I think I broke his neck."

I gulped again, feeling like I might be sick. "I think he's dead."

131

We heard angry voices and heavy, pounding footsteps on the stairs above us.

No time to think, to try and make sense out of what had just happened.

I jumped off Ari's lifeless body and grabbed Angel's hand. Angel grabbed Iggy, and we started running with Nudge and the Gasman right behind us. I was aching everywhere, but I ran. I ran like the dickens, whatever that is. I saw no sign of Fang and the other mutants — they'd already gone.

"*Fly!*" I shouted, dropping Angel's hand, and she instantly leaped out over the sewer water, snapping her wings open and pushing down hard. Her sneakers dipped into the water, but then she rose again and flew off down the tunnel, her white wings a beacon in the darkness. The Gasman went next, looking freaked out and pale, and Iggy took off after him.

I heard a booming voice.

"*He was my son!*"

Jeb's anguished cry echoed horribly after me, bouncing

off the stone walls, coming at me from all angles. I felt short of breath. Had I really killed Ari? Made him die? It all seemed surreal — the sewer, the files, the mutants, Ari . . . Was I dreaming?

No. I was painfully awake, painfully myself, painfully right here, right now.

I turned and looked back at Jeb, the man who'd been my hero once upon a time.

"Why are you doing this?" I shouted at the top of my voice. "Why this game? This test? Look at what you've done."

Jeb stared at me, and I remembered clearly when he was like my father, the only one I trusted. Who had he really been back then? Who was he now?

Suddenly, he changed gears completely. He wasn't yelling anymore. "Max, you want answers to the secrets of life, and that's not how it works. Not for anybody, not even you. I'm your friend. Never forget that."

"I already have!" I yelled, then turned away, leaving Jeb behind.

"Take a right!" I shouted at Angel, and she did, swerving gracefully into a larger tunnel.

Just as I swerved after her, almost crashing into a wall because I banked too late, I heard one last, haunting cry. Jeb had changed his tone again — he was screaming at me, and I pictured his red face, red as a stop sign.

"You killed your own *brother!*"

132

Jeb's horrifying words echoed in my head again and again, the meaning and consequences seeming worse each time. *You killed your own brother.* Could that be true? How? Or was this just more theater? Part of my test?

Somehow, we made it up to the street, where Fang was waiting. I felt faint, like I'd been hit by a truck, but I forced myself to keep moving. I remembered what was stuffed in my pockets. Names, addresses, pictures — of our parents?

"Where are the other kids? The mutants?" I asked Fang. So much was going on now. It was hard to keep it all straight, but it had to be done, so I did it.

"The girl with wings took them." He shrugged. "She didn't want to stay with us. Wouldn't take no for an answer. Sound like anyone you know?"

I waved him off — I didn't want to talk about it now, didn't want to talk about anything.

I could still see Ari's eyes rolling back, could hear his neck snapping.

"Just walk. Keep walking," I said, and started to limp forward. "Walk the walk."

It was almost two minutes later that I realized Angel was carrying something besides Celeste.

"Angel?" I stopped in the middle of the sidewalk. "What's that?"

Something small and black and furry squirmed under her arm.

"It's my dog," said Angel, and her chin went stiff, like it always did when she was about to get stubborn.

"Your what?" Fang said, peering at the object in question.

We all gathered around Angel, but then I remembered how conspicuous we were. "Let's move," I muttered. "But this discussion isn't over, Angel."

In Battery Park, down at the tip of Manhattan, a small, abandoned band shell was almost completely hidden by overgrown rhododendrons and yew bushes. We huddled under its shelter as the rain washed dust off the city. I was wiped. I felt like I had absolutely nothing left.

"Okay," I said, sitting up straighter, trying to put energy into my voice. "Angel, explain the dog."

"He's my dog," she said firmly, not looking at me. "From the Institute."

Fang sent me a look that said, If you let her keep this dog, I will kill you.

"Angel, we can*not* have a dog with us," I said sternly.

The dog wiggled out of her arms to sit at her side. It looked pretty normal as far as I could tell. Its bright, black doggy eyes shone at me, and it was grinning in a friendly way. Its short, stumpy tail was wagging. Its nose sniffed the air happily, excited by all the new scents in the world.

Angel gathered the dog to her. The Gasman edged closer to look at it.

"And besides, you have Celeste," I pointed out.

"I love Celeste," Angel said loyally. "But I couldn't leave Total behind."

"Total?" Iggy asked.

"That's what his card said," Angel explained.

"Totally a mutant dog who will probably turn on us and kill us in our sleep," Fang said.

The dog cocked his head to one side, his grin fading a moment. Then his tail wagged again, insult forgotten.

Fang looked at me: I got to be the bad cop and lay down the law.

"Angel," I began cajolingly. "We can't always feed *ourselves*. We're on the *run*. It's dangerous out here. It's all we can do to deal with us."

Angel set her jaw and looked at her sneakers. "He's the most wonderful dog in the whole wide world," she said. "So *there*."

I looked at Fang helplessly.

"Angel," he said severely. She looked up at him with wide blue eyes, her face grubby, clothes filthy, cornrows all fuzzy.

"The first time you don't take care of him, boom, he's *out*," Fang said. "Understood?"

Angel's face lit up, and she threw herself into Fang's

arms while I gaped at him. He hugged Angel back, then caught my expression. He shrugged and let Angel go.

"She made Bambi eyes at me," he whispered. "You know I can't resist it when she does Bambi eyes."

"Total!" Angel cried. "You can stay!"

She hugged the small wiggling black body, then drew back to beam at him. Total gave a happy yip, then made an excited leap.

And our jaws dropped. We all stared in disbelief. Total almost hit the top of the band shell, about sixteen feet above us.

"Oh," said Angel, and Total landed, almost bottomed out, then jumped up again and licked her face.

"Yeah, *oh,*" I said.

133

That night we made a small camp fire and sat near the water in a part of New York called Staten Island. We were licking our wounds. Especially me. I hurt all over. But I was also unbelievably excited about what I'd found at the Institute.

"Okay, we're all safe, all together." I took a deep breath and slowly released it. "We found the Institute and *maybe* we got exactly what we went there for. Guys, I found names, addresses, even pictures of people who might be our parents."

I could see surprise, shock, incredible excitement on all of their faces, but also hints of fear and trepidation. Can you imagine what it's like to meet your parents when you're somewhere between six and fourteen? I sure couldn't.

"What are you waiting on?" asked Iggy. "The envelope, *please*. Open it, already. Then somebody tell me what it says."

I felt a trembling sense of elation as I started pulling out the pages I'd taken from the Institute. Here were the answers to the mysteries of our lives, right? The others gathered around me, leaning over my shoulders, helping me smooth the printed pages flat without smearing the ink.

"Max, what did Jeb mean — you killed your brother?" Nudge asked out of the blue. The question was so typical of her — off in her own world again. "He didn't mean that Ari was your brother, did he? You guys weren't — I mean, *triple yuk* —"

I held up my hand, trying not to shriek from bottled-up emotion. "I don't know, Nudge," I said, forcing myself to sound calm. "I can't think about it right now. Let's read these pages. When someone gets to something interesting, yell." I handed out the wrinkled stacks.

"Who's your daddy?" crowed the Gasman. "Who's your mommy?"

134

Angel started reading slowly, sounding out words. "This doesn't make sense to me," she said after about ten seconds.

Then the Gasman sat up. "Here I am!" he shouted. *"Here I am!"*

"Let me see, Gazzy."

The Gasman handed me his stack and I pored over it. Sure enough, I found his name: "F28246eff (the Gasman)." My heart nearly stopped.

"Here's an address!" I said, tracing my finger down a page. "It's in Virginia!"

"I've got an address too, and some names," said Fang. "And *my* name. And, oh man, there are pictures."

"Let us see, let us see!"

Everybody gathered around Fang, and even though he's usually Mr. Calm, Cool, and Collected, he was shaking. We all were. I myself was trembling like the temp had dipped about fifty degrees.

Nudge was pointing at a photocopy in Fang's hand. It showed a man and woman who seemed to be in their thirties. "He looks just like you, Fang. And so does she. They've got to be your mom and dad! No doubt."

Her voice choked up, and suddenly we were all crying, except Fang, of course, who just muttered, "Maybe, maybe not."

Then everybody was looking through the pages, searching for their parents. Nobody made a sound. Until —

"*Here they are!* My mom and dad!" Gazzy shouted. "One sixty-seven Cortlandt Lane in Alexandria, Virginia! Angel, look! This is them. It's totally amazing. It's a miracle. They look like me! And you too, Angel!"

Angel stared at the picture silently for a moment, and then her face crumpled and she was sobbing. I instantly reached out and held her small body close, stroking her hair. Angel's usually no softie, and when I felt her shake with sobs, my chest ached with her pain. Talk about your Kodak moment. Or Fuji. Whatever.

"There's lots of numbers and nonsense printed all over these pages too," Fang said, bringing me back to the here and now.

I saw the same thing. "Why scramble just some of the information? It doesn't make sense."

"Who cares?" Gazzy yelled happily. "I found my mom and dad! YAA-HOO! I take back being mad at them!"

Fang, Gazzy, and Angel had hit the jackpot, but so far, Iggy and I hadn't. And Nudge still wasn't sure if her 'rents were out west or not.

"Iggy! Iggy! Your mom! Oh, aww —. Says your dad is

deceased," the Gasman reported. "Sorry about your dad. But your mom looks neat." He started to describe her out loud.

So then there was just one outsider, only one of us without a mom and dad in the files from the Institute. You guessed it: *moi*. I still belonged to nobody, nowhere.

I'd like to say that I'm such a good person, such a team player, that I didn't feel totally left out, heartachey, just about ripped apart and destroyed — but I really am trying to get the lying under control. I did feel all those terrible things, and a whole lot more.

But I put on a brave face, and smiled, and oohed and aahed and reread files, being happy for my guys — who, face it, hadn't had much happiness yet in their hard, short, weird lives.

But my mind-like-a-steel-trap couldn't let something go. "So why scramble this other information?" I finally asked again. Just to say something else, to put myself somewhere besides the throne of pain.

"Maybe it's information the whitecoats never wanted anyone to find out," Fang said in the hollow *Twilight Zone*-y voice he used sometimes when things got unusually weird — as opposed to regular weird.

"Like — funding," I said, thinking. "Or hospitals who gave them babies. Other messed-up scientists who help them. Like the keys to the whole Evil Empire."

"Holy Joe," said Iggy, sitting up excitedly. "If we had that stuff, we could blow them wide open! We could send it to a newspaper. That fat guy could make a movie — like *Bowling for Columbine* or something."

My heart did flip-flops just thinking about it.

"I don't care about that stuff," said Nudge. "I just want to find my mom and dad once and for all. Wait, wait! This is me!" Holding her breath, she examined the information surrounding N88034gnh (Monique). "Know what?" Nudge quickly glanced from page to page. "All these addresses are in Virginia and Maryland and Washington, DC. That's all kind of close together, isn't it? Plus, DC is where the government is, right?"

"This is the coolest thing ever," said Iggy, a far-off look coming over his face. "First we meet our parents. Joyful reunion, hugs, kisses. Then we go destroy the School, the Institute, all those sons of b — I mean, all those jerks who messed us up. That would be so great. Like, we could wipe out the Erasers, all of 'em, at once. Way cool!"

"So what are we going to do?" the Gasman asked, suddenly very serious. *"For real?"*

"I want to do whatever Max does," said Angel. "And so do Celeste and Total."

Total wriggled, hearing his name, and licked Angel's hand. Whatever had been done to him at the Institute, he didn't seem to be holding any grudges. Now he licked Celeste.

That poor bear needed a bath in a big way. We all did. I looked at the troops. We were safe, for now. We were together. A wave of thankfulness came over me.

"We go to DC," I said finally. "And take baths. And start tracking your parents down. We have all their addresses, right?"

"Woo-hoo!" the Gasman shouted, slapping Iggy high five, taking him by surprise.

I smiled at them. I loved them all so much and I wanted them to be happy. I could do this for them. But inside, I felt as if black holes were eating through my chest. I had killed someone today. Maybe my own brother. Now we were going to start finding out about our pasts, maybe the meaning of our lives, and I didn't know if that's what I wanted. And only partly because I had no idea who my mother and father were.

But none of that mattered, right? These guys were my family. I owed it to them to try to help their dreams come true.

Even if it killed me.

Very late that night, or maybe it was early in the morning, I tried to talk to the Voice. Maybe, just maybe, it would deign to answer me.

I have two questions for you, okay? Just two questions. No, make that three questions. Okay. Where are my *mom and dad? How come I'm the only one with no files at all? Why am I having these terrible headaches? And who are you? Are you an enemy that's inside me? Or are you my friend?*

The Voice came right back to me: *That's more than three questions, Max. And sometimes whether someone is*

419

your friend or enemy is all in how you look at it. But if you must know, I consider myself your friend, a good friend who loves you very much. No one loves you more than I do, Maximum. Now listen. I ask the questions, not you. You're just here, and the Voice actually chuckled, *for the ride. For the incredible, indescribable Maximum Ride.*

EPILOGUE

There's nothing in the whole wide world like flying in the early morning, say around sixish.

At fifteen thousand feet, I could still make out the colors of cars inching along the New Jersey Turnpike below us. It felt fabulous to be wheeling in the air again, stretching my wings out fully, working out the soreness. We were flying in loose formation, coasting in one another's air wakes, smiling at nothing. We were happy to be together in the sky, way above the world that held our mysteries and our pain.

Total seemed to like the wind whistling through his fur, and the altitude didn't seem to be bothering his breathing yet. I knew the others were excited about finding their parents, and I knew that I was going down that road with them, to the end of the line.

Fang glanced over at me, his face smooth and impassive, though I could almost feel the anticipation rolling off his feathers. I smiled at him, and his dark eyes lit.

Fang. I had to do some thinking about him.

Me. I had to do some thinking about me too.

When we got to Washington DC, it would be either incredibly great or a totally heartbreaking disaster. Iggy thought that meeting their parents would be our ticket to safety and freedom and happiness. I wasn't that naive.

Knowledge is a terrible burden, Max, said my Voice. I sighed. Still with us.

It's a two-edged sword, the Voice went on. *It might help you, but it might put you in danger greater than anything you've faced so far.*

Gotcha. But I had to do it anyway.

Max — you have a bigger mission than finding the flock's parents. Focus on helping the whole world, not just your friends.

I held my wings steady, coasting for a long, long way on a warm updraft. It was like floating on a cloud, the best feeling you can imagine. I wish you could try it with me. Maybe next time.

You know, Voice, I thought finally, *my friends* are *my world.*

www.maximumride.com

Remember what I said at the very beginning?
Now, I'm giving you the a choice:
You can put the book down now—
 but you'll just have <u>some</u> of the story.
Look other places for more of it.
 Dig even deeper, and you could become <u>part</u> of it.
 The web of answers is out there.
 If you can find the portal.

Be careful. And don't say I didn't warn you.

Max

P.S.— Make sure you check out the postings from Fang's blog on the next page. The discovery that he and Nudge made is hugely important.

Nudge and I are going to scout DC before the whole Flock goes down there. That way when we do leave, we can do it quietly. It would be cool to have a few days there before the Erasers know we're gone.

She's navigating, I'm the bodyguard. I think it took her all of 20 minutes on the Internet to come up with three different routes mapped out for us to test! She's only 11, people!

Max is going to stay here in NYC with Ig, Gazzy, Angel and Total. There are lots of places to hide and eat. She'll definitely have her hands full with Erasers, though. I'm actually a little worried about them with me not being there. I know we've got to "divide to conquer," but I don't have to like it.   — Fang

It was cold when we left this morning, and of course we were followed. Two of 'em! And one was much bigger than the other. I wasn't happy about them being there, but it did keep Nudge quiet. Which I have to say, I appreciated. We let them tail us until we crossed the river into Jersey. (It's amazing how long it takes ground movers to do that...) Then we went back and did it again, and again, trying different routes. Each time they would give up when we crossed the river and pick us up when we came back to the city. I was letting them see us come and go. Give 'em a little false sense of security. Man, they're stupid. On the last flight over, I found a cool little tree house in a ritzy suburb. Sweet! Mucho thanks to the dad who built this place. We might actually get a good nights sleep because of you, sir.

We've crisscrossed two different routes in one day. I'm totally exhausted. 300 miles in 12 hours has got to be some kind of record! And, the last leg of it I had to carry Nudge. She was actually nodding off while flying! I guess you can't really understand how tired you'd have to be to fall asleep while flying. It's sort of impossible. But, that's Nudge for ya.   – Fang

Here's a sketch I did of our tree house. Nudge says we should just live here because Erasers don't like the suburbs. Maybe she's right.

I woke up in a complete panic – heart racing, adrenaline pumping . . . the whole nine yards. Something woke up this huge dog in a neighbor's yard, and then silenced the beast pronto. A little bit too pronto, if you know what I mean. Nudge slept through the whole thing, but I didn't like the feeling I got afterwards. They know we're here.

After my little panic attack, nothing else happened. Nudge woke up happy and I barely slept. What else is new?

We didn't see anything following us, but every time we would get near the city limits there were choppers. So, we were forced to travel on the ground. Thank god for Nudge, I couldn't read this metro subway map to save my life. It gave me a Max-sized headache. It also led us to a nice unused maintenance station. Good spot for the night.

Washington DC is beautiful. I think America is a very good idea. I just wish I could walk into my Senator's office and say, "Senator Dude, Um, we have a problem with these sicko scientists..."

But, then again, I don't think we even have a Senator, do we? Is there a state where mutant freaks are represented? If so, let me know.

It's 4AM. We're in a coffee shop somewhere, I don't know where. I was asleep in our Metro station and Nudge was on watch. I woke up to a sickening sound. What I saw was Nudge driving herself into an eraser's abdomen so hard, he hit the wall and I heard a couple ribs crack. (Again, she's only 11.) He spat out blood, and then just hit the cement quivering. The bigger one hit her with a backhand that sent her flying, and then he came at me. I got a good hold of him and spun him around. He went over the edge of the platform and brought me with him. I tried to flip him off me, but he must have weighed 250 pounds. Nudge jumped in and put her fingers so deep in his eye sockets that he jumped up and backwards. I gave him a kick, and he stepped back onto the third rail. Exploding, flaming eraser! This is why moms tell you to stay away from the third rail, but it sure came in handy this time.

We lifted quivering guy's wallet. There was a fake driver's license, a bunch of business cards and best of all a couple hundred bucks! Score! We've ridden two busses and took one flight. It felt good to get off the ground . . . really good!

Nudge is now on her 4th doughnut, so she's pretty pleased with herself. She should be.

We still don't know why they are so hot on our trail. I need to find some answers, and fast. Max wouldn't like it, but we all know Max would go to find the answers, too.

First we'll fuel up then we'll go check out these business cards.

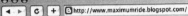

Weird. The second card in the stack led us here. The front is some electronics place, and in the back this...

INSTITUTE FOR HIGHER AERONAUTICS! The heck? It's too close to be a coincidence, don't you think? And, it would explain why there are so many Erasers around here...

We went back to the weird Institute building. At night there was a lot more activity. Erasers coming in non-stop. Nice cars, nice clothes, nice smug faces (that I wanted to smash!).

I couldn't do a whole lot with Nudge hanging in the background, but I had to get a look at what they were doing in that joint. So, I had her set off all the car alarms at the same time. It was pretty funny. Then they came streaming out of there like a cavalcade of clowns in the circus.

I slipped in the front door, crouched behind a generic reception desk, and waited for them to all come back in. When they did, I crept to the doorway and looked inside. There was this hangar-like room full of gymnastics equipment. An older scientist in a lab coat was lecturing the troops sitting on the floor. I gotta tell you, the sight of another white coat made me freeze.

I heard, or maybe felt, a breath on the back of my neck. I turned around to face wet, dripping Fangs and a foul smell. Eraser! He snapped at my face, but I turned my head and saved my nose. He started to scream, but I was too quick for him, and kicked him up between his legs so hard that he couldn't breathe. A high pitched whine came from his bared mouth. I gave him a roundhouse to the head, and dropped him. When I got to the door, Nudge was crouched on top of a beautiful silver Hummer. Her expression was mischievious.

"I called for back up." She said, "The police, fire department, paramedics and a few different pizza delivery places are all on their way."

Reader's Guide

Maximum Ride: The Angel Experiment is not only a fun read, but it's also full of thought-provoking story elements that are ideal for discussion groups or for your own exploration. Here are some questions to get the conversation going!

1) Each of the six children in the flock possesses a supernatural skill. How does each child's strength contribute to the flock?

2) When Angel is taken, the flock is devastated because they know she will be taken back to the School for more tests and experimentation. What options do they have for rescuing her? Why are they willing to put themselves in harm's way to save her?

3) What are the qualities of a hero? Discuss why Jeb had been a hero to Max. Jeb had taught Max to never trust anyone. What is the irony in this lesson?

4) Describe Dr. Martinez. At what point does Max realize that she can trust Ella and Dr. Martinez? Why is it difficult for Max to leave the comfort of their home?

5) Max and Fang are the same age, so why is Max the leader instead of Fang? What characteristics does she possess, which Fang lacks, that enable her to safely lead the flock? What are the drawbacks to her leadership? Would Fang be a better leader? Why or why not?

6) The flock's search for their parents gives them hope for a new way of life. What do they expect to happen when they find them? Do you think their expectations are realistic? Why or why not?

7) How does Max begin to lose trust in herself by the end of the novel? Do you think she stays true to herself and the flock? How do her goals shift?

8) Debate the question that the Voice poses to Max at the end of the novel: "Is it important to be right or is it important to do what's right?"

9) Because of genetic engineering, Max and the flock are able to protect themselves with supernatural skills, and make a quick getaway by soaring through air. Yet the kids also endured terrible tests in the labs and are hunted by even more advanced creatures. Overall, do you think the book supports genetic experimentation or discourages it? How do you feel about genetic engineering?

Please turn the page for a preview of

You can't study for survival.

SCHOOL'S OUT—
FOREVER

A MAXIMUM RIDE NOVEL
THE #1 *NEW YORK TIMES* BESTSELLING SERIES
BY JAMES PATTERSON

the next installment in
The Fugitives series

by James Patterson

1

Sweeping, swooping, soaring, air-current thrill rides — there's nothing better. For miles around, we were the only things in the infinite, wide-open, clear blue sky. You want an adrenaline rush? Try tucking your wings in, dive-bombing for about a mile straight down, then *whoosh!* Wings out, grab an air current like a pit bull, and hang on for the ride of your life. God, *nothing* is better, more fun, more exciting.

Okay, we were mutant freaks, we were on the lam, but man, flying — well, there's a reason people always dream about it.

"Oh, my gosh!" the Gasman said excitedly. He pointed. "A UFO!"

I silently counted to ten. There was nothing where the Gasman had pointed. As usual. "That was funny the first fifty times, Gazzy," I said. "It's getting old."

He cackled, several wingspans away from me. There's nothing like an eight-year-old's sense of humor.

"Max? How long till we get to DC?" asked Nudge, pulling up closer to me. She looked tired — we'd had one long, ugly day. Well, *another* long, ugly day in a whole series of long, ugly days. If I ever actually had a good, easy day, I'd probably freak out.

"Another hour? Hour and a half?" I guessed.

Nudge didn't say anything. I cast a quick glance at the rest of my flock. Fang, Iggy, and I were holding steady, but we had mucho de stamina. I mean, the younger set also had stamina, especially compared to dinky little nonmutant humans. But even they gave out eventually.

Here's the deal — for anybody new on this trip. There are six of us: Angel, who's six; Gasman, age eight; Iggy, who's fourteen, and blind; Nudge, eleven; Fang and me (Max), we're fourteen too. We escaped from the lab where we were raised, were given wings and other assorted powers. They want us back — badly. But we're not going back. Ever.

I shifted Total to my other arm, glad he didn't weigh more than twenty pounds. He roused slightly, then draped himself across my arm and went back to sleep, the wind whistling through his black fur. Did I want a dog? No. Did I need a dog? Also no. We were six kids running for our lives, not knowing where our next meal was coming from. Could we afford to feed a dog? Wait for it — *no.*

"You okay?" Fang cruised up alongside me. His wings were dark and almost silent, like Fang himself.

"In what way?" I asked. I mean, there was the headache issue, the chip issue, the *Voice-in-my-head-constantly* issue, my healing bullet wound. . . . "Can you be more specific?"

"Killing Ari."

My breath froze in my throat. Only Fang could cut right to the heart of the matter like that. Only Fang knew me that well, and went that far.

When we'd been escaping from the Institute, in New York, Erasers and whitecoats had shown up, of course. *God forbid* we should make a clean getaway. Erasers, if you don't know already, are wolflike creatures who have been chasing us constantly since we escaped from the lab, or School as we call it. One of the Erasers had been Ari. We'd fought, as we'd fought before, and then suddenly, with no warning, I was sitting on his chest, staring at his lifeless eyes, his broken neck bent at an awkward angle.

That was twenty-four hours ago.

"It was you or him," Fang said calmly. "I'm glad you picked you."

I let out a deep breath. Erasers simpled everything up: They had no qualms about killing, so you had to lose your squeamishness about it too. But Ari had been different. I'd recognized him, remembered him as a little kid back at the School. I knew him.

Plus, there was that last, awful bellow from Ari's father, Jeb, echoing after me again and again as I flew through the tunnels:

"You killed your own brother!"

2

Of course, Jeb was a lying, cheating manipulator, so he might have just been yanking my chain. But his anguish after he'd discovered his dead son had sounded real.

And even though I loathed and despised Jeb, I still felt as though I had an anvil on my chest.

You had to do it, Max. You're still working toward the greater good. And nothing can interfere with that. Nothing can interfere with your mission to save the world.

I took another deep breath through clenched jaws. *Geez, Voice. Next you'll be telling me that to make an omelet, I have to break a few eggs.*

I sighed. Yes, I have a Voice inside my head, I mean, another one besides my own. I'm pretty sure that if you look up the word *nuts* in the dictionary, you'll find my picture. Just another fun feature of my mutant-bird-kid-freak package.

"Do you want me to take him?" Angel asked, gesturing toward the dog in my arms.

"No, that's okay," I said. Total weighed almost half of what Angel weighed — I didn't know how she'd carried him as far as she had. "I know," I said, brightening. "Fang will take him."

I gave my wings an extra beat and surged up over Fang, our wings sweeping in rhythm. "Here," I said, lowering Total. "Have a dog." Vaguely Scottie-ish in size and looks, Total wiggled a bit, then quickly settled into Fang's arms. He gave Fang a little lick, and I had to bite the inside of my cheek to keep from snickering at Fang's expression.

I sped up a bit, flying out in front of the flock, feeling an excitement overshadowing my fatigue and the dark weight of what had happened. We were headed to new territory — and we might even find our parents this time. We had escaped the Erasers and the whitecoats — our former "keepers" — again. We were all together and no one was badly wounded. For this brief moment, I felt free and strong, as if I was starting fresh, all over again. We *would* find our parents — I could feel it.

I was feeling . . . I paused, trying to name this sensation.

I felt kind of optimistic. Despite everything.

Optimism is overrated, Max, said the Voice. *It's better to face reality head-on.*

I wondered if the Voice could see me rolling my eyes, from the inside.

3

It had gotten dark hours ago. He should have heard by now. The fearsome Eraser paced around the small clearing, and then suddenly the static in his ear made him wince. He pressed the earpiece of his receiver and listened.

What he heard made him smile, despite feeling like crap, despite having a rage so fierce it felt as if it were going to burn him up from the inside out.

One of his men saw the expression on his face and motioned the others to be quiet. He nodded, said "Got it" into his mouthpiece, and tapped off his transmitter.

He looked over at his troop. "We got our coordinates," he said. He tried to resist rubbing his hands together in glee but couldn't. "They're headed south-southwest and passed Philadelphia thirty minutes ago. The Director was right — they're going to Washington DC."

"How solid is this info?" one of his Erasers asked.

"From the horse's mouth," he said, starting to check his equipment. He rolled his shoulders, grimacing, then popped a pain pill.

"Which horse?" asked another Eraser, standing up and fastening a night-vision monocle over one eye.

"Let's just say it's insider information," the leader of the Erasers said, hearing the joy in his own voice. He felt his heart speed up with anticipation, his fingers itching to close around a skinny bird-kid neck. Then he started to *morph*, watching his hands.

The frail human skin was soon covered with tough fur; ragged claws erupted from his fingertips. Morphing had hurt at first — his lupine DNA wasn't seamlessly grafted into his stem cells, like the other Erasers'. So there were some kinks to be worked out, a rough, painful transition period he'd had to go through.

But he wasn't complaining. It would all be worth it the moment he got his claws on Max and choked the life right out of her. He imagined the look of surprise on her face, how she would struggle. Then he'd watch the light slowly fade out of her beautiful brown eyes. She wouldn't think she was so hot then. Wouldn't look down on him or, worse, *ignore* him. Just because he wasn't a mutant freak like them, he'd been nothing to her. All she cared about was the flock this and the flock that. That was all his father, Jeb, cared about too.

Once Max was dead, that would all change.

And he, Ari, would be the number-one son. *He'd come back from the dead for it.*

4

By dusk we'd crossed over a chunk of Pennsylvania, and a
thin spit of ocean twined below us, between New Jersey and
Delaware. "Look at this, kids, we're learning geography!"
Fang called out with mock excitement. Since we'd never
been to school, most of what we'd learned was from tele-
vision or the Internet. And, these days, from the little
know-it-all Voice in my head.

Soon we'd be over Washington DC. Which was pretty
much where my plan stopped. For tonight, all I was worried about was food and a place to sleep. Tomorrow I
would have time to study the info we'd gotten from the Institute. I'd been so thrilled when we'd hacked into the Institute's computers. Pages of information about our actual
parents had scrolled across the screen. I'd managed to print
out a bunch of it before we'd been interrupted.

Who knew — by this time tomorrow we might be on
someone's doorstep, about to come face-to-face with the
parents who had lost us so long ago. It sent shivers down
my spine.

I was tired. We were all tired. So when I did an automatic 360 and saw a weird dark cloud heading toward us, my groan was deep and sincere.

"Fang! What's that? Behind us, at ten o'clock."

He frowned, checking it out. "Too fast for a storm cloud. Too small, too quiet for choppers. Not birds — too lumpy." He looked at me. "I give up. What is it?"

"Trouble," I said grimly. "Angel! Get out of the way. Guys, heads up! We've got company!"

We swung around to face *whatever* was coming. Fast!

"Flying monkeys?" The Gasman called out a guess. "Like *The Wizard of Oz*?"

It dawned on me then. "No," I said tersely. "Worse. *Flying Erasers.*"

5

Yep. Flying Erasers. These Erasers had wings, which was a new and revolting development on the Eraser front. Half-wolf, half-human, and now half-avian? That couldn't be a happy mix. And they were headed our way at about eighty miles an hour.

"Erasers, version 6.5," Fang said.

Split up, Max. Think 3-D, said my Voice.

"Split up!" I ordered. "Nudge! Gazzy! Nine o'clock! Angel, up top. Move it! Iggy and Fang, flank me from below! Fang, ditch the dog!"

"Nooo, Fang!" screeched Angel.

The Erasers slowed as we fanned out, their huge, heavy-looking wings backbeating the air. It was almost pitch-black now, with no moon and no city lights below. I was still able to see their teeth, their pointed fangs, their smiles of excitement. *They were on a hunt — it was party time!*

Here we go, I thought, feeling adrenaline speeding up my heart. I launched myself at the biggest one, swinging my feet under me to smash against his chest. He rolled back but righted himself and came at me again, claws slashing the air.

I bobbed, feeling his paws whip right past my face. I turned sharply just in time to have a hard, hairy fist crash into my head.

I dropped ten feet quickly, then surged back up on the offensive.

In my peripheral vision, I saw Fang clap both hands hard against an Eraser's furry ears. The Eraser screamed, holding his head, and started to lose altitude. Fang had Total *in his backpack.* He rolled out of harm's way, and I took his place, catching another Eraser in the mouth with a hard side kick.

I grabbed one of his arms, twisting it violently in back of him. It was harder in the air, but then I heard a loud *pop.*

The Eraser screamed and dropped, careening downward until he caught himself and flew clumsily away, one arm dangling.

Above me an Eraser lashed out at Nudge, but she dodged out of the way.

Max? Size isn't everything, said the Voice.

6

I got it! The Erasers were bigger and heavier, their wings almost twice as long as ours. But in the air, those were liabilities.

Panting, I ducked as an Eraser swung a black-booted foot at my side, catching me in the ribs but not too hard.

I zipped in and dealt out some powerful punches of my own, knocking his head sideways, then I flitted out of reach.

Compared to the Erasers, we were nimble little stinging wasps, and they were clunky, slow, awkward flying cows.

Two Erasers ganged up on me, but I shot straight up like an arrow, just in time for them to smash into each other.

I laughed as I saw Gazzy roll completely over like a fighter plane, smacking an Eraser in the jaw on the turn. The Eraser swung a hard punch, landing it on Gazzy's thigh, and Gazzy winced, then launched a side kick at the Eraser's hand, which snapped back.

How many of them were there? I couldn't tell — everything was happening at once. Ten?

Nudge, my Voice said, and then I heard Nudge cry out.

An Eraser had her tight in his arms, his fangs moving toward her neck. His teeth were just starting to scrape her skin when I dropped on him from above. I wrapped one arm around his neck and yanked hard, hearing him gag and choke. Grabbing my wrist with my other hand, I yanked harder until he let Nudge drop away from him.

"Scat!" I told her, and, coughing, she swooped away from the fight. My Eraser was still struggling but starting to weaken. "You better get your guys out of here," I snarled into his ear. "We're kicking your hairy butts."

"You're gonna fall now," I heard Angel say in a normal voice. I swung my head to see her gravely watching an Eraser who looked confused, paralyzed. Angel shifted her gaze to the dark water below. Fear entered the Eraser's eyes, and his wings folded. He dropped like a rock.

"You're getting scary, you know that?" I said to Angel, not really kidding. I mean, making an Eraser drop right out of the sky *just by telling him to* — jeez.

And Iggy, said the Voice. I veered off to help Iggy, who was in tight hand-to-hand with an Eraser.

"Ig!" I called, as he grabbed the Eraser's shirt.

"Max, *get out of here!*" Iggy yelled, and released the shirt, letting himself fall quickly out of reach.

I had time to think *Uh-oh,* and then the small explosive Iggy had stuck down the Eraser's shirt detonated, leaving an ugly gaping hole in his chest. Shrieking, the Eraser plummeted heavily downward.

And how did Iggy manage to stash his seemingly endless supply of explosives on his person without my even having a clue? Got me.

"You . . . are . . . a . . . fridge . . . with . . . wings," Fang ground out, punching an Eraser hard with every word. "We're . . . freaking . . . ballet . . . dancers."

Take a deep breath, Max, said my Voice, and I obeyed without question.

At that moment, I felt a blow to my back, between my wings, that knocked the wind out of me. I rolled, belly-up, using the oxygen I'd just gotten, trying to suck in more air.

Whirling, I snapped both feet out in a hard kick into the Eraser's face, then froze in shock. *Ari!*

He wheeled backward and I floundered away, wheezing and hoping I wouldn't pass out. *Ari! But he was dead —* *I'd killed him. Hadn't I?*

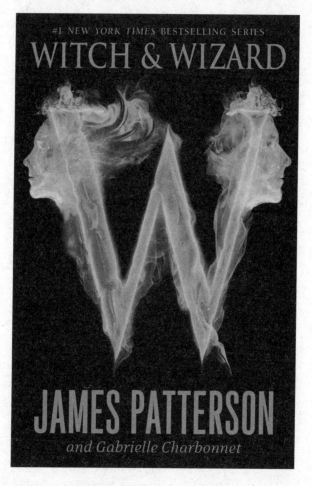

Wisty

IT'S OVERWHELMING. A city's worth of angry faces staring at me like I'm a wicked criminal—which, I promise you, *I'm not.* The stadium is filled to capacity—past capacity. People are standing in the aisles, the stairwells, on the concrete ramparts, and a few extra thousand are camped out on the playing field. There are no football teams here today. They wouldn't be able to get out of the locker-room tunnels if they tried.

This total abomination is being broadcast on TV and the Internet too. All the useless magazines are here, and the useless newspapers. Yep, I see cameramen in elevated roosts at intervals around the stadium.

There's even one of those remote-controlled cameras that runs around on wires above the field. There it is—hovering just in front of the stage, bobbing slightly in the breeze.

So there are undoubtedly millions more eyes watching

than I can see. But it's the ones here in the stadium that are breaking my heart. To be confronted with tens, maybe even hundreds of thousands, of curious, uncaring, or at least indifferent, faces...talk about *frightening*.

And there are no moist eyes, never mind tears.

No words of protest.

No stomping feet.

No fists raised in solidarity.

No inkling that anybody's even thinking of surging forward, breaking through the security cordon, and carrying my family to safety.

Clearly, this is not a good day for us Allgoods.

In fact, as the countdown ticker flashes on the giant video screens at either end of the stadium, it's looking like this will be our *last* day.

It's a point driven home by the very tall, bald man up in the tower they've erected midfield—he looks like a cross between a Supreme Court chief justice and Ming the Merciless. I know who he is. I've actually met him. He's The One Who Is The One.

Directly behind his Oneness is a huge N.O. banner— THE NEW ORDER.

And then the crowd begins to chant, almost sing, "The One Who Is The One! The One Who Is The One!"

Imperiously, The One raises his hand, and his hooded lackeys on the stage push us forward, at least as far as the ropes around our necks will allow.

I see my brother, Whit, handsome and brave, looking

down at the platform mechanism. Calculating if there's any way to jam it, some means of keeping it from unlatching and dropping us to our neck-snapping deaths. Wondering if there's a last-minute way out of this.

I see my mother crying quietly. Not for herself, of course, but for Whit and me.

I see my father, his tall frame stooped with resignation, smiling at me and my brother — trying to keep our spirits up, reminding us that there's no point in being miserable in our last moments on this planet.

But I'm getting ahead of myself. I'm supposed to be providing an *introduction* here, not the details of our public *execution*.

So let's go back a bit....

James Patterson received the Literarian Award for Outstanding Service to the American Literary Community at the 2015 National Book Awards. He holds the Guinness World Record for the most #1 *New York Times* bestsellers, including *Confessions of a Murder Suspect* and the Maximum Ride series, and his books have sold more than 350 million copies worldwide. A tireless champion of the power of books and reading, Patterson created a children's book imprint, JIMMY Patterson, whose mission is simple: "We want every kid who finishes a JIMMY Book to say, 'PLEASE GIVE ME ANOTHER BOOK.'" He has donated more than one million books to students and soldiers and funds over four hundred Teacher Education Scholarships at twenty-four colleges and universities. He has also donated millions to independent bookstores and school libraries. Patterson invests proceeds from the sales of JIMMY Patterson Books in pro-reading initiatives.

Read all the MAXIMUM RIDE **books:**